Children
of Italy

Love
Secrets
&
Betrayal

Children
of Italy

Love
Secrets
&
Betrayal

A Novel by

Christine Simolke

Bellflower, CA

Masquerade an Imprint of Hawkins Publishing Group
P.O. Box 447
Bellflower, CA 90707
www.hawkinspublishinggroup.com

Associate Editor: Michelle Dunbar
Falconi Family photos courtesy of Falconi Family Archives
Cover artwork courtesy of FabioBerti | Dreamstime.com
Cover design and layout | Hawkins Publishing Group Design Team

ISBN: 978-0-9962145-1-3
Library of Congress Control Number: 2015913980
Manufactured in the United States
10 9 8 7 6 5 4 3 2 1

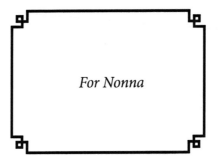

For Nonna

Acknowledgements

I would like to thank my husband, Greg, my children, Daniel and Michael, my mother, Eliana, and my friend, Karen for their encouragement and support through the process of writing this book. A special debt of gratitude goes to Martice Hawkins for taking a chance on my manuscript and for believing in my story.

I would also like to express my deep appreciation to the readers. I thank you many times over for spending your valuable time with my book. Lastly, I am eternally grateful to my great-grandparents, Luigi and Appollonia, my grandmother, Giovanna, and my aunts, Maria and Evelina, for their inspiration. This book is an homage to them and all the immigrants who helped to make America a great country.

Give me your tired, your poor,
Your huddled masses yearning to breathe free,
The wretched refuse of your teeming shore.
Send these, the homeless, tempest-tost to me,
I lift my lamp beside the golden door!

Emma Lazarus
On the pedestal of the Statue of Liberty

March 1924

Chapter 1

All men have regrets. Luigi Falconi had only one. The guilt from it had robbed him of many a good night's sleep. His transgression couldn't be undone, but he could sweep it under the rug. He would begin tonight with a clean slate, as the Americans liked to say.

He wanted to be the husband his wife, Appollonia, deserved. The father his daughters needed. Their years of being apart were over. His family was leaving Italy to join him in America. The thought of their arrival in New York in nine days filled him with hope. His dream of a good life for his family in a new country was becoming a reality. He had worked for twelve arduous years to fulfill his promise to them, but one more thing had to be done before their arrival.

In the room above the *ristorante,* Luigi laid next to Isolde. Her body radiated heat, like the embers glowing in the fireplace. He wiped his face with his calloused hands and sat up in the sleigh bed, tracing his finger over the intricate carving etched in the headboard as if it would give him the words he needed to say. Coal dust blackened his nails, though he had washed in the porcelain basin on her dresser. A trace of black powder always remained, no matter how hard he scrubbed. He closed his hand into a fist.

"This is our last night together," he said, his voice stern and commanding.

The words hung in the air over her bed, where a shadow stretched from the candle's flame on the nightstand. Isolde opened her eyes. They were dark and vacant like those of the black rat snake that Luigi had seen coiled in back of the woodpile.

"I wish it could be different, but don't worry. I won't make any trouble for you."

When she sat up beside him, the light of the moon beamed through the window behind her. She wrapped the blanket they shared around her shoulders like an open cloak, and her dark, tousled hair framed her solemn face and cascaded across her breasts. She reached up to run her fingers through his hair.

"I'm meeting my family next weekend in New York," he said in Italian, as if to emphasize they were coming from the old country.

"I know," she answered, without taking her eyes from his.

The blanket fell from her bare shoulders, and he looked away. She touched his face and turned it toward her.

"Stay with me tonight."

He had never allowed himself the intimacy of sleeping all night with her or any other woman he had used as a substitute for his wife.

She kissed his neck and then his shoulder. "Don't go yet," she whispered. Her beautiful body illuminated by the moonlight mesmerized him, and when she moved her lips from his neck to his chest, he lay back on the soft pillow and closed his eyes.

After a fitful sleep, he awoke just before dawn. A cool breeze blew the curtain away from the only window in the room. He dressed in the dark and slipped out the door without waking her. As he walked in the sobering morning air, he remembered the night two years ago when he had let her seduce him for the first time.

"I'm married," he said, as she led him to her room. He stumbled up the dark staircase, light-headed and aroused. As she shut the door and lit a candle, he whispered, "I love my wife, but I'm lonely. That's all. Nothing more."

"I understand," she said, and kissed him. He still remembered the taste of wine on her lips.

An hour remained before any of the men would stir in the boxcar at the edge of the mining camp in the small town of Covel, West Virginia. A layer of coal dust covered the ground and clung to Luigi's shoes as he walked the muddied road. Tree branches formed a canopy over him until he reached the old railroad yard. Inside the boxcar, he heard the snoring and coughing of his fellow miners. He climbed inside and snuck back to his pallet. If they had noticed his absence, they wouldn't say anything. He kept their secrets, too. Like him, some of the other men, whose wives were still living in the old country, had sex with the single women who worked as cooks, shopkeepers, and waitresses in the mining camp. It's only for affection, they said, trying to absolve their sins and convince themselves it was acceptable until their wives arrived. Mostly they didn't speak of their infidelity or the guilt many of them felt.

This was Luigi's second longest stay in America. During his first six years, while working on the railroad, he had strayed, as well. His indiscretions then had been a few one-night stands, after drinking too much wine with girls whose names and faces he no longer remembered.

He had made only one trip home to Italy and Appollonia during his time away. After that visit with his wife, he was filled with good intentions. Upon his return to America, he pledged aloud to his friend, Vincente, that he wouldn't give in to temptation. Vincente laughed. "You've had many *indiscrezione*, Luigi you're no saint. Don't make a promise you can't keep."

Though loneliness enveloped him like a gloomy fog, he stayed away from women for four years. Then his attraction to Isolde, like the intensity of the sun's rays after a storm, burned the gray cloud away and along with it, his vow of fidelity.

The other women had been one-night stands at moments when alcohol clouded his judgment. His affair with Isolde had been more than an indiscretion.

The first time he saw her, she smiled at him when she brought spaghetti to his table in the *ristorante*. Her arm brushed his shoulder. His heartbeat quickened. He couldn't take his eyes off of her.

"I made it myself. I hope you like it," she said. Her voice was seductive and her black hypnotic eyes held onto his gaze. Everything about her was inviting, her raven hair, the curve of her back, the sway of her hips when she walked away from the table, her full lips that he longed to kiss. When she arrived in the bare and lifeless camp, he was lonely for his family and struggling to save enough money to bring them to live in America. Each day was the same and his mood was as dark as the underground mine where he spent his days.

Isolde and several other women worked as waitresses at the *ristorante*, where the miners sometimes ate their evening meals. The other girls didn't tempt him. She was different. Many of the men were attracted to her, but she ignored their advances and treated him as if he were the only man in the room. He began to look forward to seeing her and the way she made him feel.

"She's got it bad for you, Saint Luigi," Vincente said.

"I don't want any trouble." Luigi said the words without conviction and watched Isolde as she moved around the room.

"She looks like trouble to me," Vincente warned.

To avoid temptation, he stopped eating at the restaurant. A few weeks later he saw her crying while reading a letter in the post office.

"What's wrong?" he asked.

She dabbed her eyes with a lace handkerchief. "It's a letter from my mother. I miss my family and Italy. My sister in New York..."

"Why didn't you stay with her?" He wondered aloud.

Again her eyes filled with tears, and she told him that her sister had died. He offered her his dry bandana, the one he tied around his forehead to keep the sweat and coal dust out of his eyes while he worked.

"You're kind," she said. She wiped her face and let her hand linger on his when she offered to give the bandana back.

"Keep it," he said, and then he put his hand on the small of her back and opened the door to the post office. Dusk had fallen on the quiet street. "I'll walk you home."

They talked about their families and the old country.

"When my sister died, I wanted to go back to Italy, but the passage was too expensive. Then my friend, Katia, wrote and asked me to come to West Virginia. She told me I could work in the *ristorante* and put money aside to buy a ticket home."

"Are you going back to Italy soon?" Luigi asked.

"Yes, I hope to go back in less than a year. I miss my family."

"My wife and three daughters are still in Italy," he blurted out.

"They'll join me before too long." He sighed as though a great weight had been lifted from his shoulders.

She touched his face and thanked him for escorting her home.

The next day, he shaved and bathed after work and went to the ristorante for dinner. Her face lit up when she saw him. He told himself they could be friends, but it quickly became more.

Sleep eluded him as he reflected, and a dull headache came upon him as he waited for morning on his pallet in the boxcar. He pulled his sheet and thin blanket up around his shoulders and folded his pillow under his aching head. His crude resting place was not as comfortable as Isolde's bed, where he had spent many hours in the past two years. Sometimes he even ate dinner in her room and dozed while she read a book by candlelight, before he left to spend the night with the other men. Their time together had eased his loneliness, but a life with his family was what he wanted.

"To do what's right will bring you real happiness." His mother's words, spoken each night when she tucked him in as a child, were etched into his memory.

Ever since Appollonia's last letter, filled with the details of their daughters' lives and their upcoming voyage, he had begun to prepare Isolde for the end of their affair. It had been their arrangement from the start that they were both biding their time; he, until his family joined him, and she, until she made enough money to return to Italy.

"Don't worry. I won't make any trouble for you." Isolde's words hadn't been said in anger. Luigi rubbed his temples and rolled his head from side to side. Vincente awoke beside him, stretched, and nodded a greeting. Luigi smiled. When the sun's rays shone through the cracks in the boxcar, he got dressed and walked to the mine. His headache was gone.

As soon as Luigi shut the door, Isolde opened her eyes. He hadn't kissed her or said goodbye. She rubbed the flat plain of her stomach. She didn't want a child, but if she found herself pregnant, she would keep it.

From the beginning, he told her their time together would end when his family arrived in America. They were his responsibility and he wanted to do what was best for them. She had hoped to persuade him that he would be happier with her. How stupid she had been, thinking that this day would never come. In the end, their moments of ardor weren't enough to break the bond Luigi had with his wife and daughters.

At the thought of losing the quiet and darkly handsome Luigi, she got out of bed and paced the room like a caged animal. She went to the window and let the cool air wash over her. An Italian man might be confused by the strong pull of *la famiglia*. She would have to make him see that she was not just a woman who could ease his loneliness, that what they had was a lasting passion.

When they first met, he told her of the years he had worked in America, saving for his family to join him. He wanted his daughters to live in the new country where they would have a chance for a good life. It was obvious how much they meant to him, and she envied the love and loyalty he felt for them. If she had been a kinder woman, she would have stayed away from him. But she didn't care that he belonged to someone else. She knew he would try to resist her, and had played along, with the hope she would wear him down. Her patience had been rewarded.

Her last seduction of a married man had been careless and ill conceived. A short time before coming to America, she had fallen in love with her brother's married friend, Vittore, a handsome fisherman with a steely gaze that took her breath away. Each day when Vittore and Giuseppe carried their day's catch home along the coastal road to town, she met them as she gathered flowers or drove her father's cart to the market to buy supplies for her mother.

"Don't come this way," Giuseppe cautioned when he saw the way she looked at Vittore. "I know what you're thinking. Only a *puttana* sets her sights on a married man."

"You can't tell me what to do, Giuseppe," she hissed at him.

Something about stealing Vittore from another woman made

him more attractive and exciting.

Soon after Giuseppe's warning, she found Vittore alone, cleaning fish outside her family's barn. Without speaking to him, she slipped inside. He followed her, closing the door behind him. She unbuttoned her dress while he watched, but when he reached out to touch her, she stepped away.

"I want you, Vittore," she said. "But maybe we shouldn't."

He grabbed her and pulled her to him. "*Bella Isolde.* You can't deny the passion between us."

She enjoyed the urgent way he kissed her and began to undress her. She unbuttoned his shirt and pulled it away from his chest as he caressed her.

One kiss was as far as they had gotten. Giuseppe threw open the barn door with a violent shove and marched toward them as if he were her angry husband instead of her brother. "Go," he said, pointing to the door. "Get away from my sister."

Vittore snatched his shirt from the barn floor and backed toward the door.

"Have you forgotten your marriage vows? Your pregnant wife?" Guiseppe shouted. His hands were balled into fists, and he took a step toward his friend.

Isolde glared at her brother. "Mind your own business, Giuseppe."

Vittore said nothing. She had been sure that he was in love with her, but he didn't defend her or even look at her. He ran from the barn like a chastised dog.

Giuseppe seldom spoke to her after that day. He only guarded her like a vigilant sentry. The closeness they had once shared began to slip away.

From her bedroom window, she watched the sunflowers wave in the fields and longed for something more. After several weeks of being held captive in her own home, Katia's letter arrived telling her of America. Vittore hadn't tried to sneak away to see her, and she was tired of her uneventful life. The stories she heard about the melting pot of immigrants in America intrigued her. Life there had to be more exciting than her pastoral village filled with old or already married men.

It didn't take her long to make plans to leave for West Virginia. When her ship docked in New York, she didn't stay there. The story she told told Luigi about her dead sister was a lie to gain his sympathy. Giuseppe was her only sibling.

Isolde's parents were surprised when she told them of her plans to go to America, but no tears were shed. Giuseppe scrapped together the money for her ticket in a few weeks time, contributing some of his own savings.

When he took her to the shipyard in Rome, the rhythmic beat of the horse's hooves tapping on the cobblestones filled the heavy silence of their long ride.

Upon their arrival, she climbed down from the cart and looked up at him as she pulled her suitcase from the back before he could help her. "You're happy for me to sail away across the ocean."

"No, but it's a chance for you to reinvent yourself and put your old ways behind you," he said. He dropped the reins and eased himself off the cart, his face tired and sad.

"I'll never come back to Italy. This is goodbye for good." She tightened her fingers on the handle of her worn suitcase.

Giuseppe embraced her. "*Addio, sorella.* I hope you'll be happy in America."

She stood like a post with her arms limp at her sides, her black eyes dry and cold. When he released her, tears dripped upon his cheeks as he handed her the envelope with her ticket and enough money to last a month or so. She took it and turned away, without thanking him or looking back.

It seemed like such a long time had passed since that day. The sound of a horse trotting and the wheels of a cart on the road outside her window startled her. She touched the glass and looked at the street below her. The cart's driver glanced up. He had curly black hair like Giuseppe. She pulled the lace curtain in front of her naked body and stepped back into the room.

Luigi wanted to be free of her as well. She looked in the faded mirror above her dresser and ran her hands along the curve of her hips. He had caressed her like this, only moments ago. He was hers now. She had no one else.

Chapter 2

Giovanna stared at the sleek lines of the *SS Roma* with fascination. Steam poured from the smoke stacks of the beautiful, luxury ocean liner. She wondered if she would disappear in America like the vapors of water rising into the clouds. Italy was like a dandelion in a field compared to the sprawling country of the United States of America. When this voyage was over, she would be able to call herself an Italian-American, the eldest daughter of Italian immigrants, Luigi and Appollonia Falconi.

As she daydreamed, she loosened her grip on her youngest sister's hand. Seven year-old Evelina took the opportunity to run ahead of their mother and their sister, Maria, who walked in front of them. Giovanna saw the flash of dark hair and the back of the severe black dress similar to her own and ran after her. Her mother grabbed Evelina's hand before she became lost in the moving throng of passengers anxious to board the ship.

"I'm sorry, Mama," Giovanna whispered.

Her mother's face softened when she heard Giovanna's apology.

At thirteen, Giovanna had many moments of wistfulness, but she didn't want her little sister to be lost on purpose.

"*Va bene,*" Appollonia said. *It's okay.*

Giovanna smiled and pulled her baby sister close. Next to her, twelve-year old Maria wasn't smiling. Her dour expression belied her gentle nature. She also wore the same black dress without a drop of color or ornamentation. Giovanna patted her shoulder and received a nervous grin.

They looked as if they are going to a funeral instead of emarking on the most remarkable journey of their lives. She had helped to sew the dresses in preparation for their trip, and hadn't thought to question her mother's choice of material. Now she saw the other ladies bustling about the shipyard in Genoa wearing colorful and fashionable attire, and she began to feel that the carefully tailored dresses were old-fashioned at best.

As she lingered on the dock, she daydreamed that when she arrived in New York, she would buy new, American style dresses. It was a fanciful dream. Buying clothes was out of the question. However, she had a talent for sewing and felt confident that she could create a dress similar to any that she saw in the store, if she could afford the material. As soon as she was old enough, she would get a job. With her own money, she would purchase handsome fabric to make beautiful clothes for herself, her mother and her sisters.

Twenty passengers or more were ahead of Giovanna as she waited to board the magnificent ship. A young boy had already taken their three suitcases and one big trunk. He gave their tickets a cursory glance and promised to place their belongings beneath their bunks in the third class steerage compartment. They had relinquished their meager belongings to him with reluctance, and only because he wore a uniform similar to the officer standing in the doorway.

The line moved at a steady pace, as the officer from the ship's staff greeted each passenger with a handshake. After the formal welcome, and once on board, she, Maria, and their mother would be required to read a passage in Italian to another officer in accordance with the Literacy Act of 1917 to prove that they could read in their native language. Evelina was exempt, but she had practiced reading, nonetheless, just in case she was called upon to perform. Giovanna knew she did not want to be excluded from any task asked of her sisters.

Restless Evelina pulled on the sleeve of her dress. "Look," she said, admiring the handsome officer who wore white gloves. "I want to shake his hand."

"We have to wait our turn," Giovanna said, though she felt the same excitement and impatience.

The officer was handsome. His hair was cropped very short under his military style hat, and his eyes were warm when he smiled at each passenger. She wondered if he were from America or Italy. He stood very stiff and tall in his pressed white shirt and black pants. His polished shoes, the color of writing ink, reflected the glint of the sun. To pass the time, she pretended to have a conversation with him, answering with a clever remark, smiling and nodding her head while he flirted with her.

She smiled into the wind and Evelina bent her head back and regarded her with amusement. Giovanna shook her thoughts away and looked at Maria, who appeared preoccupied, her eyes staring off into the distance.

"What's wrong, Maria?" Giovanna asked.

"I miss Antonio. I promised to marry him when we turn seventeen."

"You're twelve and a half," Giovanna said. She was only eighteen months older. "Why are you worrying about who you'll marry?"

"Zia Cecilia married Zio Erasmo when she was seventeen."

"You can't marry Antonio. We're going to America. Forget about Italian boys. "

"I like Antonio," Maria said. She narrowed her eyes and frowned at Giovanna.

"We'll meet some nice Italian-American boys. You'll see," Giovanna said. "Besides, Antonio isn't good enough for you."

"You always think you know everything."

"I'm just telling you the truth."

"Do you think we'll ever come back to Italy?" Maria asked.

"Maybe someday," Giovanna said. She looked away, so that Maria couldn't see her face. It was unlikely her family would ever return to Italy. He father was an American citizen now and wanted his family to stay in America permanently. There wouldn't be money for traveling back and forth across the ocean.

"My history teacher told us that some years ago, another ship, *The Titanic*, sunk on its maiden voyage after hitting an iceberg." Maria lowered her voice and grabbed the ship's rail as though speaking of an iceberg might bring them into contact with one.

"What's a maiden voyage?" Evelina asked.

"The first time a ship leaves its port for a trip," Giovanna whispered.

Maria continued. "I've had nightmares about ship wrecks every night this week."

Giovanna handed her rosary to Maria and listened with interest.

Maria clutched it for a moment and then shoved it into her pocket. "My teacher said that all of the women and all but one of the children in first class survived by climbing into lifeboats. In third class, only a third of the children and half of the women survived. So I prayed that we would be first class passengers. When the boy took our bags and trunk, I heard him mumble that it would be hard to drag our suitcases all the way to third class."

Giovanna looked to see if her mother was listening. She appeared to be thinking her own thoughts.

"Don't let Mama hear you talk about *The Titanic*," she whispered. "Pray for a safe passage."

Giovanna's uncle, Zio Erasmo snuck up behind her sisters, picked Maria up and twirled her around, causing her rosary to drop from her pocket. He placed Maria on her feet and embraced her mother. Maria reached for the fallen rosary and held it to her chest.

"When are you coming back to Italy, Appollonia?" he asked.

Her mother's brother had arrived behind schedule, but he was still there in time to go aboard with them for a few moments. He had promised his wife that he would inspect their accommodations for the long voyage; though it was too late for anything to be done if their sleeping quarters weren't satisfactory.

"Erasmo, I'm happy you're here," her mother said. "We haven't left Italy yet. How can I know when we'll return?"

"Can I talk you into staying?" Zio Erasmo's voice was light, but Giovanna could see from the look in his eyes that he was serious.

Her mother wore a brave smile and looked into the sky above the harbor.

"I'm lonely for my husband. I want my family to be together."
Zio Erasmo pulled her mother aside, but Giovanna could still
hear their whispers.

"Luigi should have tried harder to find work in Rome instead
of seeking his fortune in the United States. Why couldn't he
work at the slaughterhouse with our cousins and me? Instead
he's building railroads and shoveling coal halfway around the
world. He's a romantic fool to believe the stories of a better life
in a country full of capitalists and dreamers. Do you even feel
you know him anymore? He's only come home to see you once
in twelve years."

"Luigi thinks our life will be better in America. Try to
understand." Her mother took Zio Erasmo's hand, but it didn't
calm him. His face was red and he looked one step away from
anger.

"Luigi's been gone for most of your marriage, leaving
you to raise your daughters alone, while he chases *il sogno
Americano*."

"*The American Dream*," Giovanna whispered.

The first time her father went to America, Giovanna had been
less than two years old, but she knew the story. He thought he
could make good money in the land of opportunity, but her
mother didn't want him to go. He went anyway and didn't come
home again until Giovanna was almost seven. He stayed for a
few weeks, and then returned to America. Nine months later,
Evelina was born. Her father's two trips added up to twelve
years away from Italy and his family, with only one brief trip
home during that time.

Giovanna loved her uncle, but she felt a fierce loyalty toward
her father and hoped her mother would defend him.

Her mother didn't get angry, instead she spoke with a
confidence Giovanna had never heard from her until now.

"Today we're starting over. I trust Luigi. I'm taking my girls
to be with their father. He has his citizenship papers now. We're
going to be a family again."

"I can see this is what you want," Zio Erasmo said with
resignation.

"He misses me and wants to be a father to his girls. He's

been saving his money to rent an apartment for us. He's happy that we won't be living apart anymore. I'm proud of him for all the years he's worked hard and saved to bring our family back together."

Zio Erasmo lowered his voice "Do you think he's been faithful?"

Giovanna tried to look as if she weren't listening to him.

"I know he loves me. I hope his thoughts of me have been enough to keep him true."

"I hope so, Appollonia. I'll pray to the Virgin Mother to give you strength and to keep her watchful eye on your family. I'll pray that Luigi will do what's best for all of you."

Giovanna felt ill at ease and bent down and hugged Evelina. Her mother took a deep breath and inhaled the dank air of the shipyard. Her asthma was under control in the dry air of the countryside of their home in Valcaldara, but the humidity here in Genoa made her every breath an effort. Giovanna feared the tight quarters of the ship and the stress of the long voyage would aggravate her condition. Her mother carried a small jar of honey and a packet of cinnamon in a satchel slung over her shoulder. When mixed with tea, this soothing combination helped her breathe easier.

Giovanna looked to see if Maria had heard the conversation. She wore an innocent expression and Giovanna touched her cheek and cupped her chin in her hand. Her kind sister drew her face upward, and Giovanna kissed her forehead. Maria smiled. Giovanna relaxed, and the anxious wrinkle in her brow disappeared.

Though only a year and a half older, Giovanna towered above Maria and was tall enough to rest her chin on top of her sister's head. Unlike Maria, who was petite and fair like their mother, with beautiful blue eyes that shone with kindness, she and Evelina had their father's dark hair and eyes. Giovanna not only resembled him, she considered herself his substitute in helping her mother until they were with him again.

Her mother moved closer and gave Giovanna a weak grin, a show of courage that thinly veiled her fear.

"I'm excited," Giovanna said, and reached for her mother's

hand. "I can hardly wait for the voyage to begin."

Zio Erasmo smiled at her and tightened his arm around her mother, who sighed. Her lips trembled ever so slightly.

Giovanna turned to face the ship and noticed the tailored clothing of the family in the first class line beside her. She admired the fashionable dress and bobbed hairstyle of the little girl, about Evelina's age, who stood between her parents. Her dainty fingers adjusted a silk headband that had begun to fall out of her hair. Evelina stared at her with her mouth open. When the girl turned to face her, Evelina blushed, and the girl smiled. The child's mother wore a hat with a wide brim and a yellow satin ribbon tied in a simple bow, which complemented her white and yellow dress. Her skirt flared slightly whenever a breeze graced the impatient passengers, and she placed her hand on her head to keep her hat in place. In her other hand, she carried a frilly, delicate umbrella called a parasol. Giovanna had seen women carry them in Norcia, but never in Valcaldara. It was far too dainty to keep rain from soaking a lady. She knew that it was used more as an accessory to complement a woman's dress and could be raised to shield her from the rays of the sun.

"What a beautiful umbrella," her mother said.

She agreed, as they both stared at the woman's porcelain skin and stylish attire. By comparison they looked to be dressed as kitchen maids or cooks at best.

Giovanna assumed the man in front of the woman was her husband by the familiar way she stood next to him, not touching like young lovers who can't bear to be apart, but closer than one stood near a stranger. He wore a tailored gray, pinstriped suit with a crisp white collared shirt and charcoal tie. In his left hand, he held a fedora; and in his right, his ticket, which he surveyed with studied concentration. It looked different than their tickets. *Prima Classe* was stamped in black letters at the top. She pulled her own ticket from her mother's hand and noted the inferior *Terza Classe* stamp on the paper. As she studied his face and stature, she saw that the gentleman was well groomed, but not handsome. Her thoughts turned to her father, whom she had never seen in a tailored suit. Even in his worn work britches, his striking countenance and muscular frame were more pleasing than the dignified face and expensive clothing of Signore *Prima Classe.*

Unkind thoughts. It wasn't her nature to make comparisons or feel envy, an emotion she seldom felt in the country setting of Valcaldara, where the latest fashion was not a consideration, and there was little class distinction. Caring for children and animals, growing vegetables, cleaning and cooking did not require skirts that fluttered or matching parasols. Even though she had never had occasion to wear fancy clothing, she took note of it and admired well-tailored clothes.

Giovanna watched her mother staring at the stylish family and put her arm through hers. "When we get to America, I'll make a new dress for you."

Her mother turned her head. "You are a wonderful seamstress," she said.

Giovanna resolved that she would find a way to earn money to buy a pattern and bright, feminine material. Her mother deserved a beautiful dress and more.

"Lucia, do you have your ball of yarn ready for the moment of the ship's departure?" the girl's mother asked.

At the mention of yarn, Evelina tugged on the canvas satchel that hung loosely on her mother's shoulder and pulled out a brown ball of yarn, that had been given to her by her aunt, Zia Cecilia, Zio Erasmo's wife.

"Why do you need the yarn?" Maria asked.

"I'll hold the ball while I stand on the ship. I'll give Zio Erasmo the end of the strand of yarn and he'll hold it on the dock. As the ship moves away from the dock, the ball will unwind while everyone says good-bye. The yarn will unravel as we sail out to sea. When it comes to the end, I'll let go. The yarn will fly in the wind."

Lucia held up her ball of yarn and nodded when Evelina finished her explanation of the custom. Both girls giggled with anticipation. Giovanna sighed. She was pleased that Evelina took delight in the custom, but it was, in her opinion, a waste of a perfectly good ball of yarn.

Giovanna followed the well-dressed family up the boarding

ramp. *Signora Prima Classe* shook the hand of the ship's greeter, followed by her husband and Lucia. Evelina waited behind her and was the first to represent the Falconi family, smiling without reserve at the handsome young man in uniform. Her mother nudged shy Maria to follow her sister, and she did so. Giovanna did not carry out her imagined flirtation, but chose instead to gaze at her shoes when she offered her limp hand. The confident boy in the pressed uniform gripped her hand and held on to it. She looked up and a blush tinged her cheeks.

"I hope to see you soon." His voice was both confident and kind.

"Oh," she said with surprise. It was all she could manage to say.

He released her hand and it drifted to her side as though she wasn't sure what to do with it. Then she walked up the gangplank of the ship, and turned to look at him before she stepped aboard. He tipped his hat in her direction, and she smiled as Maria pulled her to the table where they had to pass their reading test. Though she was a good reader, her hands shook and she stumbled over the words.

Maria asked the man in charge, "May my sister start again?"

Giovanna took a deep breath and read again, with no mistakes this time. Maria put her arm around her waist and squeezed her.

Her mother sank with a heavy sigh onto a bench next to the table. Giovanna watched beads of sweat drip on her face and neck and darken the back of her dress. There would be more tests to pass before they stepped unrestricted onto American soil. After each one, she hoped the oppressive weight of worry would become lighter.

Zio Erasmo stood behind the bench and placed his hands on her mother's shoulders. He smiled at the girls, but his eyes reflected a deep sorrow. Taking her mother's satchel, he helped her to her feet as she gulped in the sea air. Giovanna observed this poignant moment with regret. Her mother might never see her brother again. The thought overwhelmed her with sadness. The notion that she would ever be separated from her own siblings wasn't something she ever wanted to contemplate.

Her mother gave Zio Erasmo a half-hearted smile, and then led the way down the stairs to the third class compartment.

With the successful completion of the reading test, the passengers were free to go to their quarters until the ship's whistle signaled that it was time for departure. They were expected to be on deck to bid farewell to loved ones. Each family had been given a schedule, printed in Italian and English, of the mealtimes, activities, and for the steerage passengers, the lights-out time. They would not have the luxury of extinguishing the lights at their leisure. Their compartment was more like a dormitory, where all passengers were expected to be in their bunks and quiet by ten o'clock.

At the bottom of the stairs were four cabins, two on each side of the hallway. Each room contained four bunks.

"One of these rooms would be perfect," her mother said.

Giovanna glanced at Zio Erasmo who examined their tickets, but he frowned and continued past the cabins to a large room filled with people speaking and gesturing in many different languages. Young children ran about and older adults sat on trunks, rolled up blankets, wooden crates, suitcases and two-tiered bunk beds that lined the walls of the low ceilinged room. Some were talking, some were fighting over a bottom bed and several others were pulling on a rope stretched from a top bunk on one side of the room to another top bunk on the other side of the room. Giovanna heard one Italian woman say to another that it must be a clothesline, and she demonstrated by taking the shawl from her shoulders and throwing it over the line. The other woman shook her head and pulled on the line to test its strength.

It appeared that claiming a bed was first come, first served. Giovanna did not see even one bunk that wasn't covered in luggage and parcels already.

Evelina darted around the room like a sparrow looking for an empty nest.

"Here," she called, and patted a top bunk, throwing her coat over its edge. "There, Maria." She pointed to another top bunk, two beds down from the one that held her dangling coat. Maria ran to the spot and threw her coat, just as Evelina had done.

Two small windows at the end of the room provided the only light, making it hard to see if there were any more vacant bunks. Giovanna hurried to the opposite side of the room. She wanted desperately to find a bottom bunk for her mother. She let out a sigh when she reached the end of the row and saw only a few top bunks left unclaimed. She placed her coat on one and reached for her mother's coat. Her mother and Zio Erasmo were standing near her surveying the chaos of steerage passengers. The room was warm and she could see sweat on her mother's forehead and a worried look in her eyes.

"We won't be sleeping close together." Her mother's words came out in a scratchy whisper.

"Not there," yelled the boy who had taken their luggage on the dock. He had come into the room from the hallway and smiled in recognition when he saw Giovanna. He motioned to her with a wave of his hand. "You're in a cabin."

She retrieved their coats, and they all followed him to the first cabin in the hallway and found their trunk and suitcases there.

"Are you sure?" Giovanna asked. He nodded and showed her their name written on a paper wedged into a metal plate on the door.

Her mother brought her hands to her face. Tears began to fall silently down her cheeks as she took in the four neatly made beds, a washbasin, a chamber pot, two white hand towels and a candle in a holder. "*Grazie, mio marito.*" *Thank you, my husband.*

Zio Erasmo clapped his hands in delight and picked Evelina up and placed her on the top bunk on one side, while Maria climbed a small ladder to the top bunk on the other side.

"I'll be damn," he muttered. "I didn't want to say anything about that other…" He made a terrified face and rolled his eyes toward the door. They all laughed. "Luigi splurged. Good for him and good for you."

Giovanna hugged her mother, who self-consciously wiped her tears. She smiled and left Giovanna's embrace to inspect the linens, stretched tightly over the thin mattresses. When she saw that they were crisp and clean, her face lit up. Giovanna lay on the bottom bunk below Maria. She felt as if she were in a tiny cave.

Giovanna cleared her voice as though she needed to make an important announcement. Then she stood and shouted, "Our adventure begins."

"We're on an adventure!" Evelina reached her hands to touch the ceiling above her head. Maria jumped down from her bunk and Zio Erasmo twirled her around and around.

"Yes," her mother said. "And your Papa is the prize at the end of our journey."

The ship's horn blew, and they hurried to the deck for the ceremonial departure. Evelina instructed Zio Erasmo to hold his end of the strand of yarn until they were out of sight.

Each of the girls embraced him. His eyes filled with tears as he held onto them without speaking. He released them slowly and turned to his sister. She closed her eyes while her own tears fell from her doleful eyes and her shoulders shook. He kissed her on each cheek and embraced her. When he let her go, they both smiled bravely and he turned away without looking back, his footsteps heavy on the wooden gangplank, the stand of yarn trailing along behind him.

Giovanna put both hands over her heart as her uncle walked away. Would they be together again before too many years passed? Her hands fell to her sides, as if her wish, like a feather, had been carried away in the wind. The sun warmed her cheeks as the ship slipped out to sea, and she closed her eyes and took a deep breath. In nine days she would be in America, and Italy would be an ocean away.

Alessandro stood close to the ship's hull and watched the passengers he had greeted during boarding hasten to the top deck of the SS *Roma*. They searched to find an open spot along the rail from which to wave. The children held their symbolic yarn, ready to release their hold as the last strand unraveled and hung in the air. Their excitement was contagious as they poked at one another and tossed around their balls of yarn.

Alessandro enjoyed their banter as he kept an inconspicuous

distance away from his friend, Mario. He had given him a few coins to arrange a meeting with the dark haired girl he had met when he greeted the boarding passengers. Should she say no to his request, his pride would be spared if Mario were the one to receive her rejection.

Mario had been more than happy to play the part of intermediary. He was always looking for ways to make extra money and would probably spend it on gambling and cigarettes. The older boys smoked and played cards in the servants' quarters below deck when they were off duty, and Mario wanted to be like them. Alessandro had taught him how to bluff at cards, but he hadn't won yet. Mario's paltry stash of coins was almost gone due to his poor skills as a gambler.

Alessandro gambled some, but quit when he began to lose. He saved all but a few dollars of his pay so that he could eventually stay in America and study to become a doctor. He wanted to be one of the immigrants who disembarked at Ellis Island instead of returning on the ship to Italia. This would be his third trip on the *SS Roma*. He planned to find a way to stay by his tenth trip or give up his dream for good. He had told his parents about his plans, and knew his father had set aside some money to give him. Once he became a doctor in America, he would send them a fat envelope with enough money to buy whatever they needed. According to the other boys in the crew, making that kind of money was easier in America than Italia. He knew overzealous dreamers exaggerated stories of fortune, but he also knew his prospects in Genoa were grim. He would soon try his luck, just as most of the ship's passengers planned to do. In the end, they all wanted the same thing, a better life.

Alessandro left the hallway unnoticed and wandered with purpose among the passengers on the crowded deck after he had overheard Mario's conversation with the beautiful, dark-haired girl, Giovanna. She would be fourteen in a few days. His attraction to her was immediate, and he had become tongue-tied. He hadn't asked how he could find her. Thankfully, Mario knew. Parting with the change he kept in his pocket to pay for Mario's help was worth being able to stand near her and hear her voice. Looking around he glimpsed her standing at the rail with her mother and sisters in their matching black dresses. They made an awkward quartet in their simple traveling clothes. He wouldn't have noticed her if he hadn't volunteered for duty at the dock in Genoa. Most days he worked in the kitchen and didn't get to mingle with the passengers. The other boys shied away from the greeter's job of shaking hands and smiling, but he didn't mind the task they found tiresome and boring. He wore a contented grin when Giovanna caught sight of him walking toward her. Their eyes met and she blushed.

"Hello, Signorina Giovanna."

"Hello, Signore Alessandro."

"You greeted us," her mother said to him. She gave Giovanna a reproachful look.

He tipped his hat to her mother, "Signora Falconi, please let me introduce myself. I'm Alessandro Pascarella. May I stroll the ship's upper deck with Giovanna after the evening meal?"

She seemed taken aback at his request. "Excuse us for a moment. I must speak to my daughter first."

"Of course," Alessandro said. He walked away until he was out of earshot, and then he turned to look at them. Giovanna stared in awkward silence at the deck while she listened and nodded her head as her mother spoke. Several minutes passed before they began to walk toward him, and he occupied the time by nodding to passengers and pretending to inspect the deck.

Signora Falconi came up behind him and cleared her throat. He turned and smiled. All three of her daughters stood beside her. "She may go with you, but her sister, Maria, will chaperone," she said.

"Thank you, Signora Falconi," he replied.

Giovanna smiled and introduced her sisters. Maria bit her lip and her cheeks turned a rosy pink.

Evelina, blurted out, "I want to chaperone, too."

"Mama," Giovanna protested.

"Yes, you may go with Maria, Evelina."

Alessandro promised to meet all three of them at eight o'clock, and then blended into the swarm of passengers to resume his duties to prepare for the ship's departure. At the end of the deck, he observed the Falconi women as they waved goodbye to the relative who had escorted them aboard.

"Zio Erasmo," the little Evelina exclaimed. She found her uncle in the multitude of well-wishers, holding a strand of yarn.

"*Arrivederci*," Her uncle shouted and waved.

"*Arrivederci, Zio*," Evelina stood on the tips of her toes and reached into the air as if she were trying to touch the clouds in the sky.

Signora Falconi bowed her head and wiped her eyes. Giovanna hugged her on one side, and Maria laid her head on her mother's shoulder as the ship pulled away from the dock. Evelina waved to her uncle and the ball of yarn unraveled in her other hand.

Their uncle's figure became smaller and smaller. When the others on the dock released their strands of yarn, so did he. The floating yarn was a festive sight.

Alessandro wondered if they would ever see him again.

He drifted through his chores; preoccupied with thoughts of how Giovanna's hand felt when he greeted her, and the way her eyes brightened when she smiled. He was eager to spend time with the striking beauty and thought eight o'clock would never arrive. When it was finally time to go to the upper deck to meet her, Alessandro saw her first and stared. She looked luminous in the waning light of dusk. His heart raced in his chest and his skin tingled as though he had been presented with a wonderful surprise. It was the greatest sensation he had ever felt. When she caught him staring, she looked down at her hands. He greeted her and she gave him a timid smile. For the second time that day, he was overcome with the inability to speak.

They strolled the deck for a full ten minutes without saying a word, while Maria and Evelina walked behind them. Mario strolled beside the sisters and nodded to crewmembers as they passed.

"Why aren't they talking?" Evelina asked Maria, her voice loud enough for her sister and Alessandro to hear.

"Shh," Maria answered.

Evelina tapped Alessandro on the arm.

Giovanna turned around and glared at her little sister. "Mind your own business or I'll take you back to Mama."

Alessandro winked and smiled at Evelina. She smiled back and Maria bowed her head.

Alessandro was comfortable around girls, but today everything he longed to know about this special girl, all the questions he had, had somehow slipped from the tip of his tongue. Then he remembered what Mario had learned. The details spun through his mind as he nervously rubbed the back of his neck, and then laced his fingers together.

"So, your birthday is in a few days?"

"Yes," she answered. Her head was down, but she turned it to the side and smiled at him. "I'll be fourteen."

He smiled back. "I'm seventeen," he said, and then his mouth froze. His mind was a complete blank again.

Evelina broke the silence. "It's a good thing I came along, because I can be Maria's chaperone. Mama will be proud that I'm helping my sisters."

Maria's face flushed red with embarrassment and she walked faster. Mario picked up his pace as well. Alessandro thought he would like to have sisters like these.

"Mario and Maria. Mario and Maria," Evelina chanted.

Alessandro saw Giovanna smile as she turned around and put her finger to her lips. Evelina stopped chanting and skipped along in silence.

Chapter 3

Back in the cabin, Appollonia wrote to her brother, Erasmo, thanking him for all he had done to help her prepare for the trip. She folded and sealed the letter, and then wrapped her shawl around her shoulders, tied a scarf around her head, and left the cabin to climb the stairs into the soft light and gentle breeze of the early evening. Once on deck, she saw Giovanna and Alessandro first, followed by Maria and Evelina, with the luggage boy, Mario, tagging along beside them. Other passengers stood along the rails where the wind blew their skirts and coats. The fresh air was a welcome relief from the stuffiness of her cabin, though she did feel grateful for the privacy the room offered. Fingering the rosary in her pocket, she paused at the railing to say a prayer for a safe passage and good health for her children, the precious trio of young women she watched with amazement as they walked along the deck.

Upon reaching the ship's railing, she stopped and stared at the glossy waves of the Atlantic Ocean, letting her mind drift back over the previous months. So much time, effort and sacrifice had gone into this day. The first step had been Luigi's naturalization as an American citizen, and then his being granted permission to bring his family to live with him. After this milestone, the Italian government had taken a long time to ready the emigration papers. Then, there were many trips to the city of Norcia to fill out applications, provide documents, and answer endless questions. In February they had abandoned their home and bid farewell to their family in Valcaldara. A family friend came to load their meager belongings onto the back of his buggy, drawn by one over-worked horse, and they rode to Norcia where they caught a train for Rome. There, for three weeks, they stayed with aunts, uncles, and cousins while more papers were shuffled and many more questions were asked. Once they were deemed of sound moral character and checked from head to toe, inside and out, by several doctors on several different days, they were declared physically fit. At last, after months of preparation and years of anticipation, this day she had longed for so ardently, had finally arrived.

Erasmo had taken the day off from his job in Rome, where he worked in the slaughterhouse, to accompany them to Genoa. Thinking of her brother, her other siblings, nieces, nephews, and the friends she had known her whole life brought tears to her eyes, and she reached for the embroidered handkerchief in her pocket. How she would miss those she had left behind and her life in Italy. She had never travelled beyond her country until this day. Now, incredibly, she was on a beautiful ship traveling across a vast and mystifying sea.

Her thoughts turned to Luigi, tall and handsome, waiting to welcome her and his daughters, who were growing into beautiful young women. He would hardly recognize Giovanna and Maria and had never seen their spirited Evelina with her lively, dark eyes and ready grin. She knew he would love her as much as he loved her older sisters.

The ship lurched and she gripped the rail of the deck, looking into the dark water of the ocean. The sudden movement startled her and her pleasant thoughts were pushed aside. A fear that nagged at the back of her brain floated into her consciousness. The voyage was still ahead of them. Anxiety took a hold of her thoughts. Her chest grew tighter and each gasp of air became a struggle to take in. Her shawl slipped from her shoulders, her eyes grew heavy, and her legs buckled as exhaustion overtook her and she dropped to the floor of the deck. Evelina ran toward her with her arms outstretched.

Alessandro sent Mario to find the ship's doctor as the Falconi sisters hovered over their unconscious mother. Giovanna took off her shawl and placed it under her head, while Maria sat near her and held Evelina close.

He bent over Signora Falconi and let out a sigh when he saw her chest moving up and down rhythmically. "She's breathing," he said.

"Thank God," Giovanna said. Her face was ashen and tears filled her eyes as she kneeled next to her mother and cradled her head in her lap.

Alessandro turned to Maria, who sat on the other side of her mother. "Unbutton the top of her dress to help her breathe easier." Maria rose up onto her knees and her nervous fingers fumbled with the tight buttons. After undoing three buttons, she sank back onto her heels and looked up at him with frightened eyes.

"Where's the doctor?" Evelina asked, her voice frantic.

Alessandro searched the crowd that was beginning to gather.

"*Il medico*," Mario hollered, as he cleared a path for the doctor along the deck where the passengers murmured with alarm.

Maria stood aside to make way for the doctor. Alessandro nodded at him, and he bent to a crouch beside Appollonia. From his black bag, he pulled a tiny jar of smelling salts and waved it under her nose. She coughed and gasped for air.

Her girls watched with anxious faces as the doctor listened to her heart and lungs with a stethoscope. When she tried to stand, he gently pushed her back into Giovanna's lap.

"Wait a few moments before rising. You fainted and might still be lightheaded."

"She has asthma. We have the home remedy she puts in her tea," Maria said.

The doctor instructed Mario to quickly bring Appollonia a cup of hot tea, while Alessandro helped her to a lounge chair. He noticed her embarrassment at being gawked at by the crowd and addressed them in a stern voice.

"Go about your evening. The signora's being well cared for by the doctor." At his command, they dispersed like bees leaving the hive in a huddled swarm.

"Thank you," Appollonia whispered with labored breath.

"You're welcome, Signora Falconi." Alessandro placed his hand on her arm and smiled at Giovanna.

"Thank you, Alessandro," Giovanna said.

He touched her arm and let his hand linger there for only a moment, before dropping it to his side. Her hand went absently to the spot where his fingers had been.

Mario returned with the steaming tea and the moment was lost. The color began to return to Signora Falconi's face, and her breathing calmed as she sipped from the china teacup.

"Is her asthma the only thing that troubles her?" the doctor asked Alessandro.

He looked at Giovanna.

"She's been working hard to get ready for the trip," she said.

"You're going to be fine, Signora Falconi. You're just overwhelmed by all you've had to do and think about. A little rest is all you need," the genial doctor said, as he took her pulse. "The color has returned to your cheeks, and your pulse is normal."

Signora Falconi smiled and in a timid voice said, "Thank you, Doctor. I'm ready to go back to my cabin with my daughters for the rest of the evening."

Alessandro's smile faded as he helped her stand.

Giovanna sighed. "Will she be alright?"

"I believe she's in good hands with you," the doctor said. "Stay beside her until you reach your cabin and tuck her into her bunk. I'll stop by to see her tomorrow. I think she'll be fine once she gets a good night's sleep. Walk along the deck three times each day." He turned to smile at Signora Falconi. "I'm certain rest and fresh air will revive you, signora."

The girls thanked the doctor again and started toward their cabin. Giovanna and Maria braced their mother with their arms around her waist. Evelina walked in front of them. The evening breeze blew their dark hair and pushed against them like a strong hand as they guided their mother along the ship's deck.

Alessandro stood at the railing with the doctor and watched them go.

"I'll make sure they have everything they need," he said.

"Very good, Alessandro. Between you and her attentive daughters, I think Signora Falconi will be just fine," the doctor said. He packed his leather case and went below deck.

Alessandro supposed he would spend the rest of his evening in the crew's quarters, playing cards with Mario and some of the other shipmen. He would rather have spent his time getting to know Giovanna. When he looked around for Mario, he noticed he wore a long face. It appeared they both had something to brood about now that their evening plans had changed.

"Let's go to our bunks until it's time for poker," Alessandro said. Mario nodded and shuffled along beside him.

Alessandro enjoyed the crew's regular poker game at ten o'clock sharp every Friday night. It lasted into the early morning hours and made for a lethargic team of young shipmen who hadn't yet learned the correlation between insufficient sleep, too much illegal hooch smuggled aboard by the American crewmembers, and a roaring headache the next morning. The older crewmen expected the young men to be slack and irritable during their Saturday morning chores, but tormented them anyway as they remembered being just as foolish in the past.

Alessandro went to his locker to change into comfortable cargo pants and a long-sleeved cotton shirt, his uniform for the long night at the card table. Mario had spread the scant haul of coins he had collected in tips for the day on his bed. Being that he was one of the youngest boys permitted at the table, he wouldn't need much money for the short time the older boys allowed him to be part of the evening's gambling. It was his practice to save half of his tips in a compact tin box hidden amongst his belongings before he started betting and drinking, a practical tip Alessandro had taught him, and he had been wise to follow.

Two bunks down from Mario, Alessandro slipped coins into his own secret reserve, a money pouch that he kept tied around his waist and hidden under his shirt. He was making a similar pouch for Mario.

"The other guys are all right, but no one is completely trustworthy, in my opinion, especially where money's concerned," he said, and then he winked at Mario.

"You're too suspicious," Mario whispered.

"I like to think I'm being cautious. Money is scarce and many of the crew members are desperate to get their hands on it. They don't care if I'm the one who earned it instead of them."

With a wary eye Mario looked around at the men who lounged on their bunks. Some of them dozed. Some read books and newspapers while their legs dangled over the sides of their beds. Others held hushed conversations.

"I'll be careful," Mario said.

Alessandro was saving most of his money to move to Michigan where his Zio Franco and Zia Lucia lived and owned an appliance repair shop. They had an extra room in their apartment and a job at the shop for him when he was ready. With each trip he made on the *SS Roma*, his resolve strengthened that making America his home and leaving Italy was the best way to chart his future. His parents were distressed with his decision, but they knew his prospects in Genoa were limited to working at the slaughterhouse or on the ships. They were reassured only by the fact that he would be living with his mother's sister and her husband. He was learning English and wanted to go to medical school in America. Once his dreams were realized, he planned to send for them and any of his siblings who wanted to leave Italy. His mother would be happy as long as she was with her husband, her children, and her sister, his Zia Lucia. By the time he had completed his studies, he hoped they would be ready to join him.

He closed his eyes and thought of the way Giovanna had looked on the ship's deck, with her timid smile and kind eyes. Why had he taken so long to work up the nerve to begin a conversation with her? Tomorrow he would try again and promised himself not to waste their moments together with awkward silence. She had smiled at him as she escorted her mother, holding her arm with care as though it were a brittle twig in danger of snapping in two. Her dark eyes were flecked with worry, and when he saw how she felt about her mother, he was drawn to her for her kindness as well as her beauty. If he saw her in the early morning while he set up lounge chairs on the upper deck, he would speak to her without hesitation or reserve. The voyage was only nine days. He wasn't going to fritter away any more time.

Mario interrupted his thoughts. "You like Giovanna? You think she's pretty?"

"Yes," Alessandro said.

"Say, *she's the berries*," he instructed. "Since Maria's her *fire extinguisher*, I'd like to *ankle* along with you tomorrow."

"I don't speak American slang."

Mario let out an exasperated sigh. "If a girl is *the berries*, she's pretty. A *fire extinguisher*..."

"I get it, a chaperone. And *ankle* means walk. Thanks for the translation. Sure, *ankle* with me. You like girls already?"

"Only the pretty ones, but they don't usually talk to me."

"Is Maria different?"

"She doesn't think I'm a *sap*." Alessandro rolled his eyes and Mario added, "You know, *un idiota*. She's shy, but we talked a little. Her whole face shines when she smiles."

"I think maybe she likes you, too," Alessandro said. "You can walk with us."

"Thanks"

"Sure. Thanks for helping me out with Giovanna."

"You owe me ten cents."

"I thought you might've forgotten."

"I won't charge you again after today, since you're going to let me *ankle* along."

"That's good of you." Alessandro laughed.

"No problem," Mario said. Then he stretched out on his bunk and closed his eyes.

Alessandro relaxed, too, and smiled thinking of how much Mario had changed in the short time he had known him. The boy seemed older than his twelve years. Working on the ship turned boys into men quickly.

Some might say that at seventeen, Alessandro, himself was still not quite a man. He, however, felt as if he were much older, more like a father to Mario, than a friend. He remembered his first talk about drinking and gambling with the affable and stubborn boy.

"You see how the other boys get carried away when they drink. They make bad decisions," Alessandro cautioned. "In the morning, they wish they hadn't been so stupid."

"*Butt me.*" Mario reached his hand out and rolled his eyes.

"You got a *smoke*?"

Alessandro gave him a cigarette. Mario lit it and blew smoke into the air.

"Don't drink anything more than a glass or two of wine 'til you're a little older," Alessandro persisted.

"I'm almost a man. I know what I'm doing."

"You don't have to listen to me. Learn the hard way," Alessandro said.

Mario got stinking-drunk, while Alessandro watched without comment.

"I think I'm hung-over," he said the next day as he mopped the deck. "I feel like shit."

"You look like it, too, little man."

"You were right."

"Ah," Alessandro said. "I bet you wish now that you'd taken me at my word."

That day had been only a few months ago. A breeze blew in the portal window above his bunk, and Alessandro chuckled aloud at the thought of Mario's lesson.

Mario called to him from his bunk. "Are you awake?"

"Yes"

"If I win tonight. I'm going to buy a flower for Maria and one for you to give to Giovanna."

"Maybe you will win, for once. So far it's your lucky day."

"If I win thirty cents, I'll even buy one for little Evelina."

"Whoever wins the most will buy the three flowers. We can't leave the little one out," Alessandro said.

Chapter 4

Coal soot covered Luigi's body like an extra layer of skin. The black powder coated the inside of his nose, his ears, and the rims of his eyes, and traveled down his throat to settle dustily in his lungs. Each evening, when he shed his work clothes, he saw the stark contrast of his milky torso against his face and hands covered with grime; a dark reminder of his workday spent in the dungeon below the earth.

When the cramped elevator brought him up its long shaft and into the light of day, he took in the fresh air of the West Virginia foothills with strong, deep breaths. He had developed a raspy cough and knew from listening to the older miners that it was just the beginning of the ill effects his lungs would suffer if he continued to work in the dust laden coal mine.

He stripped down to his underwear and boots, grabbed a bar of soap and a worn-thin towel to wash away the dirt and smell, and walked to the creek near the boxcar where he slept. Tomorrow, he would have to do it all over again, and the next day, and the next... unless, he found another job. Even though being a miner paid well, he'd begun to contemplate other options.

Mining was a difficult way to make a living. In Italy, he had worked hard in the vineyards and on his small farm, tending the vines, plowing, planting and caring for animals. His body could tolerate physical labor. But being underground shoveling and hauling coal for ten hours each day, six days a week, was a different kind of work. The debilitating feeling of being surrounded by near darkness and the risk of suffocation, gas poisoning, collapse or explosion was sucking the life out of him.

The other men didn't talk about the danger, so he never spoke of his fears, but he thought about them, more each day. The only aspect he liked was the lack of supervision. He worked a steady pace without a foreman hovering over him.

Now that Appollonia and the girls were on their way, he wanted something better for them and for himself. He had secured a small apartment where they would live as a family when they arrived. It was an improvement over the boxcar, but still lacked many comforts. It didn't have a bathroom and there was only one electric light bulb in the main room. Appollonia had only recently installed one electric light in their house in *Valcaldara*, and her only toilet had been an outhouse. She wouldn't complain. She and the girls were used to living a rustic lifestyle without modern conveniences.

Upon settling in at the boxcar for the evening, he unwrapped a salami sandwich, cheese and an apple, and then took up his pen and wrote a letter to Appollonia's brother, Bernandino, who lived in Yorkville, Ohio, to ask about the job prospects there. In his estimation, they could save a fair amount of money if they stayed at the mining camp for one more year. During that time, maybe his brother-in-law could put in a good word for him at the steel mill where he worked.

Of course, he had another reason for leaving Covel. Isolde. Yesterday, when he had seen her in passing, she'd said, "I need to talk to you." Alone in the entryway near the mailboxes of the post office, the sound of her voice had filled him with dread. In an effort to stay away from her, he had ignored her remark and walked away without speaking. Now, he couldn't shake the feeling that he shouldn't have turned his back on her. Somehow he would see to it that Appollonia went nowhere near the *ristorante*. Thinking of Appollonia filled him with guilt and longing. She was the kindest person he had ever met. She would never hurt him. He had not been thinking of her feelings during his affair, only his own desires at the moment. His transgression and how his wife could be hurt by it, troubled him anew, each time he thought about it. He listened to the March wind whistling through the cracks of the boxcar doors and noticed his hand was shaking over the writing paper. As the other miners huddled beneath their dirty coats and threadbare blankets, he steadied himself and finished the letter to his brother-in-law.

Isolde washed the dishes from the evening meal at the restaurant, plunging her hands into the scalding water without noticing the heat. Luigi hadn't eaten there since the night he had slept in her bed and then slipped away, seemingly out of her life. She had expected him to avoid her for a day or so, as he prepared for the arrival of his beloved family, but she thought he needed her and wouldn't be able to maintain his resolve. Now that several days had passed, she was beginning to doubt her intuition. He had never said he loved her, only that he loved his family. The realization struck her like a sharp dagger that filled her with a constant ache and self-loathing.

The older women gave her no comfort or sympathy. They laughed at her when they noticed that Luigi wasn't eating at the *ristorante*. *We told you what to expect,* they said. She thought they were jealous of her youth and beauty and the attention the most handsome man in the camp had given her. She had been so sure that her relationship with Luigi was different, but it looked as though she was wrong. The same thing had happened to some of the other waitresses, and now they basked in her misery, feeling pleasure from the pain that made her one of them. Katia was her only friend, and she had gone back to Italy almost a year ago.

As she finished the dishes, she began to think about her future. Her tears fell into the water, splashing into the bubbles and dirty dishes as she released the pity she felt for herself. Living in America was no better than living in Italy. Without Luigi, she was alone. She had no family here, except the imaginary dead sister she had conjured to gain Luigi's sympathy. For a moment she thought about going to the train station and buying a ticket to somewhere far away, but the feeling passed as she remembered the one small hope she had. After drying her hands, she caressed her flat stomach and touched her breasts to see if there was any tenderness. The possibility sobered her, though it was still too early to tell. There was a slim chance that she wouldn't need to start over somewhere else. Her luck might change.

Chapter 5

Giovanna turned restlessly on the bunk waiting for the sun to rise and for her mother and sisters to awaken. Reaching for the wall behind her head. she pressed her hands against it to stretch. Though she hadn't slept much during the night, she felt wide-awake and eager for the day to begin. It was March 18th, 1924, her fourteenth birthday. She wasn't expecting any presents, but she did have something special to anticipate.

She had been at sea for almost a week and walked with Alessandro every day, getting to know and like him more with each conversation.

Tonight he was taking her to a dance in the dining room of the crew's quarters. Her mother, sisters, and Mario were going as well. Maria and Mario had become friends. She knew Mario liked her sister more than Maria was aware. Her kindness and gentle nature attracted anyone who knew her, but Giovanna thought she was too young for a suitor. Besides, they were leaving the ship on Sunday. If she were honest with herself, the same logic had to be considered when she thought of Alessandro, for it was unlikely she would ever see him again. In her heart, she hoped she was wrong.

Yesterday, as she studied his hazel eyes while he spoke, he told her of his plans.

"I want to go to America to study to become a doctor. I'm teaching myself how to read and write in English. I practice speaking with the American crewmembers, and I seem to have a knack for the language. My parents have a little money for me, and I have some saved from my job here on the ship. Soon I'll have enough to begin my education."

She looked him up and down, and said, "You seem like a

doctor to me."

"Really?" he said. His face lit up and his hand grazed hers and then fell back to his side.

Though she wanted him to hold her hand, she hadn't seen any other couples walking along the deck touching in any way, even those who appeared to be married. So she put her hands into her pockets.

"Will the training be difficult?" she asked.

"Yes," he said. "But I want to help sick people, and I love to learn about how the human body works. I've always been a good student. Hopefully, I can handle the coursework." He looked over the rail at the sea's foamy waves cresting against the ship, and then smiled at her.

"Then you will be a doctor," she said. She was surprised to see him blush.

"Thanks for that. It will help to know that you believe I can do it," he said. They walked for a few moments in silence, and then he asked, "What interests you, Giovanna?"

His question surprised and pleased her. No one had ever asked her what she enjoyed or wanted from life. "I want to be a seamstress. I especially love to make clothes."

"Then you will," he said, echoing her words to him. He touched her cheek with his hand for a moment, and then pushed it into his pocket.

She put her hand where his had been and looked up at the sun and the cotton-like clouds in the sky. It was a perfect day in every way.

His gait slowed and he changed the subject. "I'm going to Michigan soon," he said. She gave him a puzzled look, and he laughed. "It's one of the states in America."

"Oh, I haven't learned all of the states yet. How far is it from West Virginia?"

"There's a map of the United States of America tacked to the wall in the crew's dining hall where we're having a dance tomorrow night. If you'll go with me to the dance, I can show it to you."

"What about my sisters?" she asked. "Maria and Evelina will want to go and my mother won't allow me to go without a chaperone."

"They can see the map."

She laughed. "Are they invited to the dance, too?"

"You're all invited. Your mother, too."

"Then I'll have to go with you or they'll be angry with me."

"Is that the only reason you'll go with me?" Alessandro asked, puffing his lip out as if she had hurt his feelings.

"No, I think it would be nice to dance with you," she said.

He grinned. She liked the way the corners of his mouth barely moved into a smile, as though he wanted to contain his pleasure.

"Have you been to lots of dances?" he asked.

"I've never been to a dance," she said, smiling at him.

"Neither have I. So we'll be a perfect pair."

When she told her mother about the dance, she gave her consent with the caution that dancing was to be done at arm's length. This stipulation was fine with her. The thought of holding Alessandro's hand for longer than a moment was terrifying enough.

Evelina woke up, scaled the ladder to Giovanna's bunk and then stretched out beside her sister, kissing her roughly on the cheek.

"Good Morning! Happy Birthday!" Evelina said.

"Thank you, *bambina*."

Evelina frowned. "I'm not a baby. I'm seven."

Giovanna hugged her little sister and laughed. "Shush, Mama is still sleeping. I'm sorry for picking on you."

"I'll get you back," Evelina said, as her expression changed to a mischievous grin. "I'm excited about tonight. Mario and Alessandro promised to dance with me. How will I choose? I like them both."

"You can dance with both."

Evelina placed her mouth close to Giovanna's ear and whispered, "*Sono bello*."

Giovanna grinned. "I hadn't noticed how handsome they are."

Maria giggled on her bunk and rolled over to face her sisters, gracefully holding her arms in a dance pose. "Happy Birthday!"

Giovanna saw her mother stir and turn to face her. "Good morning and happy birthday, Giovanna. What's so funny?"

"Sorry for waking you, Mama," Giovanna said. "We're talking about the dance."

"I like to hear you laugh. It makes me happy," her mother said. She tossed her blanket aside and went to the end of her bunk to discreetly use the chamber pot.

"What are we going to wear to the dance, Mama?" Giovanna asked. She had taken all of her clothes out of the suitcases and arranged them on the bed in order of best to worst. Even the best one wasn't elegant enough for a special occasion like a dance.

Appollonia peeked around the end of the bunk and answered sternly, "the black dresses."

Evelina scowled at Giovanna. "The black dresses?"

Giovanna patted her little sister. "Don't worry. Mama's making a joke."

"Good, I hate those black dresses!" Evelina sighed.

"Me, too," Giovanna said, with a laugh.

Working in the vineyard and the vegetable garden and going to a simple country school did not require beautiful clothing, so Giovanna had never questioned the dresses her mother made for her. That had been in Valcaldara, where by day, they picked apples from their orchard, grapes from the vines, and tomatoes from their garden; and in the evening, they cooked, carried wood, chased chickens or sewed, if they had the energy after their homework and chores were completed.

Meandering the deck on romantic walks and preparing for a dance had brought a new concern. Suddenly thrown into a world of style conscious women and girls, her feminine nature urged her to try to keep up with the competition.

"Why are you smiling like that, Maria?" Giovanna asked, when she saw the playful grin on her sister's face.

"She has a secret," Appollonia said.

Maria jumped down from her bed. "Can I tell her?"

"What is it?" Giovanna asked.

Appollonia nodded at Maria.

"Mama and I have been keeping a secret for your birthday."

"Is it a good secret?" Evelina asked, moving in a restless dance from one end of the room to the other.

"Yes. Mama picked out some pretty material to make into dresses for us as a gift for Giovanna's birthday. Zio Erasmo and Zia Cecilia took her to a store in the city to buy it." Maria jumped from her bunk and went to one of the suitcases. She pushed hard on the lock buttons on each side. The lid popped open with a loud clack.

"Mama," Giovanna exclaimed. "This is the best surprise."

"Why did she tell you, Maria?" Evelina asked with her face knotted into a grimace.

"She needed me to help her cut the fabric. To keep it a secret, we worked while you and Giovanna were feeding the chickens and working in the garden."

"We've finished some of the sewing, but our progress has been slow. We need Giovanna's skilled hands," her mother said, turning to Giovanna, "With your help, we can finish the dresses in time for the dance."

Evelina sparkled with excitement as she helped Maria search the suitcase where the new fabric was hidden.

"Thank you, Mama," Giovanna said. "I won't stop until each *vestito* is ready."

She hugged her mother and retrieved her sewing kit from the trunk in the corner of their tiny room. She surveyed the material that her mother had pinned together for one of the dresses and readied herself to begin sewing without even changing from her gown into her clothes.

"I'm so happy that you girls will be able to wear something pretty," her mother said. Her eyes filled with tears.

Giovanna began to glide the needle and thread through the colorful fabric. She would have to work hard to finish stitching the many pieces of material together into dresses before it was time to get ready for the dance.

"I'm glad we don't have to wear those old, black dresses," Evelina said, her face contorted into a mask of disgust.

"We'll look like ladies instead of peasants tonight," added Maria.

Giovanna saw the smile on her mother's face. It looked as if, for the moment, her worries had floated away. Her mother laid out each of their dresses in various stages of completion on her bunk and Giovanna continued to sew. She listened for a moment as her sisters talked about the dance, and then she became lost in her own thoughts.

The trip had exceeded her expectations, and she wished she could slow the passing of time. Though she looked forward to reuniting with her father, being with Alessandro and the excitement and novelty of traveling on the *SS Roma* was not a journey she wanted to end. Life on the ship had been like living in a romantic story. Each day she awoke to the smell of the salty ocean air, met interesting people, ate new and unusual foods, and talked to a boy who treated her as if she were something special, something more than a common girl from the Italian countryside. She was smart enough to realize that everyday life in West Virginia would probably consist of doing chores and struggling with schoolwork in an unfamiliar tongue. This was a time to be savored. Soon she would say good-bye to Alessandro and this fairy-tale world.

Mario knocked at their door with a message that the ship would be docking a day early. He said that when the captain had announced the new arrival date, many of the passengers had cheered. Most of them did not find the voyage romantic, only a means to get to their desired destination. Her mother was distressed at the news and appeared preoccupied for most of the day. The change in plans gave her something more to fear. Her father had to be notified, and she wondered how it would be possible.

Alessandro assured her that there was a way and took her mother to the ship's office to send a telegram. Her father would need to meet them a day earlier than planned.

After an hour had passed, Giovanna heard footsteps echo in the narrow hallway and opened the door. She was taken aback by the sight of her mother, who leaned on the doorframe with one hand and fumbled with the top button of her blouse with the other. Her face was as white as her collar.

"I can't catch my breath," she gasped. "Help me, Giovanna."

Her mother took one step over the threshold and sank to her

knees. Giovanna reached out to her and lifted her slightly so that she could wedge her shoulder under her mother's arm. Then she guided her to a bottom bunk. She had never seen her look so panicked.

Sweat trickled down the side of her mother's face and dampened her hair. Her eyes fluttered and closed. Giovanna's nervous fingers frantically worked the buttons free on the collar of her mother's blouse and pushed it away from her neck. Her sisters kneeled beside her.

"Mio Dio, Mama," Maria whispered.

"Evelina, go find the doctor," Giovanna commanded.

Evelina moved to stand, when her mother took her hand.

"Don't go. I'm fine." She opened her eyes and gave them a weak smile. "I just felt very tired. I'm better now that I'm lying down."

Giovanna found a handkerchief and wiped her mother's face. Evelina dipped a porcelain cup into the water basin and offered it to her mother, who sipped it until it was empty.

"What happened?" Giovanna asked as she sank into the thin mattress of the bed.

"I sent a telegram to your Papa. Alessandro assured me that he would receive it well before we arrive in America, but as I walked back to the cabin, I worried that we might get off the boat with no one to meet us and nowhere to go." She eased herself up onto her elbows and held the cup out to Evelina.

"Thank you." Evelina smiled as the color began to return to her mother's cheeks. "I let my fears get the better of me."

Giovanna sighed. "I'm sure Papa will be there. It'll work out. Don't worry." She patted her mother's hand.

"Are you feeling better?" Maria asked.

"Yes, I'm much better. I'm sorry I gave you a scare." Her mother stood gingerly and looked around the cabin. She saw her shawl at the end of her bunk. "I could use some fresh air. Will you go with me Evelina?"

"Yes." Evelina placed the shawl over her mother's shoulders and took her hand. "Let's walk to the chairs on the deck and sit in the sun. Maybe Lucia will be out and we can talk to her."

"Do you feel steady?" Giovanna asked.

Her mother nodded. "Go back to your stitching. There's no time to waste." She smiled at Giovanna and Maria. Each of them reluctantly picked up their sewing, while she and Evelina left the cabin with Evelina watching her every step.

Maria gave Giovanna an anxious look.

"Don't worry. Once we're in America, she'll be fine," Giovana said, as much to convince herself as her sister.

After several minutes of quiet work, Maria said, "I'm almost finished with the hem of Evelina's dress." It was small enough for her to hold it in the air above her lap so that she could examine the stitching she'd completed.

A loud knock at the door startled her, and she nearly dropped the garment.

"Who is it?" Giovanna asked, still focused on the seam of her own dress.

"Alessandro," his muffled voice replied.

Maria set aside her sewing and opened the door a crack, as Giovanna moved to stand out of view, for she was only wearing her undergarments. Her day dress was in a heap on the bed.

"Hello, Alessandro," Maria said, as she peered at him.

"May I speak to Giovanna for just a moment?" he asked.

"She'll be right out." She closed the door and made a face at her sister.

Giovanna put on her old dress and slipped into the narrow hallway, happy to have an unexpected visit from him.

He said hello, then thrust a pen and paper toward her. "Will you write your new address in West Virginia for me?"

"Yes, I think I remember it."

Her fingers shook as she wrote. He was standing so close to her that she could smell a hint of the sea in his hair and see the perspiration on his face. She hadn't expected that he would want to keep in contact with her and was thrilled at the suggestion.

In his hand, he held a postcard with a picture of the ship on one side.

"I brought you a souvenir of the *SS Roma*," he said. Then he flipped the card over. "On this side is my address in Italy at the top. I don't think I'll be living there much longer.

At the bottom is the Michigan address of my aunt and uncle where I'll live, hopefully, very soon. I'll write to you when I know my plans. Please write back to me."

She took the postcard from him. "I'll write to you."

A feeling of shyness overcame her and she looked down. When she raised her eyes, he was gone. She searched the hallway for his retreating figure, but it was empty. The encounter had been so brief, she wondered if she had imagined it. The postcard of the ship slipped to the floor and under the door of the cabin. When she opened the door to step inside, Maria picked it up and smiled as she gave it to her.

Giovanna's moment of happiness was darkened by the thought that soon Alessandro would slip away from her like the postcard that had fallen from her hand.

The crew had worked since before sunrise to ready the dining hall for the dance. The first class passengers had already had a very formal dance two nights prior. This evening's impromptu party for steerage passengers and the crew would be much less elaborate. Alessandro had set the evening up with the captain only days before.

"The crew may enjoy the dance with the third class passengers," the captain said. "Only on the condition that all the preparations will be done before daybreak. The demands and needs of the passengers are our top priority. And, Alessandro, if any of the staff are unable to report for duty the next morning, it will be the last party I'll permit below deck."

The crew had willingly set to work two hours before their morning shift began, inspired by the thought of a night of music, dancing, laughter and camaraderie. The women were in charge of food and organizing the musicians; all crewmembers, who were delighted to show off their talents as long as they were allowed a chance to participate in the dancing as well. The men set up the dining hall, pushing the tables and chairs aside to make a dance floor and rudimentary stage for the instrumentalists. Some of the younger men had unofficially put themselves in charge of the clandestine task of stealing wine from the galley, for they thought it wouldn't be a party without a sip or two of spirits to loosen up the dancers. The American laws of Prohibition were not in effect on the Italian luxury liner, but they still had to be careful. The captain wouldn't be happy if he knew they were dipping into the wine supply. There was always homemade "hooch" from the Americans if all else failed, but Italian wine was a much better choice.

The dance was set to start at nine sharp and would continue into the wee hours of the morning, if the younger shipmen had their way, and, they joked, as long as there were no complaints from the passengers in first class.

Tomorrow they would arrive in the New York harbor, a day early, due to mostly excellent weather. The passengers had rejoiced at this news, but Alessandro was dismayed. It meant one less day with Giovanna. He was more than enchanted with her. He was falling in love with her. His thoughts were consumed with holding her in his arms and kissing her, but his pining might never be realized. They hadn't been afforded even a moment alone. The way things were going it looked as if he might have to settle for a handshake when she departed the ship in the morning.

Chapter 6

The small three-room apartment was almost ready for his family's arrival. Luigi had furnished it with the bare essentials. Appollonia would find her kitchen equipped with a used kitchen table and chairs, two pots, one cast iron skillet, one wooden spoon, a large knife, a rolling pin and cutting board for making pasta, one large mixing bowl, five plates and soup bowls, five drinking glasses, five forks and spoons, several bars of homemade soap, an aluminum tub for bathing and washing clothes and a pail for an indoor chamber pot.

He didn't know much about cooking, but he wanted the kitchen ready. It had been too long since he had tasted his wife's homemade pasta and soups. The cutting board and rolling pin had been his first purchase when he began to buy what she would need to make the meals he desperately missed. An Italian signora at the mining camp had offered to sell them to him when her mother died and left her with an extra set. Before her offer, he hadn't put much thought into what they would need. Since that day, little by little he had acquired most of the supplies for their apartment from Signora Limone. She made extra money selling her mother's belongings, and he saved money by avoiding the high prices at the company store.

"You pat my back. I'll pat yours," Signora Limone had said with a laugh.

She advised him on what he would need mostly without being too insistent on what he should buy from her. The arrangement had worked out well for both of them.

Two of his friends helped him carry two double-sized mattresses up the stairs to the apartment above the supply store. It was ironic that they would be living above the store in an apartment outfitted with nothing purchased from it.

Used, but freshly laundered linens and towels, also procured from Signora Limone, were stacked on the wooden kitchen table. Each of them would have one towel and washcloth, and Appollonia would have one dishrag and two kitchen towels for washing and drying dishes. When he had scoffed at buying two kitchen towels, Signora Limone had informed him that his wife would need one towel for drying her hands and one for drying the dishes. He had given in out of respect, but he didn't like the way she had smiled at him, holding out her hand for more coins. That day she seemed to enjoy bartering with him and then taking his money.

The kitchen would serve as their cooking, dining, and living area, so that the other two rooms could be used as bedrooms. His friends had helped him set up the mattresses in each of the small bedrooms, and Luigi thanked them by giving them enough money to buy a plate of spaghetti at the restaurant.

They wouldn't have a bathroom for bathing, but would pour boiled water into the aluminum tub for a quick bath once a week. Bathing in the river might continue to be his usual practice, as he had to bathe daily and was too big to fit into the small tub anyway. The girls could use the kitchen sink and a soapy washcloth in between their weekly baths. The chamber pot, a fancy name for a tin bucket, would be used in place of a flushing toilet. There was an outhouse behind the building, as well.

Over the last week, he had gathered boxes from behind the restaurant and the supply store to use as containers to store their clothes. He didn't want to spare any more money to buy furniture, and the apartment offered only one small closet in the kitchen that would serve as a pantry. Tomorrow, he would buy enough food for a few days and the girls could gather greens from the field each evening to mix with vinegar and oil for a salad to accompany their soup or pasta, their typical evening meal. Vinegar, oil, salt, and pepper were already on the top shelf of the pantry. On the second shelf were flour, yeast, onions, and a large jug for milk. Appollonia would have to walk each day or so to a farm about a mile away for the fresh eggs, milk, and vegetables they would need. Dry goods could be gotten at the supply store.

He left the towels on the table, and then took the sheets and blankets to his and Appollonia's bedroom to fix their bed. This would be the first time he had ever made up a bed, a task, first his mother, and then his wife, had always done for him. As he did so, he remembered watching Appollonia take the sheets from the clothesline in the yard, and the way the breeze blew her dress and hair and billowed the drying linens. Once each week she smoothed the clean, stiff material over the mattress and slipped ironed pillowcases over fluffy, feather-stuffed pillows. Almost every night, when he laid down on the hard, uncomfortable wood of the boxcar, he thought of the soft mattress and downy pillow in the bedroom of his rustic house and of his wife, who lay alone in that bed. When he closed his eyes, he imagined touching her supple skin and brushing her hair away from her face.

His reverie was interrupted by the realization that he hadn't purchased pillows. Maybe he could make them out of chicken or duck feathers, another commodity Signora Limone would surely be able to supply.

When the bed was ready, he took the remaining sheets and blanket and made up the second bed for the girls. When he finished, he surveyed the apartment's sparse furnishings with a smile. It was simple, but he was proud of it and hoped they would be pleased with their modest new home.

The sun was going down, but a little light filtered through the one window in the kitchen. He was tired and hungry and sat at the table in the closest chair. Digging in his pack he retrieved his meager dinner of bread, cheese, and a green sour apple that he had plucked from a tree behind the supply store. One of the men in the boxcar had slipped him a small canning jar filled with homemade Muscadine wine, and he placed it on the table next to his simple meal. It tasted good with the crusty bread, and he sliced the apple, combining a piece of sharp Fontina cheese with each bite. He wanted to grow grapes himself and make his own wine to drink with his wife's pasta, but he hadn't yet decided whether making wine was worth the chance he took breaking the law. He chuckled at the thought; because the law hadn't kept him from drinking wine that others had given him. Appollonia would want to plant tomatoes for sauce and other vegetables as soon as the weather turned warm. They would make a garden together in a place he had already picked out behind the store.

The meal left him feeling satisfied and ready for rest. He walked to the bedroom where he would soon sleep with Appollonia and laid on top of the blanket. After only a few moments, he began to drift into a dream.

She lay beside him on the bed with her back to him. He took the pins from her hair and it fell onto her shoulders. He stroked her silken waves, and then dropped his hand to her bare back. Her skin quivered, and he pushed his fingers under the blanket that covered her hips to feel the curve of her body. Then he moved closer to her and kissed her neck.

"I love you, Appollonia. We're finally together," he said and touched her shoulder. She sighed, and he kissed her again. Then her body stiffened.

"No," she said, and turned to face him. "It's me you want." It was Islode, and she glared at him with eyes full of anger.

He stumbled from the bed to the door as though her fury were pushing him with a force all its own. There wasn't a knob, so he pressed hard against it, but it wouldn't budge. Then he stood up and banged his fists until they began to bleed.

He woke up and sprang from the bed, his legs trembling and unsteady. His heart raced in his chest, as he looked around the dark room and then down at his uninjured hands. He sat on the bed again and reached to touch the place where Isolde had lain in his dream. It was empty. A feeling of relief came over him. This was the home he had made for Appollonia and their daughters. He wanted his wife here. Isolde didn't belong in his life any longer. He got up and walked through the apartment, searching each shadowed corner. The room was cold, but he unbuttoned the front of his shirt and pulled it away from his neck.

He fumbled for the door in the darkness and jerked it open. It occurred to him that he could sleep in the apartment, but he wanted to wait. He would sleep here for the first time with his family. At last, they would be together. If he could help it, nothing would keep them apart again. He tugged the collar of his coat up around his neck and stepped out onto the small porch at the top of the stairs. The air was brisk, and the moon lit up the sky. At the bottom of the stairs, he turned and walked along in front of the supply store. He didn't look at the windows glowing with light across the street.

Isolde watched from behind the curtain of the restaurant's front window as Luigi walked. When the night swallowed him up at the end of the street, she sank to the floor and wept, and then smacked her hands until they were bruised and she could no longer tolerate the pain. He had never mentioned the apartment he was readying for his family, but she knew that's where he had been.

Signora Limone had told her, and anyone else within earshot, about Luigi's plans. "He's buying all my mother's kitchen wares and towels to make a nice home for his family."

Luigi had never given her a gift or said he loved her, but they had spent many hours in each other's arms. Somehow two years together had been erased from his memory so that he could prepare a home for his family.

She had seen Luigi on the street earlier and kept an eye on the window of the apartment for most of the evening. He stayed inside for a long time. At nightfall he didn't light a candle. The window that faced the street and the front of the restaurant remained black. She wondered what he was doing in the dark.

She couldn't stop thinking of him. The longer she went without seeing him and touching him, the more she wanted him. Each day she felt as if another cloud darkened the horizon of her life. The vastness of the future without him stretched before her like a black hole.

Exhausted, she walked from the dining room to the stairs and began to go up. As she did so, she noticed her dinner on the bar. Another waitress had brought it from the kitchen for her an hour ago. She glanced at it and turned around, going back down the stairs. She quickly surveyed the room. It was empty except for her reflection in the mirror above the back counter, highlighted by the low light of one lantern. She bent down behind the bar and pushed a sliding door underneath it until it was open enough for her to stick her hand inside. Due to Prohibition, the bar in the *ristorante* was supposed to be free of liquor, but Isolde knew the owner kept wine behind a false door in a secret cupboard under the bar. Her hand searched for a notch in the wood and slid open the hidden panel. She blindly groped several bottles until she touched one that felt like a wine bottle and pulled it out into the dim light. Through the clear glass, she saw that it was red with an Italian label. She closed the secret door and the cupboard and stood up. With her free hand she turned the knob for the lantern's wick until the flame was gone. In the nearly dark room, she picked up the plate of cold food and tucked the bottle under her arm, and then tiptoed to her room. She hadn't bothered to take a glass with her. She would drink it all, straight from the bottle, and hoped it would help her sleep.

Chapter 7

"Have a nip," Mario urged.

Alessandro took the flask Mario slipped from his coat pocket. The icy wind blew along the deck as they stood at the bow and watched the ship attack the choppy waves of the Atlantic. With each thrust forward, it sailed closer to New York.

Alessandro sipped from the flask and coughed. He scowled at the younger sailor.

"What's this?" It was a rhetorical question, for he knew what it was.

"Homemade hooch from the Americans," Mario said. "The wine is locked up. Only the captain has a key."

"This tastes awful."

"Italian wine would have been much better, but it's all we've got."

"I can do without it, but the others won't complain."

The hooch did have a warming effect on his frozen body, so he took another drink, coughing again when his throat began to burn.

"Go easy, Mario. You'll feel it faster than wine," he said, passing the flask back to him.

Mario laughed and mumbled under his breath, "I know what I'm doing."

"Yes, so you've told me," Alessandro said. "Just file away what I tell you and remember how you felt the last time you were too stubborn to listen to good sense."

"Okay. I'll go easy." Mario took another pull from the flask before he replaced the cap.

Alessandro put his arm along Mario's shoulder, and they walked to the Falconi's cabin, pulling up the collars on their wool coats to cover their already numb faces.

The ship's horn sounded nine times, startling Giovanna as she finished sewing the hem on her mother's dress. Maria and Evelina stood in front of the small, round mirror on the wall next to the door to assess their reflections. Maria brushed her sister's raven hair.

Giovanna was pleased with the finished dresses and delighted that all of them would be wearing something beautiful and feminine to the dance.

"Mama," she said. "You should wear the new dress when we meet Papa at the train station."

Her mother looked pensive as she sat on her bunk and stared at the comb she held in her hand. Children ran through the hallway outside the cabin door, and their laughter seemed to snap her out of her thoughts. "I think I will. I hope he got my telegram. If he isn't there to meet us, I don't know what we'll do."

"Of course he'll be there. Don't worry, Mama."

Giovanna held up the last dress for her mother. The dresses had been cut from the same pattern with different material for each one. She was happy that her mother had chosen various colors and fabrics instead of buying only one bolt of cloth to be used for all of their dresses. Giovanna slipped into her dress and was smoothing her hair with her mother's antique brush, a cherished gift from her father, when the boys arrived to escort them to the dance.

Alessandro and Mario looked handsome in their uniforms, both smiling and holding out their arms to accommodate all of the Falconi women. Music drifted from the dining hall as they made their way to the party. In her eagerness to get back to the cabin and finish the hem on her mother's dress, Giovanna had eaten almost nothing at dinner. Her stomach rumbled with hunger and panic. She had never danced with a boy before and wasn't sure she would be able to gracefully execute the careful steps she had practiced for only a few minutes with her sisters.

The lower deck was decorated along the wall with a sash of flowers made from paper, artfully cut into delicate petals. Tables had been pushed together to make a circle around a dance floor, with a makeshift stage in the middle, crafted out of supply crates with wooden folding chairs for the musicians. Each table held a lantern and a tray of cookies dusted with bright sprinkles of sugar. Evelina gasped and looked at her mother before she reached for the sparkling treats. Her mother held up one finger, hoping to keep Evelina from taking more than her share. Evelina ate the cookie slowly, and then she took four more and gave one each to her sisters, Mario and Alessandro.

Giovanna smiled and nibbled the sugary delicacy with delight. It was delicious. Maria thanked her sister and stared at the cookie without looking up. Giovanna could see that Maria was as excited and as frightened as a gated racehorse. She had been a jumble of nerves all afternoon at the thought of attending her first dance.

Mario held his hand open and nodded at Evelina. With a giggle she took it and followed him to the dance floor that circled the musicians' stage.

"I feel safer dancing with Evelina until my feet are warmed up," he whispered to Giovanna. He grabbed a cookie from the table and ate it in two bites.

"We're all a little nervous," she said. Alessandro stood behind her chair with his hands on her shoulders. His warm and reassuring grip made her feel safe and she began to relax a little. He didn't ask her to dance or move to sit down. He only held fast to her as though she might float away if he let go.

After the third song, Mario came breathlessly to sit beside Maria. Evelina put her hands on her hips and stared at Mario with disappointment. Alessandro let go of Giovanna's shoulders and offered his hand to Evelina as an accordionist began to play a lively polka. She stood on Alessandro's shoes and held his hands as he twirled her around the floor while she laughed.

"I hope she doesn't slip on his polished shoes," Appollonia said.

Giovanna and Maria sat with their mother at the edge of the dance floor, their faces illuminated by a lantern's glow. Mario had left the table to get them something to drink.

"I don't think I can dance with Mario. I'm too nervous," Maria said, drumming her fingers on the table.

"I'm sweating all over my new dress," Giovanna answered.

"And my hands are shaking." She held them out for Maria to see.

"Evelina's happy to fill in for us," Maria said, pointing. "She's having fun."

"Good. I think it'll take most of the evening for me to work up the courage to stand up, let alone move my feet," Giovanna said.

After several more songs, the music stopped, and her mother waved to Evelina. "Take a break and have something to drink. It's time for your sisters to dance." Whether she meant for the boys to hear her or not, they took that as their signal.

"Ready or not, here we go," Giovanna said.

Mario bowed awkwardly and Maria took his hand. Then, Alessandro offered his hand to Giovanna. As he clasped one of her hands and wrapped the other around her waist, she felt light-headed and squeezed his hand until her legs were steadied.

"I have to keep you at a respectable distance, with only our hands touching, but I want to pull you close to me," Alessandro said. "I hope your mother can't read my mind."

She smiled at him, and then looked away shyly as he moved her carefully around the crowded dance floor.

"Tomorrow you'll float away from me like a leaf carried by the wind. But I won't stop thinking of you when you leave the ship. I'll sail back to Italy without you for now, but I'll find you again, when I move to America. I won't be happy unless I do. I promise," he said.

The other dancers moved around them as he held onto her gaze, his eyes full of tenderness.

He leaned close to her and whispered, "Tonight might be the last night we'll be together for a long time, Giovanna."

Giovanna knew he was right, but she didn't block out the people or the music. Instead, she wanted to remember every detail of the evening. She closed her eyes and memorized the lilting notes of the waltz, played beautifully by the violinist; the way Alessandro's hat rested over his eyes that watched her with affection, and the confident way he held her as they glided over the smooth floor as her mother and Evelina, wearing their beautiful new dresses, smiled at her from the wooden folding chairs. All these sights and sounds she etched into her memory so that she could live the night over and over again.

While she mused, Alessandro guided her swiftly off the dance floor and into a hallway near the kitchen, where women were preparing sandwiches and laughing. Taking his hands from hers, he placed them on her face and pulled her to him, kissing her with a passion that surprised and startled her. Then he whirled her back onto the floor as if they had never left.

Giovanna gasped and dropped her hand from Alessandro's shoulder. She searched his face with frightened eyes. Alessandro took her hand.

"You're upset. I'm sorry," he said, looking at her with concern.

"I'm just...," she said, turning away from him, her voice trailing off.

"You look so beautiful, Giovanna. I've wanted to kiss you since the first moment I saw you."

The room was spinning, and she thought if she looked at him, she might lose control of her emotions. The song ended and he paused, as she still clung to his hand, in the middle of the dance floor. The violinist placed his instrument on his chair and raised his bow to acknowledge the applause of the appreciative dancers. Her mother, in the dress Giovanna had sewn with such care only hours before, clapped and smiled. Giovanna felt as if she were wrapped in a dreamlike haze, and then she heard his voice as the next set of musicians began to tune their instruments.

"Please forgive me," he pleaded, placing his hand gently on the small of her back.

Giovanna didn't speak. Instead she put a quivering hand to her lips and tears welled in her eyes as she moved toward the table where her mother watched Mario bow to Maria and Evelina.

Two final songs were played and the dance was over. It was time for them to go back to their cabin.

As they all walked through the steerage hallway, Alessandro whispered to Giovanna that he would like to see her once more on the deck in the morning before the ship arrived at the harbor in New York City.

Their eyes met when they arrived at her door.

"I'll try," she answered before disappearing into her cabin with her mother and sisters.

By the light of one small candle, each of the girls and Appollonia used the chamber pot and changed into their dressing gowns. They folded their new dresses and placed them on the top of the trunk to be packed in the morning. Though the room was nearly dark, Maria could see Giovanna's face.

"What's wrong?" Maria asked. When Giovanna didn't answer, she grabbed her arm and told their mother they were going to clean the chamber pot together.

Other passengers laughed and talked as they stumbled along the hallway back to their steerage quarters. Giovanna let Maria pull her up the stairs and into the brisk night air where a low fog huddled over the deck.

"Tell me," Maria commanded.

"It's nothing."

"I know something's wrong."

Tears traced a path down Giovanna's cheeks and her brow wrinkled with uncertainty. "Alessandro kissed me. I've never been kissed before. I think I wanted him to kiss me, but not like that. He took me by surprise, and I wasn't expecting him to be so…" she said, pausing to find the right word. "Rough."

"Rough?" Maria asked. "Did he hurt you?" She checked Giovanna's mouth and stroked her hair, drying her tears with her hand.

"No," Giovanna said, "Of course not. Maybe passionate is a better word.

Maria relaxed. "Could he tell you were upset?"

"He said he was sorry. I could tell he meant it."

"He probably couldn't help himself. You looked so pretty tonight," she said. "You like him, too, don't you?"

Giovanna nodded. Maria dumped the contents of the chamber pot over the side rail into the dark ocean.

"We're leaving tomorrow." Maria stepped out of the wind and onto the stairs. "Don't be angry with him. He's probably in love with you."

The wind whistled and Giovanna stepped onto the first step with her dressing gown and robe swirling around her. Was it possible that Alessandro felt that strongly for her? She brushed her hair out of her eyes and felt a tear fall to her face. Was the jumble of emotions she was feeling, love, or just disappointment that the fairy tale would be over by this time tomorrow, when Alessandro would sail with the *SS Roma* back to Italy, and she would step onto the soil of America.

A mist of seawater sprayed the deck and Giovanna shivered. Maria took her hand and they hurried down the stairs to their cabin.

Chapter 8

Outside the boxcar, crickets scraped their wings together in their nightly song. Their noise mixed with the sounds of sleeping men and the intermittent rustle of the trees when the wind blew. It was well after midnight. Luigi and Vincente lay on thin mats only inches apart, surrounded by the chirping of the male crickets calling to the females.

"Luigi, are you awake?" Vincente asked in English.

"Italian, Vincente," Luigi whispered. Though he was learning English, he was tired and wanted the ease of his native language. It was his custom to be asleep long before this hour, but tonight he was restless.

"I want to speak English, Luigi. Let's practice, so we can work a better job than this hellhole," Vincente insisted.

"What do you want to talk about in the middle of the night, Vincente?"

"You're taking the train tomorrow to meet your family?"

"*Si*, I am."

"You're happy?"

"I've worked a long time for this day."

"You're a lucky bastard."

"*Si*, Vincente," Lugi said. He could hear the anguish in his friend's voice. "Soon your family will join you, too. It won't be long now." The wind that had been sneaking its way through the splintered cracks of the boxcar settled, and he closed his eyes. "Let's sleep."

"Luigi?" Vincente whispered. He put his hand on Luigi's shoulder. "What about Isolde?"

Luigi rolled onto his back. "It's over. She knows they're coming. I told her from the beginning that my family is everything to me."

"Just like that. *Finito?*"

"*Si, finito.*"

"I don't think it's over for her."

"She knows my family is what I want. I won't see her again."

"I see the way she looks at you. She's up to something."

"What do you mean?" Luigi asked, sitting up on his pallet to face Vincente. He was surrounded by shadows.

"Her heart shows in her eyes. It's no good."

"Don't worry about her. Go to sleep."

"*Non abbassare la guardia,*" Vincente answered before closing his eyes. *Don't let down your guard.*

Luigi wanted to pretend Vincente was wrong about Isolde, but his thoughts were filled with the notion that she might make trouble for him. He would keep his eye on her, and as soon as he heard about a job from Bernandino, he would move his family, without telling anyone where they were going.

If he wanted to leave immediately, Bernandino would have to know the truth. Telling Appollonia's brother about his infidelity and the need to get away from the woman he had turned to in his loneliness would be very difficult. Appollonia's family loved her, and Bernandino wouldn't understand how he could betray her. Dealing with his anger, however, would be easier than the fury he could expect from her older brother, Erasmo. He was lucky that Bernandino was the one who lived in America. His kinder brother-in-law would help him, if for no other reason, than to insure the happiness of his sister and her children. Luigi was counting on this and was willing to take any beating, verbal or physical, that Bernandino thought he deserved.

Any punishment his brother-in-law chose would still be insignificant compared to the suffering within his own heart. His conscience kept him awake at night long after the other men adjusted to the cold or their uncomfortable sleeping pallets. The only way he could resolve his inner conflict was to pledge he wouldn't stray again. Many nights he argued with himself, wondering if he should confess to Appollonia. The burden of the secret would lift from his shoulders, but he had convinced himself that relieving his guilt would only transfer the anguish from his own heart to hers.

He didn't think she was strong enough to handle his betrayal, and it was selfish to consider telling her. It was his load to carry, and he would lighten it by becoming a better man.

As the Americans like to say, he was *turning over a new leaf*, and the transgressions of the past were best forgotten. It was the only way to move forward, promising himself that his family would come first. In the morning, his life would start anew when he began his journey to meet them. He vowed he would make things right by being a good husband and a good father. He fell asleep thinking about the future. The past was over and he hoped Isolde realized it and would move on.

Lying in bed, Isolde opened her eyes and stretched as the sun began to come up. For the first time in days, she felt a trace of contentment. Fate had presented her a moment when she could feel the satisfaction of controlling something in Luigi's life, if not her own.

Yesterday she had arrived at the post office to find the front counter empty. The postmistress hummed as she sorted mail in the back room. On the counter, a stack of telegrams sat unattended next to the bell that customers could ring when they needed help. With her long, thin fingers poised over the ringer, Isolde noticed that the top telegram was addressed to Luigi Falconi from The *SS Roma*. She moved her hand away from the bell and instead slipped Luigi's telegram into her pocket, thinking that she would give it to him herself.

When she turned to leave, he opened the door as she pushed on the glass to walk out into the afternoon sunshine. This was her chance to speak to him after many days of unhappiness. Her fingers felt the rough paper of the telegram, and she smiled, but he didn't smile back. Instead, he looked right through her. The heat of anger rose up her neck and flushed her face as her hand closed around the telegram in the torn pocket of her dress.

With veiled anger, she tried for his attention. "I need to talk to you, Luigi."

He didn't speak. For an instant, he stood still, and then instead of going into the post office, he brushed past her and walked back to the street and on toward the boxcars without looking back. As though her hand had a mind of its own, it reached toward him, and then snapped back into her pocket, when she realized how pathetic her attempt to break his armor of detachment had been.

A cloud drifted over the sun, and darkened the street as she clutched the telegram. His moment of indifference erased any thought she had of giving it to him. When she reached the porch of the restaurant and opened the door, voices and laughter floated toward her. She went to the stairs and ignored the greetings of a waitress and several miners. All she could think of was Luigi's vacant stare. Alone in her room, she lit a candle and sat on the bed where she and Luigi had shared many nights together. Then she unfolded the telegram and read its message.

The ship will arrive one day early. Please meet us at the train station. We will wait for you. Love, Appollonia.

Feeling a moment of triumph, she crushed the paper in her fist and hid it inside her pillowcase. Luigi wouldn't know of his family's early arrival.

Appollonia. It was a melodious name. Isolde wondered about the color of her hair, the beauty of her face, and the sound of her voice. Luigi had never mentioned her by name, and she had never asked.

In the morning, she would take the matches from her nightstand and burn the message. They would wait for him for many hours. Maybe they wouldn't be able to find their way, or worse. It wasn't her problem. It was Luigi's fault for ignoring her. It dawned on her that she was being coldhearted, but she didn't care. If she couldn't find a way to have a life with him, she would shrivel up like a wilted flower and die. Life without a purpose was empty and meaningless. Having a family of her own with Luigi would be her purpose. She didn't care that he already had one.

Luigi awoke when the other men began to stir and go outside to relieve themselves in the woods. Reaching beside him for his frayed, but scrubbed, clean clothes, he dressed in the soft light of the morning, and filled his pack with the fruit and candy he had bought as a surprise for his daughters. While the other miners were shoveling and sweating in the mine for the next two days, he would be traveling to New York and back. The foreman had authorized these two days off, only because he had worked overtime for two weeks.

Some of the men were jealous of his reunion with his family, but most of them patted him on the back or shook his hand to show their support, as he walked in the morning mist to catch the train. Those who had families in the old country looked forward to the day when they, too, would be reunited with their loved ones. Some of them joked about how easy the single life was without the ties and obligations of family, but they were only making light of their situation. Even the young men longed for the comfort of being with those who knew and loved them best. Young Italian women were few and far between in the hills of West Virginia, and they were for the most part, the only women they wanted. The language and cultural barrier was too much of a struggle with American women. Italian-American men felt most comfortable with what they found familiar: Italian food, wine, women, friends, family, and their native language. Assimilating into the American way of life was best done, in their opinion, surrounded by *paesan* from the old country.

As Luigi walked, he imagined Appollonia and his daughters going through debarkation at Ellis Island. He hoped and prayed that the authorities would find no reason to prevent them from entering the country. He knew they would be asked questions, which if answered incorrectly, would destine them to deportation.

Most of the questions about their occupation, literacy, last residence, destination, type of immigration, and ports of embarkation and debarkation would be asked by a crewmember on the ship, and were routine and of no consequence. Luckily, the more serious and feared questions (Did the émigré pay for their own passage? And, did they have a job waiting for them by reason of any offer or solicitation in the United States?) wouldn't be a problem for Appollonia and the girls. These two questions, he had been told, had originated from American efforts to put an end to the *padrone* system, a practice among certain foreigners residing in the United States of importing men to work in the construction of railroads.

On his first trip to America, he made friends who worked for a *padrone*, someone who was connected with men in Europe, who had convinced them to come to the United States to work. As soon as they got off the boat, the *padrone* controlled everything about their lives and took a cut of the money they made. These laborers had no intention of becoming citizens. They were temporary immigrants who came solely for the purpose of making money to send home, where they would return themselves eventually, after being taken advantage of. The only one who came out a winner was the *padrone*.

Luigi had been subjected to these questions, himself, on both of his debarkation experiences at Ellis Island. The first time he traveled to America to work on the railroad, he had, luckily, been warned by those from his village who had come before him, not to become involved with a *padrone*. Their offers were enticing, and had he not been warned, he would've fallen into this trap set by smooth talkers with shady promises. He was an uneducated farmer, but his intuition told him to trust his *paesan*. He was thankful for their advice.

Luigi knew that Appollonia and the girls wouldn't be deported for being suspected of moving to America temporarily for employment. His worries rested on the misfortune that they might become sick during the journey and wouldn't be able to pass the physical inspection, or that Appollonia's asthma would be considered a weakness. The girls were all healthy, as far as he knew, but there was always a chance that they might contract an illness while traveling on the ship. He had cautioned his wife to hide the fact that she was an asthmatic. He didn't want her frailty to be taken as a sign of poor health. The worry of all that could go wrong between now and when their ship docked made his head ache. Their fate, he supposed, was in God's hands.

Closing his eyes, he bowed his head to pray for his family.

A chill rattled his thin frame as he came upon the train station and saw the smoke puffing into the damp air from the train's smoke stack. The mist had settled a fine layer of moisture on his topcoat, so he shook like a dog hoping to leave most of the water on the path. When he found a spot in the car with open seating, he placed his pack with the presents and his lunch on the seat next to him and laid his sodden coat beside them. The train held few passengers, and he hoped he would be able to sleep on the long ride to New York. Within minutes, the whistle blew and the ticket agent walked the aisle, politely asking for each passenger's ticket. As soon as his ticket was punched, he closed his eyes and relaxed his weary mind and body, and fell into a deep sleep.

Chapter 9

The sky was overcast and a steady rain fell as the *SS Roma* skimmed the choppy waters of the Atlantic on the last day of its voyage. The luxury liner was due to arrive at the New York harbor in less than an hour. Below deck, Appollonia finished her packing and checked to be sure none of her belongings were still in the small cupboard under the sink of the cabin. Certain that she had packed everything, she relaxed on the bottom bunk and studied Giovanna, who sat on her own bunk.

"Mario's been to the cabin three times. Each time, Maria's told him that you aren't ready yet, though you clearly are. Why don't you want to go with Mario to meet Alessandro? Are you mad at him?" she asked.

"A little," Giovanna answered, looking down at her hands.

"What's wrong?"

"Nothing," Giovanna said.

It wasn't like Giovanna to harbor bad feelings, but something had caused her to quarrel with Alessandro, she supposed. She ignored her usual inclination as a mother to press for more of an answer and instead said, "Then you should go with Mario when he returns. He said he'd be back in a few minutes."

Giovanna gave her a thoughtful look, then went to the trunk for her sewing kit and unraveled it. She took out a thimble, threaded a needle, and began to darn a pair of socks.

"I might be ready then," she said.

Evelina fidgeted on her bunk and sighed with boredom. Then she jumped into the middle of the room and said, "Mama, when Mario comes back, may I go with him? My suitcase is packed. I'm just in the way here."

"Yes," Appollonia answered. She knew Evelina was tired of watching the forlorn Giovanna. She trusted Mario and knew

Evelina wouldn't leave his side.

"Good," Evelina sighed.

Appollonia watched her troubled eldest daughter as she opened her suitcase and looked inside. Across from Giovanna, Maria dangled her legs on the edge of her bunk and kicked her feet into the air.

"What's wrong with Giovanna, Maria?" Appollonia whispered.

Maria shook her head. "Don't bother her, Mama. She doesn't want to talk about it," she said, jumping down from her bed. "I think I'll go fetch your tea."

There was too much to do so she took Maria's advice and let it go. After they were cleared to remain in the United States and had settled in at the train station to wait for Luigi, there would be plenty of time to see what was troubling Giovanna. Luigi's train would arrive sometime in the afternoon near dinnertime. She had been notified that the screening process at Ellis Island could take most of the day.

Before locking her suitcase, she took from the side pocket, the antique brush set Luigi had given her many years ago. Anticipation at the thought of seeing her husband filled her heart as she combed her hair and stared at her reflection in the mirror. She stood up straight with her shoulders back. The new dress helped her look less dowdy than the black dress Evelina found so hideous, and it cheered her. She had hidden her money in a secret pocket in the lining. Giovanna had made the concealed pouch for the little bit of money they carried with them, for they had been told tales about personnel at the debarkation station who stole and extorted money from arriving foreigners.

When Appollonia had questioned Alessandro about this possibility, he reassured her.

"Most of the people who work at the debarkation station are kind. The bad things you've heard about happened a long time ago when the immigrant receiving station was at Castle Garden. It's been converted into an Italian opera house. I haven't heard of anyone having problems at the new facility."

"That's good, but I think we should be cautious," she answered. "Luigi made me promise to trust no one completely. I'm not suspicious by nature, but I plan to do what he asked. He said to keep the girls close and the little bit of money I have tucked away."

"It's good advice. It never hurts to be careful."

Her level of anxiety increased as she touched the pocket one more time to make sure the money was there. She knew being apprehensive might aggravate her asthma, so she concentrated on the brush as it scratched her scalp, fantasizing with each stroke about how happy she and her girls would be when they were reunited with Luigi.

The years had been lonely without him, but raising her girls had filled her days with happiness. She wished her husband had not missed so much of their childhood, but while she cared for them, he worked to secure their future. All of what they had been through was for their daughters.

With each day that passed, Appollonia thought more and more about living with Luigi again. Though they had been married many years, she was closer to other family members than she was to her husband. A ridiculous thought, considering she had conceived three children with him, but he had lived in America for most of their marriage. At forty years old, she was not the fresh, attractive girl he had fallen in love with in his twenties. Her figure was thicker, after carrying and birthing three daughters. Lines were forming around her mouth and at the corners of her eyes, and her hair didn't glisten like the lustrous hair of a young woman. The worries of life and the increasing severity of her asthma made her feel tired and drained of energy. Would he notice that she was a worn version of the girl he had once longed for with passion and excitement? Certainly he would, but would he love her anyway?

Luigi would be different than her last recollection of him, naturally, but she wouldn't care as long as he was still kind and loving toward her and the girls. She had no photographs of him from the last six years, only a memory of his eyes as he leaned in to kiss her, and a faint remembrance of his figure as he climbed aboard a wagon bound for Genoa, where he would catch a ship to America. If his hair and his mustache were beginning to gray or his shoulders were stooped, she would long at first for the young man of her memory, but she was realistic about the effects of the passage of time. A man's outward appearance was not the most important quality to a woman. If his soul remained the same, holding the kind spirit that she loved about him, she would find him just as attractive as she had when they had first met. If his heart still wanted to be with her alone, she would be content. Would he still feel passion when he touched her? Would she? He was her husband. If she didn't feel close to him at first, she would in time. They would somehow rekindle those feelings from their youth.

If he had fallen in love with another woman while he was away, then he wouldn't have sent for her and the girls, she supposed. This thought eased the moments of uncertainty she experienced when she couldn't sleep, when her insecurities forced their way through her logic while she lay awake in the dark, missing him. If he wanted her to be with him in America, then he missed her and wanted to have a life together from now on. This made sense to her, and she concentrated all of her thoughts on hoping it would be so.

There would be adjustments. She was prepared to compromise. He would want to be the head of the family, so she would have to step back at times. They had never lived together with three children. He didn't know Evelina and had not seen Giovanna and Maria since they were very young. They didn't know him and weren't used to the stern voice or strong ways of a man, for they had only lived with her or other female relatives until recently when they'd spent time with her brother, Erasmo.

Everyday, she spoke to her daughters of their father, reminding them to keep him in their hearts and minds.

"Your father loves you as I do," she said each night as she tucked them into bed. "Ask God to keep him safe and healthy."

"Will we see him again?" they always asked.

"Of course, and when we do, show him respect and appreciation. He's working hard for us in America, and soon we'll join him."

She wanted them to be aware of his sacrifice and love for them.

"We'll think kind thoughts," Giovanna said.

Maria added, "And pray for him."

"And rest for him," Evelina said. "Since he's working so hard."

Appollonia had tried her best to nurture their future relationship, and her own with their father, in anticipation of their approaching reunion. She hoped it had been enough to prepare all of them for the change they would soon be experiencing.

As man and wife it would take time for them to return to living together with ease and familiarity. When Luigi had travelled to America and returned to her for a visit, it had taken many days for them to settle into a regular routine and to feel comfortable with the changes that life had wrapped around them. This time the stress of the voyage and moving to a new country layered more worry on her shoulders. Life with Luigi had to work. Returning to Italy would be out of the question. Life in America was the only future for her daughters, and she would do her best to make it a good future for them. She couldn't contemplate returning to their homeland.

Maria came into the room with the cup of tea. Appollonia smiled at her middle daughter, who was such a sensitive and dear child, and put on a brave face. With each sip of the soothing tea, she took a deep breath and tried to relax.

Each morning of the voyage, she had taken a stroll with her daughters. Her health had improved since that first day, and she hadn't experienced any more fainting spells.

The doctor passed them on several of their walks. "I'm happy to see you feeling healthy and well cared for, Signora," he said each time.

"I know I'm lucky to have such devoted children. They're better than money in the bank," she'd answered. Evelina liked to repeat this phrase whenever someone spoke of being lucky.

She smiled now, thinking of Evelina and how much she was enjoying the trip. Each day she played paper dolls with Lucia, the girl she met on the first day of their voyage. As the girls cut out and dressed their delicate paper dolls, Appollonia sat in a lounge chair and enjoyed the sunshine. She had never before relaxed in the sun doing nothing and probably never would again. Lucia's mother smiled at her, but they didn't carry on a conversation, as she always seemed busy reading or talking with her husband.

Their voyage had been filled with luck as well, until two nights ago when they had endured the only bad weather of the trip.

They were preparing to turn in for the night, when the wind assaulted the ship in powerful gusts, and driving rain pelted the polished deck and steel hull of the craft that was their only protection from the wrath of a sudden storm. The luxury liner cut through the rough waves like a plow through rocky soil, and the passengers were pitched about the ship.

They kept from sliding about the cabin and slamming into each other by hanging onto their bunks, but the swaying ship caused a violent seasickness that plagued them for half the night.

"It's going to be a rough ride," Alessandro had warned them, as soon as he learned from the captain of the impending storm.

"But don't worry, the ship can handle almost anything the sea dishes out."

The girls felt secure with this guarantee from their brave new friend, but Appollonia remained quite fearful until the fury of Mother Nature calmed. She was thankful her daughters weren't frightened by the tempest, but she felt enough trepidation for all of them.

Alessandro checked on them the next morning as soon as he was able to leave his post, one of many thoughtful gestures he had shown them on the voyage.

"Hope you ladies are alright this morning. Mario and I are here to clean your cabin."

"I can't let you clean our mess," Appollonia said, holding her hand out for the mop Alessandro leaned against.

"We're experts," Alessandro said. "You ladies wait in the hallway for a few moments, and we'll make your room ship shape."

She remebered how they had gently pushed her out into the

hallway, where she and the girls had reluctantly waited until the boys were finished with their work. She wasn't used to being taken care of in such a fashion and appreciated their kindness. They were especially considerate for young men and had watched over her and the girls with genuine concern and affection. Thinking of Luigi's words of caution, she knew that she had taken a chance putting her faith in their goodness. They had made the journey easier for her and very pleasant for the girls. She hoped she would see them again someday and could repay their kindness.

Someone knocked three times on the door, interrupting Appollonia's reverie. She opened it and peered at Mario who stood waiting in the hallway. Evelina saw him and jumped up, reaching toward Giovanna to pull her from her bunk.

"Come with me, Alessandro is waiting," Mario said. He looked around the door's edge. "All of you."

Giovanna looked at her sister and then at her mother. "I'm tired of being mad."

Appollonia was glad to see Giovanna's face brighten.

"Go on. Tell the boys thank you for everything."

Mario stepped into the doorway and tipped his hat to her.

"Good luck to you in America, Signora Falconi. It's a pleasure to know you."

"The pleasure's mine, Mario. God bless you."

"Thank you ma'am. God bless you as well."

Evelina sighed with exasperation, "We're all blessed. Now let's go see Alessandro."

Appollonia laughed at Evelina's impatience. "Yes, okay, go. I'll see you on deck."

Mario bowed and took the trunk with him, promising to return for the other bags. Appollonio offered him a coin as a tip, but he refused, closing her hand.

"Spend it in America and think of me," he said with a smile.

Appollonia took one last look at the cabin before going to the upper deck. Out of habit, she had neatly made her bed, instructing the girls to do the same. She sat on her bunk and took several deep breaths, and then stood before the mirror to pin on her green identification number that each steerage passenger was required to wear. Alessandro had prepared her yesterday. "Your first stop will be at the Lower Bay of New York Harbor. There you'll be placed in quarantine. You might have heard of the social equality of America, but when it's time for your medical examinations, you'll see that the steerage passengers don't receive the same treatment as the first and second-class passengers, or those who are already American citizens. They'll receive a quick inspection on board and will be let off at a pier at the tip of Manhattan, where they will be greeted by their friends and family."

"What about us?" Appollonia asked.

"You'll be rounded up and loaded aboard a barge for your trip to Ellis Island. There you'll have a more thorough physical exam. You'll first go to the Registry Room, a big high-ceilinged room with many lines of immigrants waiting their turn to be inspected. The physical examinations will be performed in another room, Judgment Hall, by a team of uniformed Marines," Alessandro said.

"The Marines are doctors?"

"No, they're soldiers."

Appollonia frowned.

"It's okay. They're trained for this job," Alessandro continued. "When there aren't too many immigrants waiting to be inspected, this might take forty-five minutes. If the lines are long, you could wait three or four hours. If the inspector declares you free of illness or any medical problem, you'll then be released to enter the United States of America."

"I've heard some of the other steerage passengers refer to Ellis Island as *L'Isola dell lagrime*," Appollonia said. "Why is it called *The Island of Tears?*"

It's because immigrant parents worry that they might become separated from their children while going through the inspection process," Alessandro said. " Also, suicides are not uncommon among those who are refused and ordered deported."

"Is it too late to go back to Italy?" Appollonia said, only half joking.

Alessandro laughed. "You won't have to worry about losing

your daughters. They'll stay close to you. You're all healthy as well. No reason for tears."

Thoughts of these possibilities burdened her with incredible concern, even though she had stressed the need for the four of them to stay together while going through the debarkation process. She envied the first and second-class passengers more for the ease they were being afforded to enter the country than for their wealth and status. She didn't pine for wealth or possessions as long as her family was well and happy. Today she could count herself lucky on both points and was thankful for her good fortune.

After taking one last look around, she left the cabin. As she walked to the deck, she reminded herself that only one test remained before they could officially enter the country. If they all passed their medical examinations, she could relax at the train station while waiting for Luigi.

If Luigi's train didn't arrive too late in the day, they would have their evening meal as a family aboard the next train to their new home in West Virginia. Otherwise, they might stay in an inexpensive hotel, all sleeping in the same bed. She smiled knowing that soon she would be relieved of her worries.

Alessandro stood next to Giovanna and placed his hand over hers on the railing as they watched the *SS Roma* glide into the New York harbor. She was no longer upset with him for stealing a kiss. Both of them were at a loss for words as they tried to say goodbye amidst the crowd of passengers marveling at the sight of the many ships in the harbor. Mario was making Maria and Evelina laugh beside them, but Alessandro didn't hear their voices. He was consumed with dread. Giovanna was leaving him, and he wished he could walk down the gangplank with her onto the shores of America.

A noisy group of jovial young Italian men pushed them as they crowded to the railing for an unobstructed view. He could see they didn't feel the weariness of the older men and women who appeared to be relieved to have the journey behind them. Their vitality almost guaranteed that they would pass the impending inspections. Their voices crowed with exuberance, "*Viva La Merica!*" and the crowd joined them.

"I care for you," Alessandro shouted above the cheering crowd.

"I won't forget you," Giovanna said. Then she put her hand on his shoulder and kissed his cheek. He held her and saw her mother look the other way as she dabbed her cheek with a handkerchief.

The kiss surprised and pleased Alessandro, erasing the night of chastisement he had put himself through when he had left Giovanna at her cabin. Though he still felt a lover's anguish at having to part from her, he no longer regretted his impetuous decision to kiss her. She wasn't angry. It gave him a renewed faith in the destiny he was sketching for his future. He closed his eyes for a moment in the midst of the noisy passengers full of anticipation. When he opened them, he saw the wooden deck of the pier.

The ship docked, and the American citizens and first and second-class passengers stood near the gate of the gangplank. Their friends and family waved to them from the pier as they prepared to disembark. Giovanna, her family, and the other steerage passengers would follow them off the ship where they would then transfer to the barge that would take them to Ellis Island for their examinations.

Alessandro only had a few more moments before Giovanna disappeared into the mass of immigrants arriving at the first stop of their adventure. He wanted to tell her he would move to America to be with her as soon as possible. Once she was caught up in the moving, excited throng, he wouldn't be able to touch her again.

"Be safe, Giovanna. Hold on to your mother and sisters."

"Alessandro," she shouted above the noise. The crowd threatened to swallow her up.

"I'll see you again when I come to America," Alessandro shouted. He didn't take his eyes from her.

"I hope it will be soon." Her dark eyes stared at him with longing.

Her mother, Maria and Evelina were beside her now. The

four omen linked hands, making a chain. Mario followed them to the barge, pulling their luggage on a cart.

Alessandro stayed behind at the railing as the Falconi women were swept along with the third class passengers. He straightened his coat and held his head up. He would not put off leaving Italy for America. Every day he worked would bring him one day closer to being with her again. It wouldn't be long before he had enough money saved to travel to his aunt and uncle's home in Michigan.

Mario boarded the ship with the empty luggage cart. Alessandro had never seen him look so glum.

The *SS Roma* sat quietly at the pier. The crew began to clean the ship and prepared to receive supplies for the return voyage. Alssandro hoped it would be the last time he made the trip back to the old country. If he had his way, the next time he traveled on the ship from Italy to America, it would be as a passenger for immigration to the Promise Land.

Chapter 10

The barge crept through the calm waters of the Hudson River as if the captain didn't care that the steerage passengers were impatient to reach Ellis Island and begin their lives in America. It was an uncomfortable ride. Each person leaned against his suitcase, sandwiched between others who stood on their tiptoes to get their first look at the new land.

Appollonia began to wheeze.

"Deep breaths, Mama," Maria instructed, as she watched her mother with concern.

"Yes, deep breaths," Appollonia repeated. She concentrated on her breathing.

"It won't be long," Giovanna said, as she rubbed her back.

Appollonia closed her eyes, and took controlled, deep breaths. She tried not to worry, but dark thoughts of failing the medical exam and the possibility of deportation filled her head.

"We're here," Maria said. Her face beamed with anticipation as they slowed to pull close to the dock.

The Statue of Liberty loomed on its own little island nearby, and Evelina pointed to it, excitedly jumping up and down. "Look!"

Appollonia opened her eyes to take in the majestic splendor of the statue and began to cry, her voice emphatic as she spoke to her daughters. "We've arrived in the land of the free. This is a special moment. Keep the lady of liberty in your memory. Never forgot what she represents."

As the ship docked, the girls stared at the statue, their mouths open and their eyes wide. They stood transfixed by her grandeur, while the other passengers began to gather their belongings.

"She's beautiful," Evelina said. Maria took her hand.

"I've never seen anything so wonderful," Giovanna whispered, holding her neck as she leaned back to take in the full view of the imposing statue.

"Move out of my way," a man with a stern, impatient voice yelled.

Appollonia tried to step aside, but the rude passenger pushed her as she reached for the handle of her suitcase, and she fell into her trunk, cursing his insolence. She wondered how they would carry all of their belongings without a cart or any assistance.

Evelina ran toward the man and kicked him in the shin before her sisters could stop her. He ran ahead ignoring her angry shouts. "I got him good," she declared as several passengers clapped, and her sisters pulled her back to stand near them.

Appollonia glared at her youngest daughter. "Don't run away again." Evelina pouted.

"And thank you for kicking that impolite man," Appollonia whispered, smiling at her fearless daughter.

Evelina smiled back and grabbed the handle of her suitcase. "I'll always protect you, Mama."

Many passengers began to rush by them to get in line for their medical examinations. Giovanna and Maria hurried as well, and had worked out a way to carry a suitcase and push the trunk while leaning hard against it.

"We'll probably be the last ones to reach the examination hall," Appollonia said in resignation.

There appeared to be no one like Mario to help them and no carts of any kind for moving heavy luggage.

Evelina lifted one of the suitcases. Appollonia thought it looked much too heavy and she reached to take it from her.

"I can do it, Mama," Evelina said with determination.

Appollonia let her slide the heavy bag along the deck of the barge, and followed her daughters while turning to get another look at the Statue of the Liberty.

"Look at the tall buildings," Giovanna said, as she pointed to the tip of the island of Manhattan.

"That must be New York City," Appollonia said. "We'll take a ferry there and then board a train to West Virginia."

"I've never seen so many buildings crunched together in one place," Maria said.

From where they stood, the lofty structures appeared to be too close to the water. They looked as if they would topple into the vastness of it and sink into its murky clutches.

Appollonia continued to wheeze. Her labored breathing made a whistling sound as she inhaled the cold air. She closed her eyes and breathed deeply, in and out, becoming more anxious when the rattling sound of her breath didn't subside. The rosary in her pocket was twisted around her fingers as she prayed she would pass her exam. She was filled with a desperation she had never felt before. She wanted more than anything to board the ferry to New York City and meet Luigi at the train station.

The girls pushed the trunk down the gangplank and onto a grassy area.

"Where do we go from here?" Giovanna asked.

Appollonia sat on the trunk and watched the other passengers hurry toward the building as if they were in a race to be at the front of the lines that formed at each doorway.

"Let me think," she said. The chaos around her only added to the overwhelming feeling of confusion she felt.

"I'll help you," offered a voice from behind them. A man wearing a top hat and long coat with a scarf wrapped loosely around his neck approached them.

Once he drew closer, and she could see his face, Appollonia recognized him as *Signore Prima Classe*, the fancy man who was traveling with his wife and daughter, Lucia, Evelina's playmate. They weren't with him now. He smiled at all of them and took the handle on one side of the trunk, instructing the girls to work together to carry the other side. The four of them were able to reach the last line inside the doorway with all of their belongings, and then with the same speed he had appeared, he disappeared. Appollonia shouted a grateful thank you as he melted into the crowd.

"How do you like that?" she said.

She wouldn't have guessed that he would be the only man on the barge to offer them assistance, and wondered why he had alighted with the steerage passengers.

Once inside, they waited in one of the long lines in Judgment Hall. Appollonia began to perspire and continued her effort to control her breathing. Many of the immigrants were apprehensive. Their faces were wrinkled with worry and fear. A Marine escorted several families to an enclosed area for closer inspection. Appollonia prayed they wouldn't be singled out. At least her girls had survived the crossing of the Atlantic without becoming sick or acquiring any lice or other pests that enjoyed hosting on travelers trapped on floating vessels.

"Let me check your hair one more time," she said as she grabbed Evelina's shoulders.

"No, Mama," Evelina said, squirming away from her.

"Just a quick look while we wait."

"You can inspect me," Maria offered and parted the soft curls at the back of her head.

"Come on, Ev. It'll give us something to do," Giovanna said. Evelina stuck her tongue out at Giovanna.

Appollonia rolled up her sleeves. Each of them stood still as she parted their hair and scrutinized their heads for tiny bugs.

"You're clean," she said, and sat on her suitcase with a sigh. It made her feel the tiniest bit better to know the inspectors wouldn't find any lice in their hair.

After waiting for two hours, it was their turn at the table. A man in uniform began examining Giovanna, his lips pursed and his forehead wrinkled with concentration. She was declared fit, and he moved next to Maria, who also passed without question. As he checked Evelina's eyes, Appollonia began to wheeze, and she turned to hide her troubled breathing.

The Marine stopped his exam and studied her.

She gave him a weak smile, but her discomfort was obvious.

"Just a minute," the examiner said in Italian. He raised his hand and shouted, "Translator" as he walked away from them.

"Where's he going?" Appollonia asked.

"Sit down, Mama. I think he's looking for someone to help you," Giovanna said.

He was gone for several minutes and she continued to struggle.

"I'll find a nurse or doctor," Giovanna said.

"No!" Appollonia's voice was hoarse, but firm. She wrung her hands and took off her shawl. "We stay together."

Soon two men marched toward them, one very young and the other, *Signore Prima Classe*. He came to Appollonia's side and put his arm around her shoulder. He had changed from his long overcoat and top hat into the uniform of an inspector. By his manner, he appeared to be in charge. The girls followed as he guided Appollonia to a chair in a room at the far end of the hall, where he gave her water. Then he ordered the young man to bring them sandwiches and fruit.

When the boy had gone, the *signore* reassured her. "I'll be able to help you pass through the inspection area without any trouble. Please, drink, eat and rest. I'll return soon," he said.

Soon the boy returned and they ate the sandwiches and fruit. Appollonia felt better after the meal and relaxed in the chair. She closed her eyes for a moment, rolled her shoulders back, and put her hand into her pocket, tracing the smooth beads of her rosary. Silently she prayed that they wouldn't be deported because of her compromised health. Then she sat up straight in her chair and pinned the wisps of hair that had fallen into her eyes.

After a few moments, *Signore Prima Classe* returned. "I'm an interpreter in charge of immigrant inspection. I understand how you're feeling. My wife and daughter also suffer from asthma. When I saw you on the ship, you seemed in general good health. You also seem like a very nice family. Because I know this about you, I'm going to let you enter the country, if you have someone coming to pick you up." He paused and lowered his voice, "And you mustn't tell any of the others that you've received special treatment."

"My husband is meeting us at the train station in New York City. I promise, I won't tell anyone," Appollonia said. "Thank you for taking care of us."

"You're welcome. Keep your promise and good luck in America," he answered with a smile. Then he tipped his hat and left the room. Each of them gave an audible sigh.

"We made it," Evelina said. "You don't have to worry anymore, Mama."

The young Marine escorted them to the ferry that would take them to New York City. She realized that she didn't know the name of the man who'd done them a tremendous favor. Their trip had been filled with the kindness of strangers, she thought, as she remembered the doctor, Alessandro, and Mario. All of them had been good to her and her girls.

The Marine helped them load their luggage onto the ferry and wished them *buona fortuna* in stilted Italian. Inside, the boat was oppressively warm and the fumes from the fuel were overpowering. Appollonia and the girls decided the deck was better and stood at the railing as the ferry glided across the channel to New York City. Appollonia pulled her shawl over her head as the boat floated through a cloud-like fog and a fine mist began to fall.

Once on land, they found a cab driver that understood their gestures well enough to get them to the train station, where they perched with their trunk and suitcases on a bench to wait for Luigi. The four of them sat together with their arms interlocked and their feet resting on their luggage. They weren't hungry since they had eaten the late lunch of fruit and sandwiches, compliments of the kind inspector. Within minutes, the sun began to set. They leaned against one another and fell, exhausted, into a deep sleep.

Several hours passed. Appollonia opened her eyes and took in the thinning crowd of people who were purchasing tickets and waiting for trains. She looked at the watch Erasmo had given her as a gift. Three o'clock? It wasn't three o'clock in the afternoon, for the windows in the station were dark. Looking around, she saw a large wall clock. It's hands were at nine o'clock. It had to be nine o' clock in the evening. Luigi's train should have arrived long ago. Something was wrong. She searched the faces of the travelers who rushed about, paying her no notice.

She realized that Luigi had made only vague references about where he would meet them. It was possible that his train was late or he couldn't find them. Panic sparked inside her as she wondered how she would ask about his train. The only words she knew in English were hello and goodbye. His train was coming from West Virginia, but she didn't feel comfortable enough to pronounce the name and felt it was likely she would be misunderstood.

Beside her the girls began to stretch and open their eyes.

"Will Papa arrive?" Giovanna asked.

"Go back to sleep. It'll be a little while yet, "Appollonia answered. She touched the number on her chest that labeled her as an immigrant and wondered with growing fear what she would do if Luigi didn't arrive soon.

A man stood alone near the ticket counter and watched her. She glanced at him and looked away, hoping he wouldn't bother them. Another hour passed, and he moved to sit in a seat near her. The girls had fallen back asleep, but she didn't dare close her eyes. Luigi had taught her once how to keep troubled feelings from showing on her face, and she willed herself to appear calm to keep the man from knowing her thoughts.

As the hour grew later, the benches around her began to empty. By eleven o'clock, she and the girls and the mysterious man were the only people left in the seating area near the now deserted ticket counter. Appollonia felt threatened by the man's presence, but she had nowhere else to go. She prayed over her sleeping daughters and sensed more with each minute that passed that Luigi wasn't going to appear before daybreak. It occurred to her that he might have not have received her telegram.

The train slowed to a stop at the station in Harrisburg, Pennsylvania. Luigi awoke with a start and saw the sign on the depot just outside his window. He had been dozing for most of the ride and stood to stretch his arms over his head and shake his stiff legs. It was dark, and he checked his pocket watch for the time. He had slept well past the dinner hour and his stomach was rumbling with hunger. As he sat back down on his seat, the train began to pull away from the depot. His pack and wet coat were still on the seat beside him.

He opened the pack to take out a sandwich, two carrots, a bunch of grapes, and a canning jar filled with water. Since he hadn't eaten for many hours, it tasted better than the paltry repast that it was.

The train would arrive in New York City in the morning where he would probably have to wait for half the day for Appollonia and his daughters. He had brought a little money with him to buy lunch and dinner and hoped that they could catch a train back to West Virginia before evening. He didn't know the schedule, so he would figure out when the next train left while he waited for them. Maybe someone would leave a newspaper lying around, and he could practice reading in English while he waited.

Riding the train reminded him of his first years in America, when he had worked on building miles of railroad track. Resting his head against the cool windowpane and listening to the rhythmic clickety-clack of the wheels gliding over the smooth rails, he remembered that time, years ago. He had been a much younger man, capable of working twelve hours or more each day, six days a week carrying rails and ties, then digging the hard, sometimes frozen earth. It had been grueling work, but he still preferred it to mining.

After being in America for six years, he went back to Italy for a visit. He appreciated his easy days working in the vineyards, eating vegetables from the garden, sleeping in his soft bed, and enjoying the company of his wife and daughters. When the money he brought with him was gone, spent on repairs to the house and necessities, he became restless and traveled to America again. Upon his return, he had found a job in a coal mine that paid better than working for the railroad company. Maybe now it was time to try a different line of work again.

Bernandino had written to him about the steel mills in Ohio. His brother-in-law wanted him to move there with Appollonia and the girls. At first, he had been reluctant to consider the idea, but when he had written back, he told Bernandino that maybe he was right.

Now that he had rested and allowed himself time to think, he knew going to Ohio would be the best possible move for all of them. Bernandino lived with Appollonia's godmother, *Comare* Rosie, in the small town of Yorkville, where many of his neighbors were also Italian immigrants. Several families were *paesan* from Valcaldara, and he knew Appollonia would feel comfortable surrounded by familiar faces. Appollonia was very close with her godmother, who was only a few years older than she. Luigi knew his wife would miss her family in Italy, and *Comare* Rosie would be a friend and substitute sister for her and a substitute aunt for his daughters. Bernandino planned to visit in the next two weeks. He would discuss it at length with him then.

Making Appollonia comfortable was important, but not the main reason for considering a quick change in his plans. Vincente's warning had infected his thoughts, and he had begun to feel uneasy. It was possible that Isolde wouldn't honor her end of their bargain. The more he thought about it, the less he trusted her to keep their indiscretion a secret. Appollonia was sheltered and naïve, but she wasn't stupid. If he spent any time with Isolde, to appease her until he could get away, Appollonia would know. He was the stupid one, thinking he could spend so much time with a woman without her becoming angry when he asked her to step aside. The affair had been a terrible mistake and he hated himself for using Isolde and for weakly giving in to the wanton lust he felt for her.

He kicked the seat in front of him and cursed the difficult situation he had created. His careless behavior threatened to jeopardize the new life he wanted for his family. It hadn't been his intention to turn his break from loneliness into a long-term relationship, but that's what had happened, and it was foolish on his part not to expect repercussions. He couldn't ignore that Isolde might be up to something. Though she had promised to let go, it was becoming clear that it was unlikely that was what she intended to do. He wanted to forget Vincente's words, but he knew his friend was right. If he didn't get away from her, something bad might happen.

The rhythmic hum of the train began to lull him to sleep again. His last thought before drifting off was that he would have to pacify Isolde to ensure her silence until he could slip away. He didn't want to break his vow to himself that he would remain faithful to Appollonia from now on. Somehow he would have to keep Isolde away from his wife. For a short time, he could do it. It was the only way.

He couldn't help remembering something his mother had taught him as a child: *"One lie begets another."*

Each of her daughters slept with their coats draped around them as a blanket, while Appollonia continued to search the faces of the few travelers left in the station. She hadn't moved from the bench in two hours and was thankful that her ability to breathe had improved since their arrival. Afraid to leave the spot or disturb her sleeping children, she continued to hope that Luigi would arrive at any moment and refused to move.

Her feelings were a mixture of determination and growing fear, as the man, who had had been watching and waiting, approached her bench. He smiled and spoke to her in Italian in a kind and gentle tone, but she still didn't trust him.

"Good evening, Signora."

"Good evening," Appollonia replied, placing her arm protectively around her daughters.

"Are you waiting for someone?" he asked.

"Yes"

"It's very late. Perhaps he's delayed."

"Yes," she answered again, remembering Luigi's warning to be cautious.

"I see by your number that you're an immigrant. I have a place you can stay for the night."

"No, thank you. My husband will be here soon," Appollonia replied in a confident voice, wishing she had removed the green immigrant number.

He persisted. "Please let me help you. You can sleep in a clean bed with your children, my wife makes a nice meal, and then I bring you back to the station in the morning. There's no charge. I see you're from the old country, and I want to help. I don't like to see a woman and her children sleeping in the train station."

"You're very kind, but my husband will be here any minute.

"Thank you. Good evening," she said, hoping to dismiss him.

He looked around and stepped closer. Grabbing her arm, he said, "You think you're too good to accept my help. Don't you?" Appollonia tried to pry his hand from her arm, but he tightened his grip.

"Let me go," she said. Her voice was filled with fear.

Evelina opened her eyes, and Appollonia gave her an uncomfortable look. "Papa," Evelina shouted and waved to a man who walked near the ticket counter.

"See. He's here," Appollonia said to the Italian man with as much false excitement as she could affect.

He walked away without turning to look at the man at the ticket counter, who wasn't paying any attention to Evelina.

"Is he a bad man, Mama?"

Appollonia smiled at Evelina and stroked her cheek. "Maybe, but he's gone now thanks to your quick thinking."

"I'm glad the man went away. I didn't like how he was holding your arm and you looked afraid."

"I'm okay now. Go back to sleep. It looks as if we might have to sleep on the bench all night. It's possible that your father didn't receive the telegram I sent from the ship. At the very latest, he'll be here to meet us tomorrow as we originally planned." Appollonia smiled at Evelina and squeezed her shoulder. Giovanna and Maria were still asleep. "You're very smart and brave."

"You'll sleep, too?" Evelina asked, smiling with pride at her mother's complement.

"Of course. Sleeping on a bench in the train station is part of the adventure."

Evelina nestled back into her spot next to Maria. "Mama?"

"Yes?"

"Will I recognize my papa when he arrives? In his picture, he's wearing a hat that covers part of his face."

"He's tall and thin with a dark moustache. I suppose he still has it. And he has the same eyes as you and Giovanna."

"Giovanna says that she remembers that he has a kind smile and loves to eat his spaghetti sprinkled with lots of black pepper."

"Yes," Appollonia said with a laugh.

"I tried to eat my pasta with pepper, but I didn't like it." Evelina, said.

"Too much pepper hides the flavor of the sauce."

"Mama?"

"Yes?"

"When you make spaghetti with garlic, tomatoes, and olive oil for dinner, it's my favorite meal."

"Mine, too, Evelina," Appollonia said, kissing the top of Evelina's head. What would she do without her and her sisters, she thought. "Now go to sleep precious one. Tomorrow we'll see your father."

"Close your eyes, Mama."

Appollonia closed her eyes and hugged her youngest daughter, thinking of the meal Evelina had described. Evelina would be a good cook. She was already helping her in the kitchen. Soon she would make simple, tasty meals without her help. Her sisters were learning to cook, and she wanted to do whatever they were doing and do it just as well.

As Evelina snuggled in next to her, she wondered if Luigi would be wearing the same hat he wore in the photograph. It was hard to believe that years had passed since she had seen her husband's face. She pictured him eating spaghetti with lots of pepper and it made her smile.

The station was quiet. A policeman came to stand a few feet away from her bench. Appollonia hadn't planned on allowing herself to close her eyes, but the reassuring presence of the officer afforded her the chance to give in to the overwhelming fatigue that she couldn't fight.

"Hello," he said in English.

Her eyes fluttered and she looked up at him. He motioned for her to stay seated. She was relieved that he didn't ask her to leave. Luigi had told her stories of being treated badly by American citizens who thought they were better than immigrants.

She wondered if the policeman always worked the night shift at the train station. Maybe he had seen many immigrant families forced to wait overnight for loved ones.

If Luigi didn't appear by then, she would have to trust him to help her. The morning duty officer might not be as kind.

"*New York City!*" the conductor announced, as Luigi's train slowed to a stop at his destination.

He found a restroom inside the station where he relieved himself and washed his face and hands. He looked for a ticket agent to help him, but stopped when he saw a pretty girl brushing the hair of a younger girl who sat on her lap.

Both girls looked disheveled, as if they had slept in their clothes, but there was no mistaking the pleasant countenance of the older child. She looked just like his sister and a little bit like his own reflection. He was certain it was Giovanna, and the younger girl in her lap must be Evelina. He knew he should go to them, but he took a moment to stare and take in the sight of his oldest and youngest daughters without their awareness of him. He watched them laughing and poking each other good-naturedly and smiled. Tears formed in his eyes as a ticket agent touched him on the shoulder.

"Sir, is something wrong?" she asked with concern.

He turned away and walked toward his daughters. "My girls," he whispered.

Luigi saw Appollonia a short distance away. When their eyes met, she quickened her step and pulled their middle child along by the hand. He held his hand up in a wave and sighed at the sight of them. Maria, a beautiful girl with a surprised look on her face, gave him a shy smile.

"Is that …" He heard his middle daughter say.

"It's your papa."

"Why are you crying, Mama?"

"Tears of joy!" Appollonia said.

Maria let go of her mother's hand and ran to stand near her sisters.

Luigi stopped at the bench, and his daughters looked up at him.

"I'm your papa," he said, as he reached for them.

Evelina looked to her mother, who was out of breath.

Appollonia nodded and wiped her tears with her hands.

Luigi hugged Giovanna and Evelina, then Maria, and finally

Appollonia. After pulling away from his wife, he held her by the shoulders, at arm's length, and surveyed her up and down with a smile.

"I'm so happy you're here, Appollonia," Luigi said, embracing her again.

"Yes, I'm happy, too," she answered, tears flowing.

"I've never seen a man cry before," Evelina said.

Luigi hugged Appollonia again as they smiled and cried at the same time.

He held her for a long moment as a flurry of people hurried by.

"My stomach is growling," Evelina said. She rubbed her eyes.

"Do you need some breakfast?" Luigi asked. Her dark hair made her look exotic, and her eyes twinkled with mischief. She was the most beautiful child he had ever seen.

Evelina nodded.

Maria stared at him. He reached out to touch a wisp of curly hair that framed her lovely face. As a small child, her hair had been blond. It was darker now. Her nose and mouth were identical to her mother's, but her eyes were uniquely her own. They were filled with kindness and innocence. He patted the top of her head and received a timid smile.

He moved his hand to Giovanna's shoulder, and she smiled as well. She was much taller than Appollonia or Maria. Her features were so much like his own that he felt a catch in his throat when he looked into her eyes.

He kissed Appollonia, and she blushed when he released her. Then he pulled her close to him and closed his eyes as he relaxed into her familiar embrace, stroking her hair. His wife. The woman he had loved as a young man and loved still. When he released her, he could see the girl she had been in her eyes and remembered falling in love with her. Though she looked tired and older, he still found her beautiful. He was overcome with happiness that they were finally together. There would be no more years of separation and longing.

A policeman walked toward Luigi.

"I'm happy to see you, sir. You're the husband and father of this family?"

"Yes, sir," Luigi answered.

"It's nice to see a happy family," the policeman said, tipping his hat.

"Thank you. I'm very happy to see them, even happier than I could have imagined."

"You take care. I'm going home to see my wife. I suddenly feel like kissing her."

Luigi laughed and kissed Appollonia again.

Luigi saw another man staring at them from the ticket counter. He tipped his hat in their direction.

"Do you know him from the boat?" he asked.

"No, he's nobody," Appollonia said. Her voice quivered and she glared at the man.

"He tried to get us to go home with him last night," Evelina interjected.

"He did?" Luigi asked. He looked at Appollonia with concern.

"Yes," Evelina said, "but we outsmarted him."

"Should I talk to him?" He studied his wife's face. She was smiling now.

"No, Luigi," Appollonia said. "No harm was done."

"We're hungry, Mama," Giovanna said.

"Of course you are," Appollonia said.

Luigi laughed. "Let's eat!"

Dragging their trunk and suitcases, Luigi took them to a coffee shop and ordered eggs and toast. The waitress brought them glasses of ice water to drink.

"This is too cold, Pop," Evelina said. Appollonia had written him that the girls were planning on calling him the American version of papa. He liked the way it sounded.

"Americans like to drink very cold water," Luigi said. "Now, tell me about your trip. Was the food as good as your mother's?"

"It was good," Giovanna said, "but not that good."

"We went to a dance. I danced with two boys," Evelina said.

"Really?" Luigi said. "I bet they fell in love with you."

"Both of them," Maria said.

"Were you comfortable?" Luigi asked.

"We had our own room. Not everyone did. It was very nice," Giovanna said.

"Thank you, Luigi," Appollonia said, putting her hand on his.

"I wanted to surprise you with a good room."

"It wasn't like the first class rooms," Evelina said.

"Ev," Maria scolded.

"It was better," Ev said quickly.

Luigi smiled. "Good. What about the weather?"

"It was mostly good," Appollonia said.

"Except for the storm," Evelina interrupted.

Giovanna wrinkled her nose, and said, "Please, let's talk about it later."

"Was it rough?" Luigi asked with a laugh.

"Yes, very rough, but only one night," Appollonia answered. "Now tell us about our new home."

Luigi described the town of Covel and the apartment he had prepared. Evelina asked if they could have a dog or a cat, and Giovanna and Maria wanted to know what the school was like and if there were any other children their age in the neighborhood. Appollonia looked tired, but she smiled and relaxed next to him in the booth as he answered their daughters questions.

"I've missed you," Luigi said, as they finished their meal.

"We missed you, too," Appollonia said.

"I missed you," Evelina said. "Even though I am just meeting you for the first time."

Luigi laughed.

"Mama showed us your picture every day and we prayed for you every night," Giovanna said.

"She didn't want us to forget you," Maria added.

"I looked at your picture and prayed for you each night before I fell asleep, too," Luigi said. He swallowed hard and his eyes filled with tears. Evelina smiled at him and he patted her small hand on the table. Her whole hand fit inside the palm of his.

They finished their meal and walked back to the train station. The girls took the smaller suitcases and he lifted the trunk. He heard them whispering about sleeping on the bench in the station all night.

"You slept all night on the bench?" Luigi asked.

Appollonia nodded. "You didn't get my telegram telling you that we would be a day early?"

"No," he said. "I didn't receive a telegram."

"It doesn't matter now," Appollonia said. "You found us."

He wondered what could have happened to it and was suddenly overcome with a feeling of alarm. Could Isolde have intercepted the telegram? Maybe he should have spoken to her at the post office, but her presence had made him shudder. With dread gnawing at him like a parasite, he hurried his family to the train. As they settled into their seats, he felt light-headed and opened the window. A gust of cool spring air drifted into the stuffy train car as it began to move. Appollonia and the girls watched the countryside rush by them in a blur for a short time and then fell asleep. Luigi felt restless and loosened the top buttons of his shirt. The anxiety that had plagued him since the night of Vincente's warning had turned into a real fear. Was Isolde already causing trouble?

Chapter 11

In the early monring hours at the *ristorante,* Isolde and another waitress packed lunches that the miners could buy on their way to work, but only one of them was needed to serve lunch. Today it was Isolde's turn. It was just as well. If it hadn't been her turn, she would have stayed in her room brooding over the thought of Luigi with his family. She alternated between feeling sorry for herself and seething in anger. One minute she cried and the next she plotted ways to ruin his family life, or convince him to run away with her and leave his wife and children behind.

She rubbed her back with one hand as she filled the water pitcher with the other. The soreness in her back and the cramps in her side were painful reminders that her plan to trap Luigi with a child had failed. She wasn't even sure that she wanted to have a child, so she wasn't disappointed about not being pregnant, except that it seemed the only way to keep Luigi tied to her. If she could think of another way, she would spare herself the trouble of a baby.

Yesterday, while Luigi was gone, she had visited his new apartment, sneaking up the side stairwell after nightfall. It was a risky undertaking, but her curiosity had practically propelled her up the stairs to see where he would be living with his wretched family. She had picked the simple lock with her hairpin and walked through each room feeling a knot of jealousy pulling tighter and tighter with each step. She laid on one of the beds to rest her head, closed her eyes and pretended that he was rushing around the train station looking for his wife and daughters with urgency, and then resignation when he couldn't find them. She fantasized that he would return to the apartment alone and find her waiting there, asleep on the rough cotton sheets in the cold room. In her imagination, he slipped under the blanket and whispered that he was glad he couldn't find them and told her he would never leave her again. She fell asleep there, awoke at dawn and slipped down the stairs, leaving the bed unmade.

She felt wicked and pleased that she had slept in the bed he would share with his wife. He would be unhappy with her at first, but scolding her would give him a reason to talk to her, and she could tell him of her fantasy. She knew he wouldn't be able to resist the image of her in his bed, even if it made him angry at first. If she couldn't tempt him to make love to her, then she would tell him that soon Appollonia would learn that she was his lover. Either way he would come back to her when he saw that her desire for him was too great to be set aside. Her passion was fueled by the challenge of winning him back, and she felt sure that Appollonia would be no match for her cunning or her beauty.

Luigi had shown her a picture of his family. His wife was plainer than she and at least ten years older. Her face was serious and her figure small and thick. Isolde judged her to be boring and unimaginative. In the picture, it looked as if most of the spark had fizzled from her personality. After the first day, he hadn't mentioned his family again. It had been foolish of her to think that he wasn't going to send for them. She wanted to pretend they didn't exist. Her two years with Luigi had been good, and she had deluded herself that he wanted her alone.

A month ago, when he casually declared they would be arriving in a matter of weeks, she was blindsided. Up until the last night they were together, she had convinced herself that he would change his mind. She had hidden her anger in the hopes that he would see she was the one with whom he should spend the rest of his life, but he was old-fashioned and thought he could go back to being in love with a wife and family he'd long ago left behind. She had misjudged how tied he was to them. Just as Vittore had been tied to his wife.

This time would be different. Luigi could be persuaded to see that she was worth his time. Before long she would be living in the apartment above the supply store.

Chapter 12

The weather was warmer and daylight stretched a little longer into the evening now that it was late April. Luigi hurried down the road just before darkness painted the sky an ominous black. He stopped to wash in the stream before going to his simple apartment, so that when he arrived his family could sit down to dinner without waiting for him to wash up. He had scared Evelina the first day she saw him after his workday in the mine. Wearing his miner's hardhat and covered in coal dust, he opened the door to find her alone in the kitchen. She screamed at the sight of his soot-coated skin. Though she wasn't easily frightened, she also wasn't used to a man entering the house without knocking, especially one so dirty. She ran to the bedroom to hide behind her mother. Luigi had bathed in the stream each day after that, chuckling to himself as he splashed the cold water over his skin.

He found himself content at the end of each day to come home to a hot delicious meal, Appollonia, and his three delightful daughters. The apartment was warm from the woodstove, and a much better place to live than the boxcar filled with tired, grumpy men. Having his family with him made him happier than he had been in a long time. He liked being with his wife again, more than he could have imagined. The girls laughed and played together. As each day passed, they became more comfortable with him.

Upon his arrival home from the train station, he had found his unmade bed, and knew it was a sign of Isolde's subtle trespass. While Appollonia surveyed the kitchen, he hurriedly arranged the sheet and blanket and wondered if he would ever feel at ease. For days he worried, and fitful dreams filled his sleep but the days grew into weeks and Isolde kept her distance. And so he began to relax into life with his family as though the threat he had anticipated had only been a figment of his imagination.

Appollonia's brother, Bernandino, was coming in two days for a visit. He was ready for them to move to Yorkville as soon as possible. He wasn't married, and especially missed being with his sister and her family. Since all was well, Luigi wasn't in a rush to leave. For the time being, he wanted to stay where they were. As he walked the short distance from the stream, he patted a dog that played with a stick in the road and wondered what Appollonia would be making for dinner.

In the field behind the apartment, Giovanna picked dandelion greens. Intent on her task, she looked down until her basket was filled. When she stood up, she saw a beautiful woman walking purposefully toward her. She was much older than Giovanna, but younger than her mother. Her dark hair rested in waves on her shoulders and her dress hugged the curves of her body in a very provocative way. When the woman approached her sisters, Giovanna made her way through the tall grass and stopped between them. Together, they warily eyed the mysterious stranger.

"Hello," the beautiful woman said. Her eyes were dark and serious, and she shifted from side to side as though she was agitated. "I'm Isolde. Your father told me all about you."

"You know him?" Giovanna asked, more out of anger than curiosity.

"We're friends."

The field was still, but Giovanna shuddered as if a breeze had blown in through the forest and brushed her skin.

"Tell him I miss seeing him," Isolde said. She turned abruptly and walked across the field, disappearing into the darkness of the woods in an instant. The girls stared after her retreating form, looks of confusion on their faces. It seemed as if they'd seen a ghost appear and disappear before their eyes.

Giovanna wondered if the mysterious woman were an

apparition, for she left behind the lingering presence of a spectral being.

"I don't like her," Evelina whispered.

"Why hasn't Pop told us about her?" Maria said, her eyes filled with a hint of fear.

"I don't know, but I agree with Ev. I don't like her," Giovanna added, looking thoughtfully at her sisters.

"Will you tell Pop we spoke to her?" Maria asked.

"Later, not in front of Mama," Giovanna answered. Taking Evelina's hand she walked out of the field, the fingers of her other hand clenched the handle of her basket.

At the edge of the field, she saw her father emerge from the street and walk to the top of the stairs. She looked up at him and waited for him to catch her eye.

The door to the apartment stood ajar and the aroma of their dinner drifted through the doorway. She pictured her mother standing at the stove stirring the *zuppa di fagioli* and then moving to the counter to slice hot bread. She closed her eyes and saw steam puff from each slice as it fell to the cutting board. Minutes ago she had been hungry and eager for the evening meal, but now her appetite was gone.

Her father stood on the porch landing holding his bag of dirty work clothes and the remains of his lunch. She and her sisters arrived at the bottom of the stairs and stopped. Maria put her hand on Giovanna's shoulder.

Giovanna gave the basket to Evelina and whispered, "Go inside and offer to set the table. Maria and I will talk to Pop outside about the lady in the field." Giovanna's face and voice were somber. "I don't want Mama to hear us."

"Tell Pop she scared us," Ev said. She ascended the steps without raising her eyes when she passed her father on his way down.

"Pop," Giovanna said. "Maria and I need to talk to you before we go inside."

Her father came down the stairs and they led him away, back toward the field.

"Where are we going? Isn't it time for dinner?" he asked.

"It's almost ready," Maria said. "But we have something to

tell you first."

"We met Isolde. She said she misses you," Giovanna said, not looking at her father. He stopped.

"Did she come to the apartment?" he asked, his voice startled and hushed.

"No, she came to the field," Maria whispered. "Mama was inside."

"Was she mean to you?" he asked.

"No, but I don't like her," Giovanna said in broken English. She was learning to speak her new language and wanted to use it now with her father, though it was unlikely her mother could overhear their conversation.

Her father looked away, but Giovanna could see that he was unnerved. "I'll tell her to stay away from you."

"And from you," Giovanna whispered, as she took Maria's hand and walked to the top of the stairs. Her father stood still at the bottom of the steps with his head bent.

"Don't say anything to Mama." She smiled at Maria and waited until her sister smiled back. Then they entered the kitchen.

"Girls, hurry. The soup is ready," her mother said. "Your father will be home any time now."

The greens were in the sink near the water pitcher. Giovanna rinsed and shook them dry, and then drizzled them with oil and vinegar and a sprinkle of salt. Evelina had set the table and was filling the glasses with water. Maria wrapped the hot bread in a towel and placed it in the middle of the table.

Giovanna began to wonder if her father had gone away when he walked through the doorway and stopped to kiss her mother.

I know he loves her, she thought.

Her mother smiled at him. Then she ladled the soup into each of their bowls, sat in her chair and asked, "Evelina, please say the blessing."

Giovanna nodded at her.

"Bless us, oh Lord, for these thy gifts, which we are about to receive, in thy bounty, through Christ our Lord. Amen." Evelina paused. "And thank you for letting us all be together."

Her father coughed and excused himself from the table. "I'll be right back," he said. "Start without me. I just need to visit the outhouse."

"Your soup will get cold, Luigi," her mother protested.

"I'll put a plate over it," Maria offered and leaned forward to place a plate over his soup bowl.

"I'll be right back," her father said.

Giovanna saw him steady himself at the railing before he walked down the stairs. Everything will be all right, she told herself.

"How was school today?" her mother asked.

Maria told her the new English words she had learned, but Giovanna wasn't listening. She spooned her soup into her mouth mechanically until her bowl was empty. She didn't want her mother to question her appetite.

Chapter 13

The sun rose over the horizon on a beautiful clear day as Alessandro finished his chores on deck and carried the mop and bucket to the railing to dump the dirty water into the waves of the ocean. The *SS Roma* had set sail from its homeport of Genoa only the day before, but he was already eager for the ship to dock in the New York harbor.

His feelings for Giovanna had changed everything. His love for her and his calling to become a doctor consumed his thoughts. He was desperate to get to America as soon as possible. His family, especially his mother, had been unhappy to learn of his decision to leave Italy ahead of schedule. When he convinced his father that he wouldn't be content to study medicine in Italy, that he wanted to live in America, he had given him the savings he had stashed away. It wasn't a large sum of money, but enough for him to leave his job on the *SS Roma* and start college, while working for his Zio Franco. Last week he had received a letter from his aunt, Zia Lucia, in Detroit, assuring him that his room was ready for his arrival. Most of the details were falling into place. He would arrive in the United States in a little over a week.

His morning duties accomplished, he went below deck to his bunk and took his language textbook and writing materials from his locker. Every spare moment was spent in study, and the discipline had proven beneficial. His command of the English language had greatly improved.

Once he had completed several lessons, he closed the book and began his first letter to Giovanna. He told her that as soon as he arrived in America, he would find a way to visit her, though the thought of meeting her father terrified him. He pictured her shy smile when she read of his fear. Somehow he would gain the courage to tell her father of his plans to make something of himself. In time, he wanted him to know that he wished to marry his beautiful daughter, although he didn't mention this to Giovanna. A proposal had to be done in person.

When he finished the letter, he began to calculate how long it would take it to reach her once the ship docked, and he mailed it in New York. The ship would be sailing for eight more days. Once the letter left the post office, it would take at least a week for her to receive it. It would be half a month or more before she read his words and a month before he received a reply.

He hoped she longed for him as much as he longed for her.

Chapter 14

The full moon shone through the window onto the floor of Appollonia's kitchen. When she got into bed, Luigi was already asleep. She noticed his work pants and coat carefully draped over a box that held his clothes in the corner of the room. She had stayed up later than everyone else to finish her mending. She fell asleep at once, but the creak of the door awakened her a short time later. Startled, she lit the candle next to her bed. Luigi was no longer beside her, and his clothes were gone. She walked across the icy bedroom floor to the kitchen. The moon's light drew her to the window. As she looked down to the street below, she saw her husband cross the mud-covered road and open the door of the restaurant on the other side of the street.

Though it was cold in the room, the shiver she suffered wasn't from the draft in the poorly insulated apartment. She got back into bed and picked at her fingernails. Her eyes darted around the dark room and she sat up and rocked back and forth.

Her mind raced back over the evening. Luigi had been quieter than usual, but she had attributed his silence to exhaustion. It was the end of the week. The girls had been quiet, too, subdued even, now that she thought about it. They had come back with the greens for the salad without the typical commotion that followed their spending time outside. Evelina had come in first, with Giovanna and Maria trailing along a few minutes later. They were helpful in the rush to get the meal to the table, but had eaten less than usual and left to work on their schoolwork with enthusiasm, as if it were a game and not a necessary chore.

All three of them were concerned with learning to speak and write their new language. She heard their stilted attempts at the unfamiliar words and the laughter that followed when one of them made a mistake. They had always been close, and their teasing wasn't mean spirited. As their mother, she didn't often boast of their admirable traits, but she was more than pleased with the bond they shared and the kindness they displayed. Knowing that the three of them enjoyed and cared for one another pleased her immeasurably, and she reminded them often of how lucky they were to have each other. Her heart filled with love and comfort as she thought of them.

While she washed the dishes, Luigi read the Italian newspaper given to him by one of the other miners. After she finished in the kitchen, she sat with him and darned his socks. As soon as the girls finished their work, she told them Evelina's favorite story about how she had found her as a newborn baby while working in the vineyards and picked her up, saving her from a pile of ants. Giovanna and Maria knew it wouldn't be long before their younger sister would realize that this wasn't how children came to be with their families, but they listened, without interrupting, each time she asked to hear the story. They settled down to sleep with only a few minutes of bedtime chatter. Luigi went to bed soon after that. It had been, more or less, a typical evening.

Appollonia got back out of bed and stood at the window. One low light was on in the restaurant. No one stood on the porch or walked along the quiet street. It was after eleven. Most of the town would be asleep. She walked back to the bedroom, tugged on her socks and pulled the covers up over her shoulders.

Everything had been going so well. She and Luigi were getting along. He was wonderful with the girls. They were adjusting to living with their father and seemed happy. Their new home was pleasant. She tried not to think about how much she missed her family in Italy. Being with Luigi made up for being away from them. Having her little family together was what mattered most. It was her nature to dwell on the good in her life, sweeping away the regrets and the unattainable wants like cobwebs. Maria and Giovanna were having some trouble adjusting to their new school, but she had expected it would take time for them to adjust and wasn't worried. They had each other and Evelina for companionship. More often than not, they seemed content. And soon she would see her beloved brother, Bernandino. A tear came to her eye as she thought of his upcoming visit, and how happy her mother would be if she could see them together.

During the day, Giovanna and Maria went to school. Luigi had decided that Evelina should wait until the following fall to enroll, since there was only a short time left before the children would be given a long break from their studies for the summer. He taught her how to speak English a little bit every evening so when she started school she wouldn't feel as intimidated as her sisters, when they began, days after their arrival. Her sisters were helping her, too.

Appollonia enjoyed her days with Evelina, who was smart, inquisitive and at times stubborn, but always full of vigor and enthusiasm. They walked together several mornings during the week to a farm a mile outside of town to buy milk and eggs. Ev had learned enough English to speak to the farmer's wife, but Appollonia had picked up only a few words. Evelina was with her during the day to help her at the post office and the farm, and she entrusted Giovanna or Maria to pick up what they needed at the supply store after school. Sometimes she listened as Luigi taught Ev new words in English, but she didn't have a knack for remembering what she heard, possibly because she didn't have an interest in learning a new language as long as her family would continue to speak to her in Italian. If it became necessary, she supposed she would learn, but if she could get by without it, she didn't want to be bothered with studying.

She blew out the candle. Her eyes grew heavy as she waited in the dark room for Luigi. Despite her intention to stay awake until he returned, she fell asleep.

Isolde sat at the table closest to the restaurant's window and watched Luigi cross the street. His footsteps echoed on the porch. When he opened the door, his rugged face wore a severe expression. His eyes, steely and cold, fixed on her. She placed her hands on the table and stood ready for his anger.

"Why did you talk to my girls?" He fumed like an animal ready to attack.

"English, Luigi?"

"Yes," he said, closing the door.

"I've missed you." She stepped toward him and sighed. Her hand went to the necklace that dangled between her breasts, and she let it rest there.

Luigi surprised her and sat down. The apple pie she had taken from the oven only moments ago, sat on the table. It was still hot and steam drifted the sweet smell of sugar and cinnamon into the air between them.

She had bathed and washed her hair that afternoon. The smell of soap clung to her skin. Her dress was plain, but flattering, cut low in the front and tight on her hips. The shawl she had wrapped around her shoulders, dropped to her arm, and he stared at her. She saw the anger in his face melt away, and he sank into the chair.

She imagined the fight he had planned sliding out of his body and onto the floor. It would be easier than she'd pictured.

"Let's talk in my room. Someone will see us here."

"*Per un momento,*" he answered, lapsing into Italian.

"Yes, only for a moment," Isolde whispered.

He followed her up the stairs and into her room. When he turned to close the door, she unbuttoned the front of her dress. She put her hand on his shoulder and he pulled her close to him. She smiled as he buried his head in her neck, as her dress slipped to the floor.

He had always taken his time in the past. She looked forward to his slow caress and gentle kisses. This time it was different, over in minutes.

"You wanted me as much as I wanted you, Luigi," she whispered, as she lay beside him.

"I have to go. I'm sorry." His voice was cold and abrupt. He swung his legs over the side of the bed and gripped the edge of the mattress. He looked upward and released a deep sigh. His eyes narrowed and the muscles in his back tensed.

"You and I will be together," Isolde said with quiet confidence.

She traced the muscles of his back with her index finger, and then pulled him next to her with her hands on his chest. The warmth of his body against hers made her feel happy again.

His body stiffened, and she let her arms drop. He stood and searched for his pants on the floor. Pulling them on with quick jerks, he took another deep breath, "This was a mistake."

Isolde lit the candle on the nightstand. The flame illuminated his face. It was full of shame.

"Being with me isn't a mistake." She veiled her anger and stood next to the candle. She raised her arms, pulling her hair in back of her head, her naked body before him. "We're good together, Luigi."

She dropped her hair and put her hand on his face. His jaw clenched.

"My wife and daughters are here now."

"Yes, and you still came to me." She moved closer and tried to kiss him, but he pushed her shoulder and she sank onto the bed.

"Appollonia," he said, and then paused. "My wife isn't well."

"I can give you what you want." She glared at him as though daring him to resist her.

Luigi walked to the door without turning around. He gripped the door handle, and hesitated. In an icy voice, he said, "I won't come back again."

"We'll see about that."

When he turned to face her, his eyes were full of anger. "Don't go near my family," he said, then stepped out into the dark hallway.

"You'll be back, Luigi," she hissed. "Or you'll be sorry."

He closed the door without looking at her.

Her dress lay in a heap on the floor, and she stepped on it instead of hanging it up. She stood naked at the window and watched him hurry across the street to get back to his precious family. As he disappeared up the stairs to his apartment, she yanked the curtain closed. After washing at the basin with a broken bar of soap, she put on her dressing gown and got into bed. Her anger gave way to the tiniest bit of hope.

Something was wrong with his wife. If she were ill or just

unable to satisfy him, he would come back to her again. If he didn't, she might have another reason to persuade him. One hand went absently to the pillow where Luigi had laid his head. The other traced small circles on her abdomen. The sheets held his scent and she breathed it in. Her eyes grew heavy and she slept a dreamless sleep.

In the morning, she woke up earlier than usual, dressed and went to the restaurant. The pie was gone from the table. She wondered if he had taken it with him.

No one else was in the kitchen. She turned on the brown box radio. The announcer's voice floated into the room.

"And now here's the latest Lewis James record, written by the songwriting team of Gus Kahn and Isham Jones, The One I Love Belongs to Somebody Else." Lilting notes from a horn began and the singer joined in *"I'm unhappy, so unhappy, but I can see, the one I love, don't care for me…"*

Isolde made sandwiches and filled water jars. She packed the brown paper bags and made cookies. The restaurant's owner let her bake sugar cookies for the lunches at an extra cost to the miners. The dough was stiff as she pushed against it with a wooden spoon. She dropped the spoon and worked the dough with her hands until it was smooth, and then rolled it into small balls *"…it was too late when I happened to find her. The one I love…"*

Talia, another Italian waitress Isolde's age, came into the kitchen

"You're early," Talia said, putting on her apron.

"You're late," Isolde answered. "I've already made the lunches."

"And now you're on to making cookies?"

Isolde glared at her.

"Aren't you the hard worker today."

"The men like to have a treat once in a while."

"I'm sure they do," Talia said sarcastically. She eyed Isolde with suspicion.

"I saw Luigi leaving your room last night. Are you together?"

"His family's here now."

"You didn't answer my question, Isolde."

"He wants to be with his family, but who knows what the future will hold." She hummed along with the song.

"They're a nice family," Talia said.

Isolde frowned and continued rolling the dough into little balls, and then put them on a tin sheet to be placed in the oven.

Talia continued. "His two oldest daughters go to school with my Eliana." Her words were like a taunt from a young child.

"And?"

"Leave him alone to be with his family. If he said it's over, let it be over."

It isn't over yet, Isolde thought. She smiled at Talia, who glared back and then turned and left the kitchen.

Chapter 15

Appollonia heard Luigi in the kitchen and hurriedly used the chamber pot and dressed in the dark room. She was a heavy sleeper and hadn't heard him come in during the night. Now it was morning, and he would be in a rush to get to work. The girls would be up soon for school, and she wanted to talk to him alone.

The bedroom door was ajar, and the smell of sautéed onion drifted through the crack. When she opened the door she saw a pie on the kitchen table. Apples poked through the slits in the sugared top crust.

"It's the best American dessert," Luigi said, looking up from the sink.

They rarely splurged on sugar, and Appollonia's mouth began to water at the sight of the flakey pastry and the browned apples dusted with the crystallized treat. She hadn't made anything sweet since leaving Italy. The last time she'd had any type of dessert was at the dance on the ship. She instantly regretted stopping Evelina from taking more than one cookie that night. She would let her have a big piece of the pie.

"From the restaurant, for Bernandino's visit," Luigi added.

"It looks delicious," she said. "Luigi…"

Before she could ask all the questions that were nagging her, he explained that he had gone to the restaurant after she and the girls had fallen asleep to collect the pie. He smiled at her and continued cooking his breakfast of vegetables sautéed in oil, and then pointed to his watch. She called to the girls and began preparing their school lunches and the sandwich Luigi would take with him to the mine. He was boiling water on the stove for her tea. He always made his own breakfast and heated the water for her tea, since she didn't feel well until she had been up for a little while. Her asthma was at its worst in the morning. The kettle whistled, and she took a deep breath and poured the hot water over the tealeaves in her cup.

She put her arm around his waist and hugged him. He slid the vegetables from the hot skillet onto a plate. Something about the way he turned his eyes downward gave her pause. Her fears from the night before came flooding back. He placed his breakfast on the table and took his glass from the counter. The pitcher of water was near the sink, so she let go of him to reach for it. She wanted to look into his eyes, but he stared at his plate and ate without looking up as she poured the water into his glass. Her hand trembled.

The girls came into the kitchen and ate leftover bread with an apple he had cut up for them to share. Giovanna and Maria collected their satchels and stuffed their lunches inside as they rushed to pull on their sweaters. Luigi stood at the door waiting to walk with them to the schoolhouse. Appollonia hugged her two older daughters and reminded them of Bernandino's visit. Luigi turned his cheek to receive her kiss and she thanked him again for the pie. His eyes darted away from her gaze again.

"I want to talk to your brother about a job in the steel mill," he said.

"You've changed your mind about staying here for a little while longer?" she asked. For a moment she forgot about Luigi's eyes and her mood brightened.

"I'm tired of breathing coal dust, and it isn't good for you either," Luigi said. His coat was on the back of a kitchen chair, and he inspected its collar before putting it on.

She knew he worried about her health. Her asthma bothered her more in West Virginia than it had in Valcaldara. She was always tired and short of breath at the end of each day. When she went to bed, she fell asleep almost instantly. Luigi understood, but he had to be upset that they had only made love a few times since her arrival.

"Are you sure?" she asked. It wasn't like him to have a sudden change of heart. She stood on the porch landing and waited for his answer. He paused at the bottom of the stairs, as Giovanna and Maria went on. The wind blew her nightgown around her knees and she rubbed her bare arms.

"It'll be better for all of us in Ohio," he said, and then turned to catch up with the girls who were already near the street.

Appollonia was happy that Luigi had changed his mind. Living near her brother, her godmother, and *paesan* from Valcaldara would be more like living in the old country.

"Evelina, we have a lot to do to get ready for your Zio's visit," she said. Evelina jumped into her arms and squeezed her. For the moment, she forgot her fears.

Luigi was especially eager to discuss moving to Ohio with his brother-in-law. It would make Appollonia happy and her health might improve. His daughters would be near their uncle, and his wife would be with her godmother, *Comare* Rosie. During the night he had decided it would be best to leave as soon as possible. His deception made him eager to be gone from the place where his lies threatened to smother him.

Bernandino would be arriving that evening and planned to stay through the weekend. They were all looking forward to seeing him, Luigi most of all.

When Luigi passed by the restaurant, he stole a glance at the window above the porch. He had gone to see Isolde with every intention of demanding that she keep her distance, but his anger had evaporated as soon as she smiled at him, and he remembered all of the times they'd made love. He silently cursed himself for losing his self-control when she let her dress slip to the floor.

"Are you okay, Pop?" Giovanna asked.

Luigi looked at his daughter and felt shame for his weakness. He ran to the side of the road where a patch of grass poked through the dirt and bent over to throw up the vegetables he had eaten for breakfast.

"Oh, Pop," Maria said. She searched her pockets and found her handkerchief.

"Thank you. I'm okay," Luigi replied. He wiped his brow and mouth with the delicate cloth, folded it along the crease his wife had ironed in, and put it into his coat pocket. He felt overcome with fatigue.

"You should go home, Pop. You're sick," Giovanna instructed.
"I'm okay now."

The girls looked at him with concern.

"I'll be fine," he said. "I guess my breakfast didn't agree with me. My stomach feels much better now."

The girls shifted their bags to their shoulders and walked on either side of him. Luigi held their hands until they reached the school and assured them that his nausea had passed. He stood on the path to the schoolhouse until they walked inside, and then continued to the mine. Dirty snow littered the edge of the road and his work boots were wet with mud. He was suddenly aware of how cold he felt and buttoned his thin coat. He absently stepped in a puddle. The mud splashed the frayed hem of his pants and stained it brown.

Guilt gnawed at his conscience. His sacrifices for his family didn't mean anything if he betrayed their trust. It was only a matter of time before Isolde confronted Appollonia or spoke to his daughters again. The only way to protect them was to take them away. As much as he dreaded confessing his secret, he had to tell Bernandino. He knew Isolde meant it when she said he would be sorry if he didn't come back to her. The desperation and anger in her voice told him her threat was real.

After the miners picked up their lunches and thanked her for the cookies, Isolde returned to her room. Her dirty laundry was on the dresser next to the porcelain washbasin that she had filled with water early that morning. The room was dark, so she took the matches from her nightstand and lit two candles. Fending off a sudden feeling of exhaustion, she took a bar of soap and began to scrub her white apron in the basin. With each stroke on the cloth her arm grew heavier. The water turned gray, and she felt unbearably tired. Her hand became limp and the material slipped into the water that was as dreary as her soul. She watched the soap sink to the bottom of the basin. Her knees buckled and she fell to the rug. Tears flowed from her eyes and her heart felt as if it had been pierced with the point of a knife.

For a moment, Luigi had been in her arms again. But it was over before she could appreciate the sweetness of it. How could he tell her to stay away? It had been easy to seduce him, but even easier for him to dismiss her as if she meant nothing to him. The anger she'd felt when he left had turned to despair.

She sat up and reached for the edge of the bed, pulling herself up. Luigi was just confused, she told herself. He thought his family needed him more than she did. She would help him see that she was more deserving of his love.

Her hands rested on her stomach as though she could beckon a pregnancy through sheer will. Though she didn't long for a child the way many women do, a baby would serve her purpose. If she were pregnant, she would almost certainly lose her job, and Luigi would have to take her in. He was a decent man and would take care of her if she carried his child. Possibly Appollonia would leave him and go back to Italy. It appeared to be the only way she might convince Luigi to abandon his family to be with her. He seemed very fond of his daughters and determined to preserve his family.

Isolde leaned into her feathered pillow and let sleep engulf her into a fitful dream. *Luigi called to her from the street below, her name floating into the room through the open window, "Isolde." She rose from the bed and reached for him, hoping he would come to her. Instead, he drifted farther away until a fog surrounded him, and then she fell, her hands still extended into the air.*

When she awoke from her nap, the early morning darkness was gone. Sunlight shone through the curtain and brightened her room. She got out of bed and put on a clean blouse and skirt. Her reflection in the mottled glass of the mirror was like that of a stranger. She painted her lips and pulled a brush through the waves of her raven hair. The smell of simmering soup wafted into her room from the kitchen when she opened the door. With a feeling of confidence, she went down to the restaurant to begin her shift.

In time, Luigi would come around. It was the only thought she could conceive of. If he didn't, she knew what she had to do.

Chapter 16

Bernandino walked from the train station carrying a small bag on his back with a clean shirt and underwear, a toothbrush, and some candy for his nieces. It wasn't far to the mining camp, and he hoped to arrive there in time to meet Luigi on his way home. The sunshine that had started the day was gone. Dreary clouds hovered low in the sky. Rain had already turned the dirt to mud, and he had to look down to avoid the puddles that had formed in the potholes. From what he could see of Covel, so far, it wasn't a scenic place. Yorkville wasn't picturesque either, though the river that snaked along the edge of the quiet town gave it a bucolic appearance with its rushing brown water. The small houses were plain and well kept in the neighborhood that surrounded Main Street. Smoke from the stacks of Wheeling Steel Mill singed the air, frequently obscuring the sun's light. The landscape wouldn't lure his sister and her family to the Ohio town where he lived, but his description of the colorful Italian, Polish, Romanian, Greek and French immigrants who lived there might.

His job was not inside the sweltering oven of the mill where the oppressive heat from the molten ore was almost intolerable. He was the caretaker of the grounds surrounding Wheeling Steel. If he could convince Luigi to leave West Virginia, the labor supervisor had promised him that he would have a job for his brother-in-law. A move would mean Luigi would trade the damp mine for the hellacious inferno where a labor gang, comprised of mostly immigrants, manufactured steel.

His stubborn brother-in-law probably wouldn't be impressed with this job description. Being a coal miner was less than ideal, but Luigi liked the pace of the steady, unsupervised work. His job in the mill would be different in that respect.

The boss of the labor gang monitored the workers closely, and this wouldn't set well with Luigi. Bernandino would have to convince him that a position at the steel mill would be the better job for different reasons. The other Italians who worked at the mill considered it somewhat safer than the mines, and they had better benefits. For his sister's sake and the sake of her family, he hoped the promise of a good future would sway Luigi. He thought it was the best opportunity for all of them, and he selfishly knew he would be happier to have them close. He missed his family.

The voices and laughter of men brought him out of his thoughts. He was close to the mine now. Miners pushed open the gate of a chain link fence surrounding the mine property and walked on the road ahead of him. He saw Luigi open the door of the elevator that had brought him up from the underground mine. He squinted at the daylight, removed his hard hat, and walked toward the creek, probably to bathe. He wondered if this was his brother-in-law's custom every day before he strolled home. When Bernandino approached Luigi from behind, he seemed to be absorbed in his own thoughts.

"How the hell are you?" Bernandino asked, as he slapped Luigi on the back.

"Bernandino," Luigi said. He hugged him. "It's good to see you."

"You, too."

He hadn't seen Luigi since the last time he'd been in Italy, six or seven years ago. He thought he looked tired and troubled.

"Come this way. I have to stop for a wash in the creek. It won't take long," Luigi said. He walked toward the water, removed his suspenders and tugged his shirt loose as he went.

"I'll wait for you over by the rocks," Bernandino said.

Luigi stripped off his blackened shirt, pants and socks and let them fall to the ground. He took clean clothes from a canvas bag he carried under his arm and laid them on a dry rock. He hurriedly rubbed a bar of lye soap over his body, followed by a a quick splash in the creek water.

Bernandino pulled his coat around his shoulders, sat on a

large rock and pondered his visit.

Appollonia was an excellent cook and would have a nice dinner when they arrived. Daydreaming about the upcoming meal made his stomach growl with growing hunger. Knowing his sister, there would be plenty of pasta with a simple but delicious sauce and a salad. While Luigi dried with a ragged towel and dressed, Bernardino languished in the thought of food. Each day his landlord, Rose prepared his evening meal, and though she was an adequate cook, he preferred his sister's cooking, because it was like his mother's. He also looked forward to seeing his nieces and was glad that he had remembered to bring them a treat.

Food was not his only preoccupation. He had a secret that was suffocating him. Now in his late thirties and still unmarried, he had no desire for a wife. Until now he might have lied about why, hoping Appollonia would buy his story that he wasn't able to find a nice Italian girl, and that Luigi wouldn't suspect that he wasn't even interested in marriage. He had only begun to face the truth about his sexuality, himself, when he left Italy for America. The clarity of accepting, instead of pretending, had given him a new lease on life. Now he was ready to tell his sister and brother-in-law.

In Yorkville, he rented a room upstairs in Rose's house. Another lodger, Henri, an amiable Frenchman who worked at the mill, lived in the other bedroom across the hall. He was enamored with all things American. Like many of the immigrants Bernandino had met, Henri, preferred to use the American version of his name. Henry. Soon he was calling Bernandino, Benny. They were close in age and became fast friends, practicing their English together in the evenings after dinner while drinking coffee and eating Rose's *biscotti* cookies. Benny secretly wished for a more intimate relationship with Henry, but he settled for the fact that they were nothing more than kindred spirits adjusting to life in a new land and never hinted of his feelings to him.

One night, after countless evenings in the dull and proper setting of Rose Amici's living room, Henry said, "Let's forget our English lesson tonight and go to Antonio's for some wine."

Even the police chief liked Antonio's wine, he made in his basement out of the grapes he grew on his small dairy farm on the outskirts of town. The hillbilly bootleggers weren't the only ones who knew how to get around the eighteenth amendment by keeping the local law enforcement bribed with complimentary alcohol.

Together they walked to the dairy farm, a little over a mile from the center of town. Inside the cow barn, they waited for Antonio to bring them a bottle of wine. Holstein cows with udders full of milk swished their tails and regarded Benny and Henry with mild interest as they stood in their stalls. The smell of hay and feed was pleasant and helped to mask the foul odor of the animals' waste. Henry walked to the closest cow and rubbed her gently. She blinked her eyes lazily at him and continued to eat. When Benny rubbed the back of the cow next to her, she snorted and startled him. He took his hand from her hide and jumped back.

Henry laughed and joined him when he sat on a bale of hay. Soon Antonio appeared with the wine, and Benny paid him and hid it in his jacket.

Antonio put the money in his coat pocket, and said, "Go through the woods back to town. It isn't safe to be seen on the road at this time of the evening. You might be questioned about why you're out here."

Benny thanked him, and he and Henry made their way to the woods, taking turns drinking the wine as they headed back to Rose's. For most of the walk, Henry joked with Benny about work, and how Benny was lucky to have a job outside as a grounds keeper. When they came to the edge of the woods, Henry lowered his voice and moved closer to Benny. It seemed he was about to confide a great secret and was having trouble finding the right words.

"I've wanted to talk to you about something for many weeks now, my friend, but I haven't had the courage until tonight," Henry said.

Benny laughed. "The wine's loosened your tongue."

Henry hesitated for a moment, and then pressed on. "Did you see the new girl who works in the mill office?"

Benny was practiced at talking about girls as if he were attracted to them.

"Yes, nice."

"You think so?"

Benny was confused by Henry's question. "Sure. She's pretty."

"I didn't think so. In fact, I barely noticed her." Henry twirled the almost empty wine bottle and watched the liquid go round and round. Then he looked up at Benny, his eyes filled with tears.

Benny stopped. It was too dark to see Henry's face clearly, but he could hear the catch in his voice. His pulse accelerated, and as he waited for Henry to continue, he looked past him into the night. The road ahead of them was flat and barren. The town was only a few minutes walk away, and the lights from the houses sprinkled the darkness.

"I'm not attracted to women," Henry said. He paused and took a deep breath. Then he continued, his words spilling out. "I care for you."

"Let's get home," Benny whispered. He could hardly take in what Henry had said. Was it possible that he wanted to be companions?

"I've offended you, Bernandino," Henry slurred as they staggered their way along the quiet road.

Benny stopped and sighed as though a great weight had been pressing on his heart that was now lifted. He put his hand around Henry's waist, and smiled. Henry sagged next to him and gave him a fearful look.

Benny tightened his grip and resumed his stride. "I feel the same way."

Henry's face flooded with relief, and he smiled. "For a moment, I thought you were going to drop me." Benny laughed.

The stars above him shone with a brightness he had never noticed before, and along with the crescent moon, they lit the way as they came upon the hamlet of Yorkville. Rose's house was dark, and Benny opened the front door as quietly as he could. When they reached the top of the stairs, he helped Henry to his bed and removed his shoes and coat. Henry smiled at him and closed his eyes.

"I was afraid to tell you," Henry whispered as his body relaxed into sleep.

"And I was afraid to admit how I felt," Benny answered, as he closed the door.

They no longer had to pretend with one another, but each of them knew he had to keep his feelings hidden from everyone else or there would be hell to pay.

Luigi cleared his throat, and Benny shook away the memory. "I have something to tell to you," Luigi said.

"What's wrong, Luigi?" Benny asked. The dire tone of his brother-in-law's voice made him stop in his tracks.

"There's no way to paint what I've done in anything but a bad light," Luigi began.

He looked up at the sky as if he were asking God for the strength to tell Benny what he'd done.

Benny stood in the waning light of dusk and waited. Other miners walked past them and spoke to Luigi. He nodded his head and remained silent until they were a good ways down the road, out of earshot.

"I've been unfaithful to Appollonia," he finally said, his voice filled with pain.

Benny felt his back stiffen. His fingers tightened around the package he'd brought for his nieces. He took a deep breath, but didn't speak.

"I'm sorry for what I've done. It was wrong. I was lonely," Luigi said. "But it's no excuse."

"Why are you telling me this?" Benny asked. He felt angrier than he had been in a long time and willed himself to keep his hands from grabbing Luigi's neck.

"I love your sister and my daughters," Luigi said. "I want to make it right. I have to leave this place to do that. I need your help." He paused. "I broke it off, the affair, but I let it go on too long. She's threatened me. I'm not sure what she'll do."

Benny stared at him.

"She seems desperate," Luigi said. He told Benny about his last conversation with Isolde. "I want to keep her away from my family."

They arrived at the mining company's supply store as Luigi finished speaking, ending with his request that his brother-in-law help him escape his grave situation.

"Why did you stay away so long?" Benny asked.

"From Italy?" Luigi said.

"Yes, from Appollonia and your daughters."

"There's no future in Italy for my daughters. I wanted to be able to bring them here, to America. I had to save money and become a citizen. It took all this time..." Luigi's voice trailed off.

Benny's news would have to wait for another day. Luigi's secret was more urgent than his own.

When Luigi opened the door, Appollonia turned from stirring the sauce that simmered on the wood stove. Benny remembered to smile at his older sister though he was still taking in the news of Luigi's infidelity.

The sight of his nieces cheered him, and he tried to put aside his anger. Giovanna was setting the dishes on the table. She looked so much like her father. Maria was pouring boiling water and pasta into a colander in the sink to drain. She was the closest in size to Giovanna, so Benny presumed it was Maria, though he hadn't seen her since she was very young. She was beautiful, on the cusp of becoming a woman. Evelina squeezed him around the waist and led him to sit in a chair at the table.

"Sit down, Zio! Mama doesn't like our food to get cold," she said in English.

"Speak Italian, Evelina," Appollonia commanded.

"Sorry, Mama," Ev answered. She whispered to him, "She doesn't like it when we speak English, but I like to practice."

"She isn't learning?" Benny asked.

"No, but Pop is teaching me. My sisters help me, too, so I won't look stupid at school."

Benny laughed. "No one will mistake you for stupid, dear niece. I can see that you're very smart, like your Zio Benny."

"Thanks," Evelina said. She gave him a mischievous grin.

Appollonia placed a large bowl of field greens on the table. Then with tears in her eyes she hugged him. When she let go, she kissed him on each cheek and held him at arm's length, surveying him up and down.

"It's been a long time. I'm so glad to see you. Mama would be happy to know we're together."

He kissed her cheeks and smiled at her. "Almost as happy as I am."

"Sit down," Appollonia said. "I borrowed a chair for your visit. We only own just enough for us."

"I carried it up from the store downstairs," Evelina said. Her eyes twinkled.

"It must have been heavy," Benny said. "Thank you."

"She's strong for a little girl," Giovanna said, winking at her sister.

Evelina narrowed her eyes and frowned, but not for long. Benny patted her on the back and her anger was forgotten.

"Let's eat, before the food gets cold," Appollonia insisted.

When the dishes were finished and the girls had gone to bed, he sat at the kitchen table with Appollonia and Luigi.

Luigi spoke first. "As I told you this morning, Appollonia, I want to move to Ohio. I think it would be good for all of us."

Appollonia sighed and closed her eyes. When she opened them her shoulders relaxed and she sat waiting. Bernandino took her hand. "I'll do everything I can to help."

"*Comare* Rosie is close to you?" she asked.

"I rent a room from her, and there's a small house for rent on my street. If you want, I'll tell the owner that you're coming soon. Maybe he'll hold it for you."

"Can we afford it, Luigi?" Appollonia asked, putting her hand on top of Luigi's.

"Yes, I think so," he said. The corners of his mouth turned upward in a weak smile, but his eyes were forlorn.

"If we move this summer, Evelina can start school there in the fall," Appollonia said. Her face lit up as she looked back and forth from Bernandino to Luigi.

"If Bernandino can arrange a job for me, we can move in a month or so," Luigi said.

"Oh, Luigi. That would be wonderful," Appollonia said. She smiled at her husband.

Benny squeezed her hand. "I'll make the arrangements

then."

"Yes," Appollonia said. She put her arms around his neck and rocked back and forth. He encircled her waist and laughed.

Luigi nodded at him.

"Consider it done," he released one hand from his sister's waist and shook Luigi's hand.

"Let's get some sleep now," Appollonia said. "I'll get some blankets for you." She turned to Luigi and kissed him, and then busied herself with getting ready for bed.

Benny stretched out on the pallet made of borrowed blankets and reflected on Luigi's guilty tale of transgression. His brother-in-law's secret was buried deep within him to spare his sister's tender heart. He would make sure Luigi kept his promise never to jeopardize his family's happiness again.

The heat of the fire was soothing. He closed his eyes and relaxed. Tomorrow would .be soon enough to explain his relationship with Henry. The weight of living a secret life would be easier if he could be himself when he was with his family. It would make pretending in front of everyone else bearable. In Yorkville, they would be together, just like in the old country. Bernandino closed his eyes and thought of walking in the fields of sunflowers in Italy with Henry by his side.

April 1925

Chapter 17

The house in Yorkville was similar to Giovanna's rustic country home in Italy in all the important ways. It was neat, comfortable and smelled of her mother's cooking. Unpainted wood covered the outside, and inside was a kitchen, living room and two bedrooms. It did not have indoor plumbing, but neither had her other home in Valcaldara so she hadn't expected it. It did have a porcelain, claw-footed tub in a small room off the kitchen, where they bathed with water poured from a pot that had been heated on the stove. They each took turns having a bath on Saturday afternoons so that they would look their best for church on Sunday. The front porch had a swing and was her favorite place to daydream and rest once her chores and homework were finished. The house had been built so close to the neighbors on each side, that if one of them yelled in anger, she could hear every word of the argument that usually followed, which frequently disturbed her respite on the porch swing. Just about every European nationality was represented in the neighborhood, and Giovanna sometimes wondered if she were in America or Europe.

Her father and Zio Benny had orchestrated the move to Yorkville in a hurry. She and her sisters had been told to pack their few possessions one afternoon, and then they left the next day. Giovanna considered the trip with her kind uncle another adventure, a much simpler undertaking than the journey from Italy. The excitement her mother felt when they arrived in the new neighborhood, which included many Italians, was infectious. *Comare* Rosie and Zio Benny lived down the street. Her father had his job at the mill. Evelina was learning English and had several freinds at school. All these changes were good and she went along without quarrel or question. But she wasn't altogether happy.

Though Giovanna liked her second home in America, she and Maria didn't like their new school.

On a sunny afternoon, Giovanna came home from school filled with frustration, laid her books on the kitchen table, and sat with a sigh in the chair where she usually did her homework. Her mother got out her rolling pin and cutting board and placed them at the other end of the table, along with a bowl of dough.

"I'm not going back to school. Tomorrow I'm going to the mill to ask for a job," Giovanna announced.

Maria stood behind her. Together they waited for their mother's response. "I hate school, too, Mama.

"Mama?" Giovanna said. Her mother appeared to be either preoccupied or ignoring her.

She gave Giovanna a look of concentration and didn't answer right away. Instead, she placed the bowl near her and rubbed a handful of flour on the wooden board she used for making pasta. Her hands expertly kneaded the yellow dough until it moved smoothly under the heels of her palms. When the dough became pliant, her mother went to the sink to wash and dry her hands. She came back to the table and sat down before she spoke.

"I'm listening," she said, and gave them her full attention.

The girls sat across from her. Giovanna was surprised that her mother didn't seem angry, and she continued with the words she'd prepared to defend her decision.

"Our teacher doesn't help us. She expects us to keep up, and she's rude when we get confused. Most of the time we can't understand what she's saying, so we aren't learning anything."

"I know studying a new language is difficult," her mother said with understanding.

"And, the other children in our class are only a year older than Evelina. It's embarrassing to be in an elementary class instead of with the other students our age," Giovanna continued.

"The principal thought you should start with the younger students, because you're just beginning to learn the language."

Giovanna studied her face. Wisps of dark hair flecked with grey had fallen from the bun she wore when she cooked or cleaned. Her eyes looked tired and she rested her head in her hands. Giovanna softened her tone.

"The teacher told us today that we won't be moving up to the next grade at the end of the year. Our English isn't good enough."

Her mother sighed. "But you practice every evening."

"Some of the students call us stupid," Maria added.

"Who's calling you, stupid?" her mother asked. She sat up straighter and looked appalled.

"It doesn't matter. I don't want to go to school anymore. My stomach bothers me every morning when I think of how the other students will make fun of my accent and laugh at me when I speak."

Her mother looked sad and Giovanna was sorry she and Maria had spoken about their humiliation, but they had to give her a compelling reason for leaving school, and it was the truth. But, it wasn't their only motive.

"We have another reason for quitting school." Giovanna continued. "Maria and I want to work. Lots of girls our age have jobs. We can help the family. Pop's paycheck isn't enough. We're barely getting by."

"Your father works hard," her mother said defensively.

"I don't mean any disrespect," Giovanna said. "We know he's doing his best, but immigrants are poorly paid. We think it's time for us to work as well." She paused, and waited for her mother to protest.

"Go on," her mother said.

She hurried on, the words tumbling out. "If we get jobs at the mill, we can buy our own things, and I can pay for fabric to make clothes for all of us. We're ready to go to work. Aren't we, Maria?"

Maria nodded. "We've been thinking a lot about this, Mama. In Italy, we would've been working at the bakery or for the big vineyard owner by now."

Giovanna braced herself for a confrontation with her mother. She might be angry with her for suggesting Maria give up her education, too.

To her surprise, she didn't protest. "If that's what you want to do, I won't stop you. You're right. If we were still in Italy, you might be working by now."

"You aren't mad?" Giovanna asked.

"It's a good idea," her mother said. She placed her hands on the table's edge and stood up.

"No argument?"

"No argument. I'll talk to your papa. You can go with him to the mill in the morning."

"May I go with her?" Maria asked. She smiled and squeezed Giovanna's hand.

Her mother took the rolling pin and pushed against a ball of dough, her face set in a preoccupied glare, as though she were pondering her answer with care. With each turn of the long wooden pin the mound became flatter. When the dough turned into a sheet, she cleaned the pin and began cutting it into strips for noodles. Her focus seemed to be on her work, and Giovanna wondered if she had forgotten her sister's question.

"Mama?" Maria said.

"Yes, you should work, too." She looked up from her task. "Now wash your hands, both of you, and help me cut the noodles, so dinner will be ready when your father gets home. Here, take the pail and fill it."

The girls took the pail without another word and walked to the backyard. Maria moved the pump handle up and down while Giovanna held the bucket under the stream of cold well water. She stopped pumping when the pail was full, and each of them lathered their hands with soap and rinsed them under a new stream of water.

"I thought she'd say no. Aren't you surprised?" Maria whispered.

"Yes and no," Giovanna answered. "It would be better if we learned more of the language, but she thinks we know enough to get by. She won't ever say it, but we're struggling. The money will help a lot."

"What about Pop?"

"If Mama thinks it's a good idea, Pop will, too."

"I feel better already. Every morning I hope that I'll do better and every afternoon I feel bad again. I'm glad we aren't going back," Maria said.

"Tomorrow we'll walk with Pop to the mill and get a job," Giovanna said with confidence.

She and Maria didn't get a job at the mill the next day or the next week or the next month, but she didn't give up. Each morning she returned to the mill supervisor's office with determination, hoping her persistence would wear him down, and each day he told her he didn't have any available positions for women.

They found part-time jobs. Maria swept and did odd jobs a few hours each morning at the corner grocery store, making less than a dollar each day. Giovanna took in sewing for the few women in town who didn't know how to sew well and could afford to pay someone else to do it for them.

Several months passed. Early on a Monday morning, the mill supervisor's wife, Mrs. Polanski, knocked on the front door. Giovanna was in the backyard. She could hear her mother's startled response through the open kitchen window.

"Ev, a Polish lady is on the front stoop with her arms full of clothes and a bolt of cloth. Go greet her in English for me."

"Who is it Mama?" Ev asked.

"Mrs. Polanski, the mill supervisor's wife."

"Do I have to, Mama?" Evelina whined.

Giovanna was proud of how well her sister spoke English. Their mother often used her as a translator when they went out and when someone who wasn't Italian came to the door. Ev wasn't fond of the responsibility.

Giovana smiled and listened as she pulled the last of the early spring weeds out of the backyard garden.

"Hello, Mrs. Polanski. Would you like to come in?" Ev said.

"I'm looking for Giovanna," she said. Her face was twisted into a puzzled snarl.

"I'm Evelina."

"I need Giovanna," she said, exhaling an impatient sigh. "If she's here, I'd like to speak to her about doing some sewing for me."

"She's a very good seamstress," Evelina said with pride.

"So I've been told. May I speak with her?"

"She's in the garden. I'll get her for you. Would you like to come in and wait for her?"

"No, I'm fine right here on the porch."

"Suit yourself," Ev said. She walked to the backyard and pulled on Giovanna's skirt.

Giovanna stood up in the last row of the garden where she was pouring water on the newly sown tomato plants.

"Mrs. Fancy Polanski is here with some sewing for you," Evelina said, hands on hips.

"Ev," Giovanna scolded.

"She can't understand me. She doesn't speak Italian. She's on the front stoop. Too good to come inside."

Giovanna rushed around the side of the house, wiping her hands on her apron and then untying the strings.

"Hello, Mrs. Polanski. I'm Giovanna," she said, holding out her hand, which Mrs. Polanski chose to ignore.

"Finally," the rude woman said with a huff.

Giovanna could see Maria standing in the living room behind Mrs. Polanski, rolling her eyes, while her mother stood in the kitchen, anxious, she was sure, about what the mill supervisor's wife wanted.

"I have some mending and hemming that needs to be done. I also would like a dress to be made out of this pattern and material," Mrs. Polanski said, handing Giovanna a dress pattern and a bolt of beautiful cloth. "Is that something you're capable of doing?"

Giovanna surveyed the pattern and touched the expensive cloth.

"She can make anything, better than anyone," Evelina stated, coming to stand next to her sister. Mrs. Polanski handed a cloth bag stuffed with clothes in need of mending to Ev, and clapped her hands to her hips.

"I can follow this pattern and make a dress for you. The mending, of course, is easy," Giovanna said.

"Well, thank you," Mrs. Polanski replied. It seemed, for a moment that she'd remembered her manners. "I need the dress in two days. I know that's short notice. Can you do it? How much do you charge?"

"The going rate," Giovanna said. She heard Ev sigh with disappointment, but she wasn't finished. "I can have the dress ready for you, but I'll have to work until late in the evening to do so."

"Wonderful!"

"I have one condition."

"What is it?" Mrs. Polanski said. "I'm desperate to have the dress ready for the ladies' luncheon hosted by the mill owner's wife."

"I want you to ask your husband to find a job for me and my sister in the mill," Giovanna said, pointing to Maria.

"What if he says no?" Her impatient tone was back.

"I'm more desperate to have a job in the mill than you are to have this dress in two days. Every day, for many weeks, I've asked your husband for a job, and he says he can't give me one. If you'll do this favor for me, I'll make sure this dress is ready for you in two days time, and it'll be beautiful. My sister is right. I'm a very good seamstress."

"You're quite the negotiator, and very sure of yourself, aren't you? I could find another seamstress…" Mrs. Polanski frowned and closed her eyes. When she opened them, she puckered her lips and stared off into the distance.

Giovanna stood patiently as though she had nothing else to do and watched her neighbor's dog dig a hole near the fence. She could feel the eyes of her mother and sisters on her. Beside her, Ev shifted from one foot to the other, balancing the bag of clothes on her hip.

Mrs. Polanski took a big gulp of air and blew it out slowly. "Alright. It's a deal, but you'd better be as good as your word."

"I'll do my best," Giovanna replied. She took great pride in her work.

"I'll be back just as soon as I speak to my husband."

"And I will begin as soon as you return."

"I see," Mrs. Polanski replied, stomping off in the direction of the mill.

"Still disappointed in me?" Giovanna asked Evelina.

"No, but do you think she can convince him?"

"She'll find a way."

Giovanna patted the top of Evelina's head and stuffed the pattern and beautiful bolt of cloth into the bag her sister was holding. "Now, explain my conversation with Mrs. Polanski to Mama, while I finish with the tomatoes in the garden."

Evelina smiled. "You know Mama and Maria will be worried until Mrs. Polanski returns."

"I'm not worried," Giovanna replied. "She looks like a woman who's used to getting her way."

The next morning, Giovanna didn't go to the mill to speak to the supervisor. His wife came to see her just as her father was leaving for work. She pulled the curtain aside to wave goodbye to her father and watched with surprise as Mrs. Polanski walked past him down the sidewalk to the porch and then knocked on the door. Her father stood in the street, staring at her as she marched to his front door. Her brisk knock thundered through the house. Giovanna had finished dressing, but she didn't hurry to answer the door. After combing her hair, she turned the knob and peered at the mill owner's wife.

"Hello," she said.

Mrs. Polanski wore her usual look of impatience. "It's done. Will my dress be ready by tomorrow evening?"

"What did he say?" Giovanna stood in the doorway and smoothed the front of her blouse.

"You and your sister have jobs in the lithograph department, starting on Monday."

"Thank you. Your husband won't regret hiring us," Giovanna said.

"Yes, yes. Well, you might regret asking for a job. The lithograph department isn't the most desirable place to work."

"We'll make the best of it. How much does it pay?"

"Twenty-nine cents an hour. You'll work a nine hour day, starting at seven- thirty, with a thirty-minute lunch."

Giovanna quickly multiplied in her head- a little less than two dollars and seventy cents a day for each of them. That would be over five dollars a day and twenty-six dollars a week that she and Maria could add to their family's income. It seemed like a fortune.

Mrs. Polanski was talking, but Giovanna was thinking about all her mother could buy with the money, such as chickens, milk, and sugar. She and her sisters would love to have sugar pizza more than once a week or maybe even an apple pie, and cloth, thread, and buttons. She could make each of them a new dress and some britches for her father.

"Giovanna? Did you hear me?"

"No, I'm sorry, Mrs. Polanski," Giovanna apologized. "Could you say that again?"

"I said, do you need me to come for a fitting?"

"Of course, of course. Can you stop by about eleven o'clock? I should have the fabric cut out and pinned together by then."

Mrs. Polanski breathed an exasperated sigh. "Do you know where I live? Could you possibly come to my house?"

"Yes, it isn't far."

Giovanna couldn't wait to begin her new job, but her excitement was short-lived. Mrs. Polanski had been right. A job in the hot lithograph department, standing, setting type all day, was one of the most undesirable positions for a woman at the mill, but Giovanna didn't complain right away.

Several months passed before she approached Mr. Polanski, this time for a better job in the administrative office. There were windows and fans in the heat of summer, and a heater in the winter for the comfort of the female clerks and secretaries. He seemed to delight in telling her "no," though she knew there was an opening. He shook his head and laughed at her, enjoying the power he had over her.

Just as Giovanna began to give up the thought of ever getting a better job, Mr. Polanski made a careless mistake. It gave her an opportunity, and she took advantage of it. If he'd been fair with her, she might have looked the other way, but he hadn't been, so she confronted him.

"Good morning, Mr. Polanski," Giovanna said when she arrived at work the morning after catching him in a romantic embrace with his secretary.

His arrogant face was solemn, and he rolled his shoulders and brushed a piece of lint from his lapel. "I'll save you the trouble of asking," he said, as he walked past her toward his office.

"No."

"You might want to check, just to be sure. I think there are two openings in filing that my sister and I would be happy to take."

"I don't care if there are two openings or not. I will not move you and your *guinea* sister to the office. Don't ask me again." He stopped with his hand on the doorknob to his office and paused.

Giovanna stood tall and straight, tilting her chin up and pushing her shoulders back. She walked to stand near him and whispered,

"If we aren't promoted to the secretarial pool and given a raise to the forty cents per hour that the other girls in the office are making, I might have to tell Mrs. Polanski what I saw yesterday, when you forgot to close your office door."

"Are you threatening me, Miss Falconi?" His warm breath assailed her and she stepped back.

"I happen to know that Mrs. Polanski is on her way to your office." She kept her voice steady under his glare.

"It's your word against mine," he said. He took his handkerchief from his back pocket and wiped his face, then looked nervously down the hallway at the entrance to the building.

"True, but I'm not the only one who saw you kissing your secretary."

Mrs. Polanski opened the entrance door and marched down the corridor toward them with purposeful steps. Mr. Polanski began to sweat and mopped his brow again.

"Alright. You can have the job." He opened the door to his office.

"And my sister?"

"Yes, yes. Now go away," he whispered, his voice full of anxiety.

"As you wish," Giovanna answered. She smiled at Mrs. Polanski, who gave her a curt nod and proceeded to walk ahead into her husband's office.

The next day she and Maria began their new jobs. Fortunately, her duties as a file clerk did not require interaction with Mr. Polanski. She did, however, continue to make dresses for Mrs. Polanski, who was not in love with her husband anymore and would have loved an excuse to divorce him. Giovanna kept her promise to Mr. Polanski, and never told his wife what she had seen that day. She and Maria were much happier working in the mill office. It seemed they had all gotten what they deserved.

When she told Evelina about her new job and how she'd convinced the hateful Mr. Polanski to promote not only her, but Maria as well, her little sister replied with a laugh, "You just might be my sister after all."

October 1927

Chapter 18

Orange and red leaves blew onto the windowsill of the attic window in the bungalow of Franco and Lucia Venezio. Alessandro watched them settle, then swirl away. His desk was piled with books, papers, and the notes he had scribbled during his morning anatomy lecture. His test tomorrow would come from the notes and the three chapters he hadn't finished reading, but he looked out the window and thought about Giovanna instead of studying. The letters he had written to her lay in the top drawer of his desk, unopened, still looking as they had on the days he had sealed them. Each was marked *return to sender, address unknown*. After ten attempts, he stopped writing to her.

His first emotion had been anger, which then grew into desperation. Thinking of her kept him up at night and diverted his concentration from his studies. His mind was like a train out of control, careening off the track and over a cliff. Sometimes he had to read passages in his textbooks two and three times to comprehend the information, his mind was so preoccupied with where she might have gone and how he could find her. Three and a half years had passed since the time he had spent with her on the ship. In that time, he had moved to Detroit, and enrolled at Wayne State University. After completing his degree in biology, he had begun his first year of medical school.

His Zio Franco and Zia Lucia hadn't understood his unhappiness when he began living with them.

"You have your whole life ahead of you. There'll be other girls." Zio Franco said.

But his mood didn't improve, so his uncle drove him to West Virginia to see if they could find out where Giovanna had gone. They had questioned her father's co-workers, her family's neighbors and the postmistress. No one knew where or why she and her family had gone.

When he inquired at the restaurant in town, a waitress had whispered to him in Italian as she rubbed her pregnant belly, "They've vanished from the face of the earth."

After he finished his drink and prepared to leave, the same girl, who was both beautiful and pathetic, had begged, "Send me their address if you ever find them." From her apron pocket, she pulled a torn envelope and scrawled her name and address across the front in pencil.

When he returned to Detroit, he placed it under the unread letters in his desk drawer. He wasn't sure why he kept it, except that she seemed as desperate to see them again as he was.

No letters came from Giovanna. Endless reasons danced through his thoughts. The postcard he had given her, with his aunt and uncle's address, was small and thin. It could've been lost. Her father might've forbidden her to write. It wasn't unreasonable to think that he might not permit his daughter to engage in a long distance romance with a suitor who was a stranger to him.

Of course, the most intolerable possibility of all was that she wasn't in love with him. She had just turned fourteen when they were together; her thoughts about love and life would have changed over time. She was almost eighteen now. He wondered if she had many suitors and tried not to think of her with another man. His chest tightened at the thought of someone else holding her and looking into her beautiful eyes.

During his first year at the university, he brooded, walking sullen and unapproachable along the paths of the campus. He made a few friends, but didn't date and rarely ventured from his attic room except to go to class and his uncle's shop to work. Sometimes he ate with his Zio Franco and Zia Lucia, but their well-intended questions tired him and tried his patience. In his second year, to appease them, he dated several different girls, even having sex with one of them. It was quick, mechanical, and unfair to the young co-ed who was obviously infatuated with him. He had ended their romance not long after that night. Being with a woman he wasn't in love with seemed like a waste of time to him. He preferred to be alone.

It was better this way. His studies absorbed every hour of the day that he wasn't sleeping, and he slept very little. For the time being he would focus all of his efforts on his medical training. It was the only thing that mattered to him, if he couldn't have Giovanna, but he couldn't stop thinking about her.

Soon he would be employed full-time. When he was able to spare some of his wages, maybe he would hire a private detective. For now, he was broke. The money his father had given him was gone. He had taken out a loan to pay for the rest of medical school. If his aunt and uncle hadn't generously allowed him to live and eat with them, he might've given up on his dream of becoming a doctor. He was thankful for their help. They weren't well off and providing for him was a strain. Someday he would repay them for their kindness.

When he wasn't being introspective, daydreaming of his lost love, he was enthralled with the study of medicine. Most of his classmates complained of the long hours spent burning the midnight oil, but he didn't mind. His determination to become a doctor gave him purpose. Though he found some of his studies in college, like mathematics, deplorable, his enthusiasm for learning had been rekindled at the start of his anatomy class on the first day of medical school. His lab partner, Sam, found probing and examining the lifeless human cadavers a bit morbid, and the two other students who "shared" their cadaver joked about working with a dead body to ease their discomfort. Alessandro, however, found this captivating as each day of dissection brought new insights into the fascinating complexity of the human body.

His intense interest in hands-on learning reminded him of a quote he had once read by Maria Montessori, the first Italian woman to become a doctor, who later went on to become an innovative educator. *"Education is a natural process spontaneously carried out by the human individual, and is acquired not by listening to words but by experiences upon the environment."*

Dr. Montessori impressed him and he agreed with many of her theories about learning. He had received a smile from the one female student in his class when he referred to Montessori as an admirable female Italian doctor and educator, quoting her on an occasion when several of his classmates had met to study together in the basement of the medical school. They were having an impassioned discussion about why different personalities entered different fields of study. Several of them had claimed that those studying medicine were possibly more logical and less imaginative than their peers in the disciplines of art or literature. Alessandro had disagreed.

"According to Maria Montessori, 'we especially need imagination in science. It is not all mathematics, nor all logic, but it is somewhat beauty and poetry."

"Well, tell that to my girlfriend, the artist. She thinks we're from two different planets," Sam added, laughing.

"That's because you're a man and she's a woman," Alessandro said. To him it was the most obvious reason for their differences.

"Touché," Sam acknowledged. "You're probably right, my friend."

The discussion ended. As their studying resumed, the female student smiled at him again. To be polite, he smiled back, but he didn't talk to her after the study group broke up for the evening.

Sam asked him later, "Why aren't you interested in going out with her? She's not bad looking and is obviously impressed with you."

"I'm in love with someone," Alessandro said.

"I've never seen you with a woman."

"I met her when I worked on the ship. She was coming to live in America with her family. I haven't seen her for over three years, but one day I'll find her." His voice trailed off wistfully.

"Three years," Sam said. "That's a long time to be away from someone you love."

He didn't want to talk about her. It only made him miss her more.

As long as Alessandro maintained his reserve, his friendships would be little more than acquaintances. He didn't need close friends now. Between studying and working in Zio Franco's shop, his days were full. And soon he would begin his clinical rotations at the hospital. Then he would try again to find Giovanna. It was what kept him going.

Chapter 19

Most days, Giovanna thought of Alessandro, but she had no way to contact him. The postcard of the SS Roma lay blurred by rain and obscured by dirt and leaves where it had fallen on the road to the train station. Years had passed since her family had made their surreptitious way out of the town of Covel.

A few days after their arrival in Ohio, she thought to look for it. Maria and Evelina had helped her search all of their belongings in their new home to no avail. Giovanna hadn't memorized Alessandro's address in Michigan or Italy, and had no idea if he lived across the Atlantic Ocean in the old country, or only three hundred miles away in a state that bordered her own.

Her time on the ship with him had been romantic and magical, a hopeful beginning. If she could've stayed in that world forever, she might have, just to be with Alessandro. When she closed her eyes at night, he appeared before her, smiling and wearing his perfect uniform. Her mouth formed a kiss as she relived the dance over and over in her mind.

Sharing a room with her sisters left her no privacy. Evelina wanted to know everything she was thinking, and Giovanna was not good at hiding her feelings.

"Why do you go to sleep with a smile on your lips? And why do you keep humming the same song?" Ev asked one evening while the three of them were drifting off to sleep.

"It's the music from the very last song, when Giovanna danced with Alessandro," Maria said.

"Are you dancing in your mind?" Ev asked. "Do you dream of him?"

"It's a pretty song. That's all," Giovanna replied. "I don't want to forget it."

Sometimes she fell asleep thinking of the dance and her walks on the deck of the ship with Alessandro. She could only wonder if he had written to her and was resigned to the fact that even if he had, she wouldn't have received his letters after their furtive departure from her first American home.

Her family hadn't seen or spoken to anyone from Covel in almost four years. She and her sisters were certain that their father had made sure not to leave a trail that could be followed by the mysterious woman who claimed to be his friend. Her father had been on edge the evening Isolde had introduced herself in the field. He remained so until they were traveling on the train to Ohio. Giovanna's intuition told her that journey, so quickly planned and carried out under the cloak of darkness, had just as much to do with escaping from Isolde, as it did with living near Zio Benny and *Comare* Rosie. She was glad to be away from the woman who frightened her and disturbed her father. Her parents were happy together in their new home, and she didn't want anyone or anything to jeopardize their relationship. They had waited so long to be together, and though their life was far from perfect, they were happy. If leaving Covel meant she would never hear from Alessandro, it was worth it. She couldn't bear to see her mother's heart broken.

"You might see him again one day," Maria said, interrupting her thoughts.

"I'm sure he's forgotten about me, and it isn't likely I'll ever see him again," Giovanna said. "Besides, I might meet a nice guy here."

"Orlando," Ev said, with a knowing grin. "I think he likes you."

"He's been asking Zio Benny a lot of questions about you," Maria said.

It seemed to Giovanna that her sisters were able to read her mind.

"I like talking to him," Giovanna said. Orlando had spoken to her many times in the last few months on his visits to Yorkville from a neighboring town where he lived.

"I've seen you talking. He's flirting," Ev said. She twirled a lock of Giovanna's hair between her fingers.

"Zio Benny told Mama that he's twenty-five," Maria said.

"He's much nicer than the boys in the neighborhood."

"He's very handsome, but he's kind of short," Evelina teased. Giovanna waved her hand at Ev, dismissing her comment. She didn't mind that she was a little taller than Orlando.

"Oh, I forgot to tell you. He left a letter for you on the table," Ev said, jumping out of Giovanna's reach.

"When?" Giovanna said, as she rushed to the kitchen. A vase of wildflowers sat in the middle of the table. Leaning against it was an envelope with her name printed on it. She picked it up and stared at it, but didn't open it.

"Read it to us," Evelina said.

"Ev," Maria said. "It's personal."

"Please," Ev begged. "It might be a love letter."

"I hardly know him," Giovanna said. She carried the letter to their room and sat on the bed.

"Aren't you going to read it?" Ev asked.

"Not with you breathing down my neck. Roll over and let me read the letter without your prying eyes peering over my shoulder."

"Come on, nosey," Maria said, pulling on Ev's arm.

Giovanna smiled at Maria and stuck her tongue out at Evelina.

"You're no fun," Ev said, as Maria pushed her onto her side and away from Giovanna.

The candle on their night table was still lit. Giovanna moved close to the flame and opened the letter with trembling fingers and read the neat handwriting.

Dear Giovanna,

I hope this letter finds you well and that you don't think me too forward for writing. Though we've only spoken on a few occasions, I would like to ask your permission to call on you so that we might get to know one another better. I'm quite taken with your beautiful smile and your kind manner and hope you find me agreeable as well. From the moment I first saw you, my heart danced in my chest, and I fear it will not be quieted unless I see you again. I've spoken to your father about my wish to court you if you agree. I'd like to take you on a dinner date. I leave the decision in your hands and wait with anticipation for your reply.

Fondly,
Orlando Flamini

Giovanna had never read such eloquent writing. And certainly no one had ever written a letter to her before. She read the letter two more times. It had been at least two weeks since Orlando had spoken to her at lunch after church. She remembered the way his kind eyes held her gaze when he talked. Something else about him had impressed her as well. He never stopped smiling.

His letter touched her and his intentions surprised and thrilled her at the same time. Though she spent many of her thoughts on Alessandro, she had begun to dream more and more of Orlando.

She blew out the candle and placed the letter under her pillow with her fingers wrapped around it, just in case Ev tried to sneak it away after she fell asleep.

The next day, as soon as she opened her eyes, she read the letter again and then hid it in the pocket of her dress. Every few minutes she touched it to make sure it hadn't disappeared. Her stomach fluttered with excitement when she thought of Orlando. What would she say when she saw him again? She was glad she had been reading the newspaper to practice English and stay informed about what was going on in the world. Still, she could tell from Orlando's writing that he was more educated than she and hoped he wouldn't think her common and ignorant.

One of her biggest regrets was giving up her formal education, but whenever she considered her decision to quit school, she remembered the insults of the other children who laughed at her accent and called her derogatory names: Dago, Guinea, Grease ball, Wop, and she felt the sting of their taunts again. She didn't know what these slurs meant, only that they were delivered with scorn and a mean laughter filled with ridicule.

The teasing confused her, because she had never uttered an unkind word to anyone who dogged her with callous jeers.

Some of them were also immigrants, from other European countries. She thought they should stick together, but there was little camaraderie amongst the various nationalities, only a fierce competitiveness. She wondered if Orlando had ever been childish or mean enough to pick on his schoolmates and tried to picture him as a young boy. Somehow she didn't think he could ever be unkind.

As she daydreamed through her morning chores, she thought about his easy manner and the beautiful words of his letter. When the laundry was folded and put away, she was suddenly tired of keeping her growing excitement to herself. She called for Maria, who ran into the room.

"What is it?" she asked. Her face was flushed and her apron was dirty where she had wiped her hands after washing them at the pump.

"Orlando wants to get to know me better and take me on a dinner date."

"Well?" Maria said. Her eyes twinkled and she stood on her toes like a ballerina poised for the next cue of the music.

"I don't know what to do."

"May I read it?" Maria reached toward her with unreserved excitement.

Giovanna gave her the letter. Maria's eyes darted over the paper and she sighed.

"He's crazy about you, Giovanna," Maria said. "Do you want to see him?"

"I think maybe I do, but what about Alessandro?"

"You have no way to get in touch with him. I don't think you can put your life on hold for a guy you might never see again."

"I know. You're probably right."

"I like Orlando. I think you should give him a chance."

"Maria," Giovanna said. "What's a dinner date?"

"I'm not sure. Maybe Pop invited him here for dinner."

Evelina poked her head around the doorframe. "I know what a dinner date is."

"You were spying on us," Maria said.

"Yes, I was. Do you want to know what a date is?" Evelina gave them her best impish grin.

Giovanna nodded.

"The man comes to the lady's house and takes her somewhere, like a restaurant or to a picture show, and they go alone."

Giovanna had never been to a restaurant or a picture show. The idea excited her, but she didn't think it would be possible for her to go.

"Without a chaperone?" Maria asked.

"The Americans call it dating."

"Pop will never go for that," Giovanna said.

"What if he says it's okay? Will you go on a date with Orlando?" Ev asked.

"I don't know," Giovanna answered. She sat down on the bed and placed her hands on top of her head.

"You're eighteen. I would if I were you," Evelina said, as though she were much older than her eleven years. She sat next to Giovanna.

"You would, would you?" Giovanna said and gave her a hug.

"That's not how they do things in Italy," Maria said.

"This is America. In America, young people go on dates. Chaperones are old- fashioned. That's the old country way," Evelina said. "I've seen Pop talking to Orlando. They laugh a lot. He might let you go. If he does, you should go. It's about time someone had some fun around here."

"Fun? " Giovanna said and made a frown. "What's fun?"

"This," Ev said, and jumped on the bed. Maria held out her hands and Ev pulled her up. Together they bounced on the bed until their mother saw their bobbing heads through the window and hollered for them to stop.

If Evelina was right, there was a slim chance her father would say yes. Even though he was old-fashioned, he wanted her to be happy. If he gave his permission, she would go.

December 1927

Chapter 20

"Where's your boyfriend, fag?" The words hit Benny like a hammer as he walked alone in the early darkness of the cold winter evening.

He didn't turn around. A dog barked and he stumbled over a crack in the sidewalk. It was only two more blocks to his place. Every nerve in his body began to tingle with fear. The two men who walked behind him laughed loudly and moved closer. The smell of alcohol drifted from their skin and clothing. They must have slipped in behind him while he was lost in his own thoughts. One of them yelled something he couldn't make out. He flinched and picked up his pace. Rose's porch was within sight.

He tried to appear nonchalant. When he reached the porch, they were right behind him. One of them kicked at his foot to trip him, but he stepped over it and walked into the hallway, locking the door behind him. Their laughter assaulted him as they went on, away from the house. His knees buckled.

"Benny, you look as if you've seen a ghost," Henry called from the top of the stairs.

Benny stood straight and put on a smile. He knotted his trembling hands behind his back. "I'm fine." Telling Henry would only worry him.

Henry hurried down the stairs and took his hand. "Rose left our dinner in the oven. She's gone to play bingo at the church." He ushered him into the kitchen, and then went to the sink to fill their glasses with water. "I have something important to tell you."

The smell of roasting chicken awakened his appetite and he realized he had eaten very little all day. He opened the oven door, and let it drop when Henry's arm brushed his.

"What's wrong?" Henry asked. He put his hands on Benny's shoulders and then embraced him. Benny relaxed into his arms. His troubles could never be hidden from Henry for long.

"Some drunks followed me home. They were rude. It's nothing."

Henry pulled out a chair for Benny and sat across from him. Taking his hands he announced, "You won't have to put up with idiots like that much longer. I have some good news."

Benny sat down and waited. Henry squeezed his hands.

"The City of Lights is a haven for all kinds of people from all walks of life. We can live there without the constant stares and whispers of those who don't approve of our lifestyle."

"Are you saying what I think you're saying?" Benny asked.

"Yes."

"We're going to Paris?" Benny smiled and embraced Henry, and then pulled away. His face clouded over.

"I've finalized the arrangements. It'll be easier for us there, Benny. You'll see," Henry said. "Still, I know leaving America will be bittersweet."

"I'll miss Appollonia, Luigi, and the girls."

Henry got out of his chair and sat on the floor at Benny's feet. He looked up at him with sympathetic eyes and held onto his arms. "I'll miss them, too, and America. I wanted to live here, just as you did, but Paris is a better place for us. We won't have to hide how we feel."

Benny closed his eyes and pictured a place where he and Henry could walk freely outdoors without being bullied and criticized. Henry was right. Here, the bullying wasn't going to end. Though he tried to hide his feelings for Henry from everyone, his fondness for the affable Frenchman was apparent. He advised his nieces to remain strong and oblivious to the criticism they received whenever other children taunted them, but he wasn't taking his own advice very well. He and Henry had resolved that they wouldn't continue to live in Yorkville. Henry knew that in France, they might find a place more tolerant of their affair. In Yorkville, the men at the mill were beginning to treat them badly. They wanted to be companions, but here, they couldn't be together without consequences.

Luigi had protected Benny on several occasions, and while he was grateful for his brother-in-law's help, he knew that Luigi only defended him because they were family. Luigi, too, had been repulsed at first to learn that Benny was in love with a man. Over time, he'd come to accept it, but it had been a struggle for him to come to terms with what he thought was "unnatural."

The insults had increased in recent months, and they made him weary. Each day he felt as if he were walking on the edge of a cliff and one stiff wind would send him into a canyon of despair. He had come to America for a better life, not one of lying and sneaking around. Living with Rose was becoming awkward, too. She appeared to know what was going on between Henry and him and treated them like patients with a contagious disease. He was tired of receiving her distasteful scowls and mumbled criticisms. Each night when they walked or studied after dinner, Henry talked more and more of Paris, where the opinions of neighbors and coworkers were more likely to be charitable.

They ate their dinner, and Benny tried to focus on Henry's words as he described the wonders of Paris. His winsome portrayal painted such an enchanting picture that Benny forgot, for a moment, there was a price to pay in leaving America. Henry's mood was infectious until he left the table and headed upstairs to begin packing. When he was gone, his enthusiasm vanished with him. While Benny scrubbed the plates and pans and dipped them into the warm water, he thought of how he would tell Appollonia his news. His heart struggled between feelings of elation at the prospect of a new and better life with Henry, and dread, at telling his sister that soon he might never see her again. She and his nieces were the only other people in his world that unconditionally accepted him for who he was.

With Luigi's help, he had explained his sexuality to Appollonia during his visit to their apartment in West Virginia. She had taken the news very well. She wasn't as naïve as he had assumed.

"I've always wondered if you felt that way," she said. Throwing her arms around him, she told him, "I love you. You don't have to worry about this Bernandino. You're my brother. I want you to be happy."

Leaving her would be very difficult. He doubted he would ever see her again, for he would most likely never return to America, and returning to Europe was not in Luigi's plans. He was very fond of his three delightful nieces as well. They didn't question his relationship with Henry, whom they treated as a family member. He hoped that Henry would always love him. Once they left for Paris, he would be his only family.

His thoughts were interrupted by a knock at the door.

"The girls. They're coming to help us pack," Henry yelled.

Benny opened the door. "Hello, my *bellas*," he said. A phony smile pulled at the corners of his mouth.

"Zio Benny, we've come to help you," Giovanna said. Maria and Evelina stood beside her on the porch. Appollonia, who dabbed at her eyes with a handkerchief, walked up the sidewalk behind them.

"Come in."

"I'm up here," Henry yelled from his room.

Benny followed his nieces as they raced to see Henry. Appollonia clasped his hand and they ascended the stairs. Henry had obviously broken the news to his sister and nieces for him. He was glad that he didn't have to tell them.

Henry closed the lid to his trunk full of books. The clasps wouldn't lock into place, so Giovanna sat on one side of the lid and Maria on the other to force it into position. Ev crouched in front of their dangling legs to lock the clasps and buckle the leather straps on the sides of the overstuffed chest.

"Paris is so far away," Giovanna said. "We'll miss you."

Henry's bed was covered with the clothes he had laid out to pack. He moved the clothes aside and patted the bed. The girls jumped up from the trunk to sit beside him. Benny searched the faces of his sister's children. Evelina was serious and quiet.

"Don't be sad, little *fleurs*," Henry said. He placed his hand, one by one, under each of their chins and tilted them upward.

Benny smiled. They were like little flowers, gentle and delicate. He knew Henry would miss them, too.

"Let's see if you're small enough to fit in my trunk," Henry said, pulling on Evelina's hand.

"We don't want you to go," Ev said. Her usual, mischievous grin was replaced with an angry scowl.

"Can't you stay?" Maria asked. Her plea was so sincere that Benny put his hand over his heart for it felt as if it were breaking in two.

He stood in the doorway, watching them. Giovanna came to him and wrapped her arms around him. He squeezed her, wondering if he could be happy in Paris without his sister and her daughters. In the short time they had lived in Yorkville, he'd become very close to them. They understood the reason he wanted to live in France with Henry, but it didn't make his leaving any easier.

Giovanna bent her head to rest it on his shoulder. He laid his head on hers and then let go of her to move into the crowded room to speak. His eyes filled with tears as he chose his departing words.

"It's good we were together in America. I'm happy that we had these days to help each other in this new place. I didn't know before you came here how happy you would make me."

Maria wiped her face as tears flowed down her cheeks.

"I'm happy when I'm with you, but in many other ways I'm miserable. I do my best to be kind, but others treat me with hatred because they think I'm different. It isn't a good life here for Henry and me. We deserve to be treated with respect. I'm sad to go away from you, because I love you. I regret that leaving America means leaving you, and I'll miss your papa, as well. I know you understand why I'm going. It's what I have to do, but I do so with regret."

Appollonia came into the room from the landing outside Benny's door. "Your words tear a hole in my heart. Even though I don't want you to go, I can't stand to see you stay here and be mistreated. Maybe you've suffered this way most of your life. If you can be happy in Paris with Henry, living where people will treat you with decency, I want you to go. I'll miss you, but I'm happy for you."

Ev stood up, pushed past her mother and darted down the stairs. Benny went to the top of the staircase, and Rose came into the hallway. Ev stopped on the bottom step, red-eyed, her face wet with tears.

"*E 'bene, piccola,*" Rose whispered. It's okay, little one

"No, damn it. It isn't," she said, running out the front door.

Benny ran down the stairs to go after her. Rose followed and stared at him with hatred in her eyes.

"I'm not upset that you're leaving. Your love for Henry is repulsive. If you weren't Appollonia's brother, I would have thrown you and Henry out as soon as you started spending time together. You thought you were so clever, studying English together and pretending to be just friends. God will punish you for your disgusting affair. No one wants you here, except for Appollonia and her pathetically tolerant daughters and husband. If it hadn't been for Luigi, you and Henry would've gotten the beating you deserved from the other men at the mill. Goodbye and don't come back. We don't want you." She waved her hand as if to push him away. "I've already rented your rooms."

Benny felt his whole body burn with anger. It was all he could do not to run at Rose and knock her down. He walked to the door with controlled steps.

Evelina threw it open and said, "I heard you."

Rose's wrinkled face puckered in a sour expression.

"If only I could put you on a boat to Paris and keep Zio Benny here," she said, running back outside and down the steps before Rose could smack her with her raised hand.

Benny climbed the stairs two at a time and closed the door to Henry's room.

He wouldn't give Rose the satisfaction of a fight.

While his family said their goodbyes to Benny and Henry, Luigi sat outside the back door of the mill at a graying picnic table. His only time to be off his feet was the thirty minutes he was allowed for lunch. Even in the cold winter months, when snow covered the table and bench and his shoes became wet as he walked across the cement, he still preferred to eat outside. Sometimes the bench was soaked with moisture that seeped into his thick cotton work britches, but he didn't mind. They dried quickly when he reentered the hot mill. His backside relished the cool bench, and his skin tingled with the brisk air that was a welcome relief from the oppressive heat that drifted in waves over him as he worked.

He drank water from a ceramic jug, savoring the liquid that quenched his thirst and eased his parched throat. Usually he was thirsty and ravenous by lunchtime, but not today. He opened the sandwich that Appollonia had wrapped in a thin linen towel and took a bite. Feelings of melancholy overwhelmed him, and he choked on the soft bread and sharp cheese. Benny and Henry ate lunch with him each day, and he would miss their easy camaraderie. His brother-in-law's decision to move to Paris was going to be hard on his family and a difficult adjustment for him as well.

Much to his surprise, Benny and Henry had become his friends. There was once a time when he would have disapproved of their feelings and behaved accordingly. When he was a younger man, if someone had told him that he would be a friend to two men who were in love with one another, he would've laughed. But his youthful ideas had changed due to his brother-in-law's kindness. Benny had helped him escape his difficult circumstances, overcoming his own anger to help Luigi settle in Ohio, without ever breathing a word to Appollonia about the real reason for their hasty departure. He hadn't thought to condemn Luigi; he'd only wanted to help. Luigi was forever indebted to him.

Though at first he was repelled by Benny's revelation, over time he'd done his best to put his feelings about homosexuality aside and accept Benny and Henry's relationship. It was the least he could do for Benny. Luigi knew his betrayal of Appollonia sickened Benny, but his brother-in-law had not chastised him for his mistake. Even without his feelings of gratitude and his family connection, he would've chosen Benny as a friend, because he genuinely liked his kind brother-in-law. He had defended him many times, coming to blows when necessary, when callous men had bullied him.

As he thought of all that Benny had done to help him, he

remembered the gloomy day Benny had arrived in Covel, recalling their conversation with sadness and regret.

"Bernandino, I betrayed your sister. I was with another woman many times. I'm sorry it happened. I want to leave this place, to be away from her. I know this makes you angry, and you have every right, but I need you to help me for the sake of my family," Luigi had blurted out, overcome with emotion and shame.

"Appollonia doesn't deserve to be hurt by your mistake, so I'll keep your secret and help you escape the trap you've made for yourself." Benny had responded with quiet control instead of the anger Luigi expected.

Benny had been as good as his word, helping his family slip from the hills of West Virginia to Ohio without a trace. Luigi owed their happiness to him and had tried to repay him by shielding him from the harsh words and cruel actions of many of the other immigrants in their small town. It had helped in a small way, but it wasn't enough. By the time he returned home this evening, Benny and Henry would be gone.

He didn't plan to return to Europe, and he knew Benny had lost his desire to be in America. He resigned himself to the fact that he wouldn't see him again. His choice to stay in this country had cost him the comfort of many extended family members. It was one of the countless sacrifices he had endured for the sake of his daughters.

Truth be told, he missed Italy. Sometimes he dreamed of the vineyards, the farmland, and the language that he still preferred to the English of his new homeland. The sights and smells of the old country still lingered when he closed his eyes in the bed he shared with Appollonia. But he didn't want to go back.

Through all the hardships and regrets he had suffered and the pain of all the years he was apart from his family, he still felt that America was the place where his daughters had the best chance for a good life. He never wavered in this feeling, even if it wasn't always the best life for him. He didn't want his daughters to be children of Italy. It was better for them to be Americans.

Chapter 21

Isolde hated working on Saturday night. The kitchen had closed hours ago, but the *ristorante* was open until eleven as a gathering place for the miners and other locals. The other waitresses finished at nine, but she had to stay until closing to serve coffee, root beer, ginger ale and tonic water. She took orders, carried drinks from the bar, and endured first flirting, then groping as the night wore on, the women left, and the men became rowdier. Even if she swallowed her pride and flirted back, the tips were small.

Her three year-old son, Giuseppe, slept alone in the bed they shared in her room upstairs. He was big enough now to climb out of the bed and walk down the stairs if he needed her while she was gone. Once he fell asleep, he rarely woke up and probably didn't even realize she wasn't in the room with him. The other women, who called him Jesse, told her how lucky she was to have such a pleasant child who stayed out of the way and seemed happy to entertain himself.

Lucky was not a word she would use to describe herself. She didn't appreciate that Giuseppe was happy and healthy, qualities most mothers longed for in their children. To her, he was a constant reminder of Luigi and the life she wanted, but didn't have. Caring for him was a burden. Having him had been a mistake in judgment on her part.

Having Luigi or any man who would take care of her had been her desire. When he had gone, and her pregnancy was evident, none of the other men wanted her. After Giuseppe was born, and she still couldn't find Luigi, she no longer took care of her appearance. Her once voluptuous figure and beautiful face were heavier now, and she rarely fixed her hair. She didn't have any desirable qualities other than her looks that would attract a man. She wasn't kind or generous or patient. Her bitterness painted her face with a cold, undesirable mask that frightened the men who had once considered her attractive. Her beauty had camouflaged her constant scowl and weak character in the past. Now it was gone, and she had nothing to offer but a resentful disposition and another mouth to feed.

Mostly men huddled in small groups playing card games, checkers and backgammon at the tables. One of them motioned for Isolde to come to his side. He wasn't a regular. She knew him vaguely for she had considered seducing him in hopes that he would tell her where Luigi had gone. His name was Aldo, and he worked as a ticket taker at the train station. He had been barely seventeen on the day she'd visited there four years ago, but he was in his early twenties now. She wondered if he remembered her.

"Hey, waitress," he called to her in Italian.

She took her time, taking slow and deliberate steps until she stopped next to his chair.

"Don't I know you?" he asked, squinting his eyes as he turned to look up at her.

Isolde smiled faintly without answering.

"I do. I do know you," Aldo continued. He slurred his words and rocked back in his chair. He had obviously been drinking homemade wine or hooch before he arrived at the *ristorante.*

"You asked me about Luigi, a long time ago, at the train station. But I didn't tell. I didn't tell, because I made a promise. I made a promise to Luigi." He placed his index finger on his lips.

Isolde pulled his arm, and he stood up as his chair fell with a thud to the floor.

"Let me help you." She got him to his feet as he winked at his friends and walked with her.

Isolde's heart raced as she guided Aldo to an empty table in the corner by the stairs. He sat across from her, and smirked.

"How are you, Aldo?" she asked him, as she reached toward him and stroked his full head of dark hair.

"A little drunk."

"You deserve to have fun with your friends."

"I know why you're being nice to me," Aldo said. He pulled away from her.

She moved her hand to the table. "I'm nice to everyone."

"No, you aren't," Aldo said. He pointed his index finger at her. "You were only nice to Luigi, but he didn't want you to know that he was moving to Ohio." Aldo paused and smacked his forehead with his hand. "I've said too much."

Isolde wasn't a patient woman, but she smiled at Aldo and slid her chair around the table until her leg touched his. She stroked his arm.

"You're very handsome," she whispered

Aldo laughed. "You're almost my mother's age."

Isolde frowned and took her hand from his arm. She wanted to slap him, and tell him that once she had been young and desirable, but instead she said, "I could be your older sister, maybe, but I'm not old enough to be your mother. Would you like to come up to my room for a little while?"

Aldo leaned close to her and wagged his finger in her face.

"What do you want from me?" he asked.

"You're a perceptive little shit. Aren't you?" she whispered. He smirked at her, but held her gaze. Calming herself she continued, "Maybe we can make *un affare*."

"A deal?" Aldo asked with interest. "Let me guess. You want to know where Luigi Falconi went? Maybe he went home to Italy. It's been a few years."

"You said Ohio. Will you tell me the name of the town?"

"Why should I? I made a promise to Luigi, and I'm a man of my word," he answered.

Isolde traced her index finger over her lips and then bit her finger while she stared at Aldo. His eyes grew wide and his expression turned thoughtful.

"I want to write a letter to him and his family, if you know his addess." She paused to rub her neck and unfastened the top button of her blouse.

Aldo watched her. Rising from his chair, he whispered, "I think you might persuade me to make *un affare*."

Isolde glanced around the room. She saw Luigi's friend,

Vincente. He appeared to be in a heated conversation with one of the other miners. The dinner hour was over. No one would notice if she was gone for a short while. She got up and quickly went to the steps.

Aldo waited until she reached the top of the stairs and disappeared down the dark hallway. Then she heard the echo of his heavy footfall on the staircase.

When Isolde opened the door to her small quarters that consisted of a bedroom and tiny sitting room, she heard Giuseppe's gentle breathing. She lifted him from the bed, carried him to the couch in the sitting room, covered him with a blanket and closed the door that adjoined her bedroom. He continued to sleep, his auburn curls matted to his forehead by sweat, and a ragged teddy bear clutched under his arm. Aldo was standing behind her when she turned. If he had seen her carrying Giuseppe, he didn't say so. He unbuttoned her blouse quickly.

She placed her hand on his chest to slow him down and handed him the pad and pencil she kept in her apron for taking drink orders. "The address."

"I don't remember the number, just the street and the town."

"That's enough," she said, as she watched him write.

He gave her the pad and pencil, and then pulled at her apron strings clumsily as she read his handwriting. *Main Street, Yorkville, Ohio*

April/ May 1928

Chapter 22

When the five o'clock whistle sounded, it could be heard on every street and in each corner of Yorkville. Housewives and merchants, alike, knew when the flood of workers from Wheeling Steel would begin their tired walk home from the mill. Most of the men and women walked to their jobs, lunch pails and purses in hand. Only Mr. Polanski and the executives owned cars. The laborers had to spend their money on necessities. There was little to none left for luxuries. Each place of business: *Severini's Grocery store, the post office, Piciacchia's Drug Store, Del Vecchio's Furniture, DiNapoli's Gas Station,* for those lucky enough to own a car, were all within walking distance.

Giovanna and Maria gathered their sweaters and purses. It was Friday, and they had big plans for the weekend. On Saturday they were taking Evelina shopping for fabric, so that Giovanna could make her a new dress for church. After shopping they would stop for lunch and an ice cream soda. On Sunday, Orlando was coming for dinner. As soon as she'd read his first letter, Giovanna wrote back and asked him to come for their Sunday evening meal. He had accepted. Their first date would actually be with her entire family. Then, when she was comfortable, and more importantly to her father, after he knew Orlando well enough, they might be permitted to go out unchaperoned.

"What are you wearing for your date on Sunday?" Maria asked. She seemed as excited about her sister's new romance as Giovanna was.

"The blue dress, I think, but it's not really a date. He's coming to have dinner here, with all of us." Giovanna shook her hair loose of the braid she'd worn all day and the wind blew it into her face.

"Mama's making gnocchi and meatballs. She only makes that for special occasions," Maria said. She put on her sweater and raised her eyebrows.

"Hmm," Giovanna sighed, smiling at Maria.

"Pop likes that Orlando's from the old country. You like him, don't you?" Maria asked.

"Yes, I like his smile, and he's sweet," Giovanna said, blushing.

"I like his wavy hair. He's handsome." Maria stroked her own wavy hair and looked dreamily at her sister. She had not met anyone of interest. The boys she knew behaved like ruffians, and those who had tried to charm her had not yet been successful.

Giovanna sighed, again.

"Do you think he's handsome?" Maria ran in front of Giovanna and stopped to get her attention.

Giovanna paused. "I do."

"You don't sound so sure," Maria said.

"I can't help comparing him to someone else with a nice smile."

They walked up the hill on Main Street and could see their father a block or so ahead of them. He was alone. Most days, the girls would have hurried to catch up with him, but not today. Their conversation wasn't meant for his ears.

"Do you think there's any chance we'll ever see Alessandro again?" Maria said. She frequently read Giovanna's thoughts.

"He's probably forgotten all about me. I did like him though," Giovanna said, doing her best to act as though he had been just a passing fancy. "He made me feel special."

"He was madly in love with you."

"We were too young to know if we were in love." As she said these words to Maria, Giovanna felt almost disloyal to Alessandro. How could she be attracted to Orlando when she still held a glimmer of hope that one day she would see Alessandro again?

"I think it was love at first sight," Maria said. "A very romantic shipboard romance, a kiss, a heartbreaking good-bye." She batted her eyes at Giovanna and pretended to swoon.

Giovanna rolled her eyes and gave Maria a light push.

"Sometimes I wonder if it really happened. Was it just a dream?"

"It really happened. I am your witness. What if you saw him again? How would you feel?" Maria asked with excitement. She was a hopeless romantic.

Giovanna put her arm around her sister and whispered, "I think I would feel as I did when I saw him standing in the ship's doorway, like it was the first warm spring day after a long, frigid winter."

"Orlando has a tough act to follow," Maria said, laughing.

Giovanna grabbed her sister's hand. When they rounded the top of the hill, they saw Evelina, who sat in a rocking chair on the porch, and their father, who climbed the steep stairs, raising his legs with a slow, tired effort.

Tomorrow was Saturday. Two Saturdays a month Pop went with a friend to the nearby town of Wheeling. She knew her mother thought her father was selfish for going "out on the town" without them every other Saturday. Her mother didn't say a word, but her bitterness was apparent in the way she watched him, standing on the porch with her lips pursed, her eyes narrowed, and her hands on her hips. He never turned around to look at her as he made his way to the bus stop dressed in nice pants and a carefully ironed shirt. Her mother didn't leave her spot just outside the front door until he was no longer visible. Her day would be spent making pasta and hanging work britches on the clothesline to dry in the sunshine. Giovanna wished her mother and father would go out together, but they never did.

Evelina ran to meet her sisters. "School was boring. I'm tired of it. That pain in the ass, Guido, pestered me on my walk home." She grabbed Maria's hand and stopped. "What are we doing tomorrow?"

"It's a surprise," Maria said. "You'll see."

"Tell me. Please. I'll keep asking 'til you tell me."

"I'll tell you this much," Giovanna said. "We're taking you to Wheeling on the bus."

"What're we doing there?" Ev asked, dancing a circle around her sisters.

"That part is a secret, but you have to be presentable and ready to leave the house by nine o'clock," Giovanna said in her primmest voice.

"Presentable? Are we going to church?" Ev guessed. A look of disappointment darkened her face.

"Do you think your surprise is an extra day of church?" Giovanna asked.

Ev shrugged her shoulders.

"You'll have to wait until tomorrow to find out where we're taking you."

"Will you tell?" Ev asked Maria.

Giovanna shook her head in back of Evelina.

"If I tell you, it won't be a surprise," Maria said, pretending to lock her lips and throw away the key.

"Shit," Ev mumbled.

"Ev," Giovanna scolded, as her little sister ran into the house.

The girls set the table and helped their mother with the dinner preparations. Tonight they would have pizza for dinner, their mother's delicious dough ladled with tomato sauce and topped with melted mozzarella, paired with a salad. Later, just before bed, a second pizza of crispy dough brushed with oil and sprinkled with sugar would be their only dessert for the week. It was their Friday night tradition.

Her father washed his hands and sat in the chair at the head of the table. Her mother brought the pizza and cut the first slice for him, while Giovanna passed the salad to her sisters.

"So," her father began. "I guess Orlando's coming over for spaghetti on Sunday."

"Gnocchi," her mother said. She took a long drink from her glass.

Giovanna thought she looked tired.

"Going to a lot of trouble," her father said. "Do you like him, Giovanna?"

"He seems nice," she answered. Her sisters giggled.

"I like him," he said. "He's a hard worker, from what I hear. He owns his own business, a restaurant. And..."

Her mother took a deep breath, but didn't interrupt.

"And," her father continued. "He's from the old country."

"He has nice hair," Evelina said.

Maria laughed. Giovanna bowed her head and bit her lip.

"I don't know about that, but he seems like a good man," her father said. He smiled at Evelina.

"We'll see if he's good enough for Giovanna," her mother said.

"We'll see," her father agreed.

"Maria and I are taking Evelina to Wheeling tomorrow," Giovanna said. She hoped to turn the conversation to other topics. "We'll ride the bus with you, Pop."

"Can we get ice cream?" Evelina asked.

Giovanna nodded and Ev smiled.

"Why are you going to Wheeling?" her father asked.

"We want to do something fun," she answered. "I have some money from sewing." She knew her father's next question would be about the cost. "You should come with us, Mama." Giovanna put her hand on her mother's arm and looked hopefully at her.

Her father glanced at her mother.

"No, I'll stay home. I have things to do here to prepare for Sunday's dinner."

Giovanna sensed that her mother didn't want to be pushed. She rarely left the house and only went into the yard to pick vegetables from the garden or pump water at the well. "We won't be gone long. We'll bring you back a treat," Giovanna said.

"That would be nice," her mother said, as she stood to clear the table.

"We'll do the dishes, Mama," Maria said.

"Okay. I'll sit on the porch for a while," her mother said. Her father was already making his way to his chair outside.

Giovanna and Evelina picked up the plates and glasses.

"I'll put the sugar pizza in the oven for you," Giovanna said.

When her mother was outside, Giovanna whispered to her sisters, "Let's find something nice for her tomorrow. She seems so tired."

"I wish she would come with us," Evelina said softly.

"She won't," Maria said. She crept to the window and peered at her parents, who sat in silence on the porch. She closed the front door.

"We can make the gnocchi with her on Sunday," Giovanna said. "Otherwise, it'll take her all morning. I think her asthma is wearing her down."

"She needs to get out of the house," Evelina said. "I would go crazy staying here day after day. She doesn't even go to the store, and the only person she talks to besides us is grumpy old *Comare* Rosie."

"If she doesn't want to go out, we can't make her," Maria said.

"I wish she would," Giovanna said. "She might feel better."

"I don't think it's right for Pop to go without her," Evelina said. "What does he do there on Saturdays with his friend?"

"I don't know," Giovanna said. "Whatever it is, I don't think he wants her to come along."

Standing in Signora Limone's yard, Isolde tried to conceal her impatience. She bit at her nails and breathed a heavy sigh like a leashed dog ready for a run. The old woman was making her beg, though she already knew what Isolde wanted.

"Please, Signora Limone. It'll be hard for Jesse to sit still on the long train ride. I know he would be happier here with you. He loves your cooking and can play in the yard while you do your chores. See how he smiles when he sees you?" she implored with the kindest voice she could muster.

"Jesse's a good boy, Isolde, but I have work to do."

"He won't get in the way. He's happy entertaining himself."

"I don't know..."

"I'll cook a meal for you and do a week's laundry." Isolde knew that Signora Limone loved Jesse and wondered why she wouldn't take care of him without bartering.

"I suppose I could save some of my laundry until you get back, and I do like the apple pie you make for the restaurant. Where are you going?" Signora Limone asked.

"It's none of your business." Isolde's charm was short-lived.

"I'm good enough to care for your son, but not good enough for you to tell me where you're going? Why is it such a big secret?"

Isolde was tired of talking to the meddlesome old woman. "It's not a secret, but I'm not in the habit of telling anyone my business."

"Yes, well…?"

"I'm going to Wheeling, West Virginia. I'm thinking of getting a job there. It's in the Ohio River Valley. There are more people there and plenty of nice restaurants. Maybe the tips will be better."

"If you're tired of Covel, why not go home to Italy?"

"There's nothing there for me," Isolde mumbled.

"What?"

"I want to stay in America."

"I see," Signora Limone looked contemplative. "Ok, Jesse can stay. How long will you be gone?"

Her innocent child smiled at Signora Limone.

"No more than two days." She turned to leave and remembered her manners.

"Thank you."

"Certainly," the old signora replied, turning to look at Jesse as he sat down in the yard and began to pull the yellow dandelions that were sprinkled amongst the blades of grass.

Isolde didn't kiss or hug him, but instead adjusted the strap of the bag that rested on her shoulder and unclenched her jaw. Jesse didn't look up as she began to walk away or notice that she neglected to tell him goodbye.

"Will you even bother to come back, Isolde?" Signora Limone's eyes searched Isolde's face when she turned to face her.

"Of course I will," she answered, and then gave her son a pat on the head. He reached up and put his small hand on top of hers. She pulled away and walked to the road, her heels clicking on the cement of the sidewalk.

The sun was finally shining on the dismal little town, but Isolde wasn't aware of the pleasant spring day. She walked along lost in thought until she came to the train. The small tote she carried was filled with tips she had saved for more than three years and a change of clothes. Its strap strained her shoulder. The train was almost empty, so she took the first seat by a window and wedged her bag safely between the wall and her leg, and then covered it with her sweater. She hoped she had enough money to secure a boarding house room or a small apartment in the steel mill town of Wheeling. After sleeping with Aldo, she had slept with several other men for money. This money, combined with the tips she had saved, pushed her moving stash up to five hundred dollars. Wheeling was a big town of more than sixty thousand people. Rooms and apartments would be expensive, but she was determined to find employment and a place to live in the next two days.

She folded her legs beneath her lap and pulled the sweater over them. For the first time in many years she felt anticipation. After finding a job and settling in, she would contact Luigi. The town where he lived was less than ten miles from Wheeling. Once he knew about Jesse, everything would work out. She was almost certain Luigi would take care of them, and if he didn't want to see things her way, she knew what to do. Resting her head against the glass, she fell asleep as the train traversed the rails.

Chapter 23

Luigi dipped his comb into a cup of water and ran it through his hair and mustache. He used the same cup of water to wet the stubble of his morning beard. When his cheeks and neck were covered with shaving cream, he ran the sharp straight edge over his face with quick strokes.

Evelina sat in a kitchen chair a few feet away and watched with rapt attention. She, like her father, was dressed and scrubbed for her Saturday excursion.

"It would be nice if you asked Mama to go to Wheeling with you," she said.

"You heard her. She doesn't want to go. She has too much to do here," he whispered.

The older girls were at the pump getting water. Appollonia was still asleep in the bedroom. He pulled the door closed so she could rest a while longer. Her rest during the night had been fitful as usual, and he hoped she would sleep until they were gone.

"I know she doesn't want to go, but it would be nice to see her in a beautiful dress with her arm wrapped around yours. You could escort her to the bus stop and whisk her off to a fancy restaurant with tablecloths and crystal wine glasses. She'd laugh at clever things you say and eat something expensive like veal or fish served on a white plate by a polite waiter. Best of all, someone else would do the cooking and wash the stack of dishes. Someone else would fetch the water from the pump and lift the heavy cast iron pot to heat on the stove. Someone else would grow the vegetables and clean and chop them."

"You've been reading too many stories," Luigi said. He wiped his face and put his razor in the cupboard. "Your mother is a wonderful cook. Why would she want to eat the food in a restaurant?"

"She's always so tired."

"She looks the same to me," he said. He finished his grooming and patted her head. "You look very pretty, Evelina. "

"Thanks, Pop."

"You'll have a good day with your sisters."

"Pop, I forgot to give you something last night."Evelina jumped up and went to her room. When she returned, she gave him an envelope.

"What's this?"

"It came in the mail for you. I put it in my school bag and forgot about it until now."

Luigi glanced at the return address. *Vincente, Covel, West Virginia*

"Is it from your friend from the mine, Pop?"

"I think so."

"Aren't you going to read it?" Evelina asked.

Giovanna and Maria came up the porch steps with the water pail.

"Later," he said, and tucked it into his pocket. He thought it odd that Vincente would write, as he never had in the four years since he'd last seen him.

"Good morning, Pop." His daughters greeted him and placed the water in the sink so their mother would find it when she awoke.

"Good morning. Let's go. We don't want to miss the bus."

"Will you get something special for Mama today?" Evelina asked, as they walked out the door.

"Yes, I know just what to get her," he answered, smiling at his persistent child.

Ev was right. Appollonia deserved a surprise. He remembered a man who sold roses from a street cart on the corner of Main Street in Wheeling, near the bus stop. If he didn't have a drink with his lunch, he could afford to buy a rose for his wife.

He spent the day walking around downtown Wheeling with his friend. The girls left him to do their shopping until it was time to catch the bus to go home. He remembered to stop and purchase the flower before boarding the bus. His friend sat across the aisle, instead of in the seat next to him, so he could lay the rose there.

Inside the bus the air was warm, so Luigi lowered the window. On the short ride back to Yorkville, he would enjoy the breeze. The bus was parked in front of a coffee shop. A waitress stood inside wih her back to the window. She seemed familiar to him. She talked to the owner and gestured with her hands. Luigi rested his head on the back seat and stared at her. The woman pushed her hair away from her face. When she lifted her arms to do so, her back was still to the window, but Luigi knew who she was.

The bus pulled away from the curb, and a breeze drifted in through the window. It tempered the air inside, but it didn't soothe him. He took off his jacket.

His friend said, "Your face is sweating Luigi. Are you all right?"

He nodded and pulled his handkerchief from his pocket to wipe his forehead. Then he remembered the letter from Vincente. Across from him, his friend closed his eyes as the bus moved into the street. He reached into his back pocket and took out the folded envelope. His daughters sat two seats behind him laughing and talking. Sliding lower in the seat, he opened the letter. His hands began to shake.

My Dear Friend, Luigi,

I'm sorry to tell you this bad news. Sometime ago, Aldo told Isolde where you are living. The word is that she'll be coming to find you. She wants you to be her man and a father to her son. That's right, Luigi. You have a son. I hope you receive this letter in time to decide what to do before she finds you.

Sincerely,
Vincente

Tears filled his eyes and ran down his cheeks. His sin was finally catching up with him.

Chapter 24

Alessandro was deep in thought while he navigated the winding mountain roads in his uncle's car. An occasional vehicle passed him, but he barely noticed. It had been more than three years since his last visit to West Virginia, but he remembered the dreary coal mining camp and the small, weather-beaten houses along Main Street. He was ready to investigate for several days and speak to everyone in town if that's what it took. Someone had to know where Giovanna had gone.

The wrinkled envelope from the waitress lay on the seat beside him. It was possible she knew something about Giovanna's whereabouts now. He remembered her determination and decided his first stop would be the restaurant. When he entered the town of Covel, his memory took him there. It was even more tired-looking than he remembered.

Once inside, he asked the first waitress he saw if he could speak to Isolde.

"She's gone with her boy, Jesse. She doesn't live here anymore," she answered.

He quelled his impatience and asked, "Where is she now?"

"I don't know the name. It's a big city north of here, very close to Ohio."

"Why did she leave?"

"Are you a relative?" she asked, suspiciously.

"A distant cousin," he lied, trying to make his voice sound calm and easy.

"She wanted to live in a bigger city and make more money. That's what she said anyway." The waitress set her empty drink tray on her hip and studied Alessandro.

"I was hoping someone could tell me where she is. All I

have is her old address," he said, and showed her the envelope printed in Isolde's handwriting.

She shrugged her shoulders. "You can probably find out from Signora Limone. She lives in the white house at the end of the street."

Alessandro thanked her and left the restaurant. An older lady sat on the front step of the white house, snapping beans and throwing them into a terra cotta bowl painted with sunflowers that was similar to one his Aunt Lucia had. A feeling of hopefulness overtook him as he went up her front walk.

"Good day. Are you Signora Limone?" Alessandro put on his best smile and extended his hand.

"Yes? Do I know you?" She looked up and sat a little taller as she continued her task.

"No, let me introduce myself. I'm Alessandro Pascarella. I'm looking for the Falconi family. Do you know where they are?" She shook her head, and he added, "What about Isolde Caldara?"

"You want to know about both of them?" She dropped the bean in her hand and gave him her attention.

"I'm looking for the Falconi's, but if you don't know where they are, I believe that possibly Isolde might," he said and sat beside her on the front porch.

"Why do you want to know?" Signora Limone eyed him with suspicion and rested her hands on the edge of the bowl.

Alessandro gently took the bowl from her and took up her task of readying the beans for cooking. Though she let him do so, she continued to stare at him.

"Are you from the old country?" She asked.

"Yes, but I've lived in America for almost four years now."

"Why do you think Isolde knows where the Falconi's live?" She asked him in Italian, as he continued to snap her beans.

Alessandro finished the last bean and placed the bowl on the porch beside Signora Limone before he spoke. Then he took the envelope from his pocket and showed it to her. "When I was here to look for them three years ago, she gave this to me, so that I could contact her if I found them. She seemed desperate. I think she wants to know where they are just as much as I do.

"Do you know why?"

"I have a reasonable guess. Why are you looking for them?" She looked into his eyes, and he didn't look away.

"I fell in love with Giovanna Falconi four years ago when I met her on the *SS Roma*. I want to find her and marry her."

"You fell in love with her on the ship from Italy?" Signora Limone said, her voice full of surprise.

"Yes," he said with a smile, remembering the moment he first saw Giovanna.

"I'll be damned. I believe you," she said. Her face relaxed and she gave him a small smile.

"Can you tell me where Giovanna and her family have gone?"

"No, I'm sorry to say, I can't. They snuck away like thieves in the dead of the night without telling anyone where they were going."

Alessandro stood up.

"That's strange." He wondered why they'd left in such a secretive way. "Can you tell me why Isolde is looking for them and where she's gone?"

Signore Limone opened her front door. "I have some fresh coffee."

Alessandro felt a glimmer of hope. He sat at her kitchen table and took a deep breath. She poured him a cup of coffee and opened a cookie tin, offering him homemade biscotti.

"Thank you," he said, taking a bite. The cookie was dipped in chocolate and tasted of pistachios. "Delicious."

The wooden chair creaked when Signora Limone sat in it with a sigh. Smoothing a strand of gray hair away from her forehead, she said, "She didn't tell me that she's looking for the Falconi's, but I think that she is and that she moved away from here because she found them."

Alessandro's mood brightened. "Will you tell me what you know?"

"Do you truly want to marry Giovanna?"

"Yes, Signora, I do."

"Then I'll tell you what I know."

Alessandro put down his coffee cup.

"Isolde is in Wheeling, West Virginia in the Ohio River Valley. She's working at the *Cafe Italia* coffee shop." She stood and gave Alessandro a slip of paper. "Here's her address. She has a little boy, Giuseppe. We call him, Jesse. He looks very much like Giovanna's father."

Alessandro hesitated for a moment before taking the paper. He began to see why the waitress had been so desperate to find Giovanna's family.

"I understand. Thank you for the coffee and the information." Alessandro stood up and his chair fell to the floor. He picked it up with shaking hands, and backed toward the door. His knees buckled and he gripped the doorframe. "I'd better be going," he said. For the first time since he had received his letters back, unanswered from Giovanna, he was filled with anticipation.

"Are you going to Wheeling?" Signora Limone asked, as she followed him out onto the porch.

He looked into the clouds, and felt buoyed by the thought that there was at least a possibility his most fervent wish could come true.

"Yes. I'll find Isolde and maybe she can tell me what I need to know."

"*Buona fortuna*, young man."

"You're my good luck charm, Signora. Thanks for your help."

"Be careful. Isolde doesn't care who she hurts as long as she gets what she wants." Her voice was like ice when she spoke of Isolde, and she wrapped her shawl around her shoulders, though it was a warm day.

"I'll do what's best for Giovanna and her family," Alessandro promised, as he walked to his car and waved.

"I hope you aren't too late to keep that cold-hearted snake from causing trouble," she yelled, waving back.

Alessandro spread out his map on the car's front seat and found the city of Wheeling. There was a good chance Giovanna was there. In his estimation, it would take close to six hours to get there. He would need the time to think.

Assuming Signora Limone's intuition was correct, it wouldn't be long before he found the woman he loved, but there were complications. The signora's warning troubled him. It seemed

Giovanna's father had conceived a child with a vengeful woman. His mood dampened as he considered the devastating news. Her revelation would be especially hard on Giovanna's mother. He wondered if there was anything he could do to keep the woman, Isolde, from hurting Giovanna's family. She might be desperate to get what she wanted, but he was desperate, as well. As he drove along the mountain roads, he thought about Giovanna and the four long years he had waited to see her again. A tangled web of deception and hurt might stand in the way of their reunion.

When Isolde and Jesse arrived at their dilapidated garage apartment after walking several blocks from the *Café Italia*, a young man greeted them on the sidewalk between the street and the garage. She eyed him with wariness.

He smiled and held out his hand. The evening breeze blew his dark hair. He was quite handsome and familiar. Isolde stared at him and searched her memory.

"Hello, I met you several years ago in Covel. I'm Alessandro Pascarella," he said.

"You'll have to refresh my memory. You're from the old country?" Isolde couldn't place him, but she knew he was telling the truth.

"Yes, do you prefer Italian?"

"No. English is fine. What do you want?"

"I'll get right to the point. I'm looking for the Falconi family, and…"

He had been looking for Giovanna. She closed her eyes and pictured the lovesick look of the young boy who had come to the restaurant in the mining camp.

"I remember now. You came to the restaurant. I gave you my address in case you found them."

"Yes, I'm still looking for them."

"They aren't here in Wheeling. How did you find me?"

"I have to confess. I lied. I told one of the waitresses at the restaurant that I was a relative. I had the envelope you gave me with your address written in your handwriting. When I showed it to her, she believed me and told me how to find you."

"Well, the Falconi's aren't here, only Giuseppe..." She looked at her son.

The young man bent down on one knee to speak to him. "Hi, my friends call me Alex," he said.

"I'm Jesse," her son said. He smiled and his eyes sparkled.

"Have you had dinner?" Alessandro asked.

"No, and I'm hungry," he answered.

"I just finished my shift at the *Café Italia*," Isolde said. "We were on our way home."

"Can I take you to dinner? I have a car," Alessandro said.

"Please, Mama. Can we ride in his car?" Jesse begged.

Alessandro laughed, and he heard Isolde's stomach rumble.

"Dinner would be nice, but I don't know where the Falconi family is," she lied. She really didn't care if he found Giovanna.

"That's okay. I'll leave after dinner to go back to Michigan. At least you can keep me company while I eat."

She looked him over and peered in the car's window. "You must be doing well."

"Oh, the Ford. No, it's my uncle's. He works for a car company in Detroit. He let me borrow it."

"I see. Well, you seem harmless. Get in the car, Jesse. We'll have dinner with the man with the borrowed car."

Alessandro smiled again. Her eyes lingered on his handsome face.

Jesse scrambled into the front seat and sat next to Alessandro. Isolde sat by Jesse and ran her hand over the vinyl upholstery. She directed Alessandro to the closest restaurant. When they arrived, he opened the door for her. Jesse left her side and ran to a booth in the back. Suddenly she was self-conscious. She hadn't brushed her hair since early in the morning and wore very little make-up, which was all but gone after her long day of waitressing at the café. She looked down at the front of her uniform. It was stained with grease and a smudge of ketchup. She pulled her coat together to cover it.

"I want a hamburger," Jesse said.

"Yes, if it's okay with your mama," Alex said. "Every America kid should eat a hamburger at least once. They're almost as good as pasta."

Lost in her own thoughts, Isolde didn't notice the kindness Alessandro showed her son.

The waitress came to the table and took their order; soup for Alessandro, a hamburger and fries for Jesse, and the meatloaf special with extra biscuits for Isolde.

"I wish I had a glass of wine," she said, when the waitress went to the kitchen. "Damn prohibition."

"I have a bottle of homemade in the car. It's hidden under the front seat. I can come up for a drink when I take you home."

"I'll think about it," she said.

He made small talk. "How do you like your job? Does Jesse like it here?"

"We haven't been here long," she said. She wasn't going to say too much and give away her plans.

"Mabel takes me to the park," Jesse offered.

Isolde put her hand on his arm, and he looked down. "His babysitter," she said.

The waitress brought the food. Isolde had been too busy with customers to eat lunch. She devoured her meal without talking. Jesse's little hands managed his hamburger without her help.

"This is good," he said, ketchup dripping onto his chin.

"I like hamburgers, too," Alex said. He took the corner of his napkin and wiped Jesse's face.

He finished his soup and looked at Isolde. His dark eyes changed in intensity. A lock of hair fell across his forehead. She found herself staring at him and said, "You can come in when we get back to my apartment. Hide the wine in your coat."

He waved at the waitress for the check and paid with a five-dollar bill, leaving her a good tip. She thanked him and gave Jesse a peppermint.

They drove back to the garage apartment, and Alessandro followed her up the stairs, with the wine under his coat. She would send Jesse right to bed and see what Alessandro had to say. Though she didn't care if this handsome boy found Luigi's daughter, she wondered if he could help her meet with Luigi.

Darkness began to fall, and crickets sang outside her small

garage apartment. Once inside, she invited Alessandro to make himself comfortable while she looked in the sink full of dirty dishes for two glasses. Under the sink, she found an almost empty bottle of dish soap and cleaned them. Jesse showed Alex his trucks, the only toys he had besides a ragged teddy bear. She finished drying the glasses and set them on the coffee table next to the wine bottle.

Jesse yawned.

"Brush your teeth and get into your pajamas," she told him.

He frowned at her and walked to the bathroom. After he turned off the water, she could hear him talking to his teddy bear. Dressed in pajamas that were too small for him, he poked his head around the bedroom's doorframe and grinned.

He smiled often, a trait he hadn't inherited from her. A smile seldom graced her lips. Life had given her so many disappointments. It wasn't Jesse's fault that she resented being a mother, but she wasn't cut out to take care of a child and didn't treat him with the kindness he deserved. Sometimes she realized how harsh she was with him and made an effort to be pleasant, but mostly she was too absorbed in self-pity to think about her child's feelings.

"Mr. Alex, your car is swell, and the hamburger and fries were swell, too," Jesse said. He sounded just like a little American child.

"I'm glad you liked your dinner, Jesse. Sweet dreams," Alessandro said.

"Can I stay up?" Jesse asked.

Isolde shook her head. "No, it's late. I'll be in to sleep soon. Get in bed."

"Please," he pleaded.

"I won't be staying long," Alessandro said.

Isolde glared at her child, and he retreated. She heard him bounce on the bed and snap out the light

Alessandro poured the wine, while Isolde held the glasses. She stared at him as she sat down on the couch and lifted her glass to her lips. She drank all of the delicious burgundy in one long gulp. After taking a small sip, he refilled her glass, and she drank most of the second glass. He took another sip and she motioned for him to keep pouring.

"Thirsty?" he asked.

"I haven't had wine in a long time, and I like it," she said.

"Yes, Prohibition." He clinked his glass against hers. "To the old country and good wine."

Isolde drank, and he filled her glass again.

"I'm drinking all of your wine. Are you trying to get me drunk?"

"Why would I do that?" He smiled and took a quick drink.

"You're a good looking man," she commented, as though it had just occurred to her. "Do you want to sit by me?" It had been a long time since she'd been with a man. She wanted to feel his body next to hers.

He took a drink from his glass, but didn't answer her.

"What're you doing here?" she said.

"I think I know why you want to find the Falconi's," he said. He stared at her, and she moved restlessly and looked down at her nails.

"I don't remember telling you my reason." She patted the couch and smiled.

Alessandro ignored her invitation again. "You want Signore Falconi to see his son."

She resented him for ruining the mood and the relaxing effect of the wine. Her eyelids felt heavy and she closed her eyes instead of confirming his guess.

"Maybe I can help you," he said.

"Do you even know Luigi?" she said, laying back against the couch and opening her eyes to look intently at him.

"I've never met him, but I want to marry his eldest daughter. I fell in love with her on her voyage to America. If you tell me where they are, I'll convince Signore Falconi to come here to see you."

"How romantic," she said. "Why do I need your help?"

"If you show up on his doorstep, Luigi will be angry. It would be better if someone else breaks the news to him. He'll have time to think about it before he sees you and Jesse. I can bring him to you. He'll be calmer, and it'll be better for you."

"Why do you want to get in the middle of this? What's in it

for you?"

"I'm hoping if I do this favor for you, that you'll tell me where I can find them." He paused and held her gaze as though he was willing her to do what he wanted. Isolde stood up to pace around the room.

"You're still in love with a girl that you haven't seen in all this time? How sweet. What if she doesn't love you? Have you thought of that?"

"Of course. I won't know until I see her. If she doesn't love me, then I'll go."

"Well, it seems you went to a lot of trouble to find me, but I don't think I can help you."

"I think you're lying."

"I think you're lying, too. You don't want to help me. Tell me the real reason you want to bring Luigi to me."

Alessandro looked down, and then stared at Isolde without smiling. "I want to keep you from bringing his bastard child to him. I don't want you to upset his family."

"Now we're getting somewhere."

"If I help him, I'll have a better chance of gaining his permission to see his daughter."

Isolde laughed. "Why do you need his permission?"

"I'm old-fashioned."

"I'll think about it. Maybe after I sleep, I'll remember where they are."

"I'll meet you at the *Café Italia* in the morning at seven o' clock. Maybe we can help one another."

"Why do you think Jesse is Luigi's son?" she asked.

"You didn't deny it, and he looks very much like Giovanna," he answered.

Isolde watched Alessandro leave. A fire burned in her chest when she thought of how angry Luigi would be when he saw her. It was what had kept her from going to him even though she knew where he lived. She locked the door and finished drinking the wine straight from the bottle, then sank into the old sofa, too tired and drunk to walk the few steps to the bedroom. She quickly fell asleep.

She dreamed of kissing the good-looking Alessandro,

but when she opened her eyes after the kiss, he turned into an angry Luigi who shook with rage. When the first light of morning streamed through the window, she woke up feeling sick to her stomach and ran to the bathroom to vomit. Perhaps Alessandro was right. She would need him as a buffer.

Chapter 25

Pop had been preoccupied on the bus trip home from Wheeling on Saturday. As Giovanna and her sisters laughed in the seats behind him, she saw him take a paper from his pocket. His face was pale and he wiped his brow with his handkerchief as he read it. Evelina and Maria noticed he didn't seem to be feeling well and wanted to go sit with him, but she stopped them. When she asked if they knew what he was reading, Evelina said it had to be the letter she had given him at home and that the return address in the top corner had been Vincente's.

After reading the letter, her father wiped his cheeks and closed his eyes for the rest of the short bus ride. In their hurry to get off the bus, he left her mother's rose behind. She picked it up and gave it to him to carry home. It was the only thing he held in his hands, and he placed it behind his back to keep her mother from seeing it until he reached the porch. Her mother's face lit up when her father presented the flower to her. Maria thought it was romantic, but Giovanna wasn't thinking of the rose, only about the drop of blood left on his finger from the prick of its thorn. The blood reminded her of how troubled her father was on the bus and she wondered what disconcerting news Vincente had written in the letter. If Pop had left it on the table when he went to the pump to wash before dinner, she would have read it, but she never saw it in the kitchen or in her parents' bedroom on the night table where he kept his wallet and the change from his pocket. She had checked when he fell asleep in the chair after dinner. Whatever was in the letter was between him and Vincente. He didn't speak of it, and she was afraid to ask.

This morning she had forgotten about it. Orlando was coming for dinner and her thoughts turned to his visit. All week she had been forgetful and preoccupied as she wondered what the dinner would be like. Her experience with boys was limited to the infrequent and short conversations she had with the Italian boys in the neighborhood and the encounter she'd had with Alessandro four years ago. It seemed like such a long time had passed. So much had changed since then that her memories of that time seemed like a fairy tale story she'd invented instead of real-life. It was hard not to compare the boys she knew to Alessandro. The dashing uniform, the serious expression he wore, and the way he looked at her made him seem like a different species all-together next to the immature boys of her neighborhood. None of them made her heart flutter the way it had when she was with Alessandro, until she met Orlando.

Orlando arrived early with a small bouquet of wildflowers. A cigarette dangled from his lips. Giovanna saw him through the window as he stood on the porch. He looked dashing, a little nervous, and nothing like a boy. He was a twenty-five year old man dressed in a suit and tie with a flat cap or newsboy cap, as her father called it, on his head full of dark, wavy hair. The only other man she knew who wore such a hat was her Zio Benny's friend, Henry. He wore a beret tilted to the side like the Frenchman that he was. Orlando's flat cap rested on the top of his head, and his twinkling eyes gazed out from under its brim. He hesitated at the door and appeared to be gathering his nerve. She watched him take the cigarette from his mouth and blow smoke into the air, and then he crushed it on the bottom of his shoe and kicked it onto the grass.

After taking a deep breath, he knocked. She steadied her shaking hand and opened the door.

"Ciao," Orlando said.

"Hi," Giovanna said. The knob of the screen door was the only thing keeping her from falling to the ground. When Orlando smiled at her, she clutched it, as her knees grew weak. Her sisters ran up the porch steps with wood for the stove, and she sighed with relief.

"Aren't you going to let him in?" Ev asked.

"Yes, sorry," Giovanna said, looking up. She had been staring at her shoes.

He smiled again and she introduced him to Maria and Ev. They said hello and walked past her into the kitchen where their mother was cutting the *gnocchi* dough into small squares and tossing them into boiling water. Orlando introduced himself to her mother, speaking in Italian. Giovanna relaxed a little when she saw her mother smile and put her wooden spoon down to greet him.

"Welcome, Orlando. It's nice to meet you," she said.

"My mother made *gnocchi* for me the last time I was in Italy. It's my favorite meal," he said. "It smells great."

"We're having meatballs, too," Ev said. "Giovanna made a dress for the butcher's wife."

Orlando gave Giovanna a puzzled look. "I'm a seamstress. They paid me in meat," she said.

He laughed. "I thought you worked at the mill?"

"I do, but I also sew."

"She's a hard worker," her mother said. "Please sit down, Orlando."

"Thank you," he said.

"I'll get Pop," Ev said. "He's in the garden."

Giovanna was glad her family was with her for her first evening with Orlando. She was overcome with a shyness that bordered on fear, and imagined it was how an actress felt the first time she was on a stage in front of an audience.

Her mother stood next to her and bent her head close. "Sit with him," she whispered. "And thank him for the flowers."

She sat next to Orlando at the table. He took off his hat and stared down at the flowers in his hand. After a moment, he said, "These are for you." He held them up for her.

"Thank you," she said. "They're beautiful."

"I thought of you when I saw them," he said.

She smiled and looked at the flowers. Her hands trembled as she took them from him. Slowly, she stood to place them in a glass full of water. Maria grinned at her and poured tomato sauce over the *gnocchi*, then placed the large bowl of potato dumplings in the middle of the table. The steam from the sauce floated into the air. Giovanna placed the flowers near her plate and glanced at Orlando. He smiled and she smiled back before looking away.

"Here's Pop," Ev said, as her father opened the front door and came in.

"Nice to see you, Orlando," he said.

Orlando stood and shook her father's hand. "Thank you for having me, Signore Falconi."

"Luigi," her father said, as he walked to the sink to rinse the lettuce he'd picked for the salad. Shaking the water from the leaves, he tossed them into a bowl and doused them with olive oil and vinegar. Her mother added a pinch of salt, and then announced that it was time to eat.

Giovanna loved *gnocchi*, but she ate almost nothing. She felt like tiny birds were flying around in circles in her stomach. Orlando, however, ate with relish and complemented her mother, saying her cooking was just as wonderful as his mother's. It was the best praise he could give. Her mother wouldn't have believed him if he said her cooking was better than his own mother's.

He didn't seem nervous anymore and talked through dinner about a recent trip he had taken to Italy. Giovanna and her family hadn't spoken to anyone who had visited the old country in the four years they'd been gone, and they were eager to hear what was happening there.

"The National Fascist Party is in power. Benito Mussolini is the dictator. Many Italians like him, but I'm not fond of him or his politics. His party will soon be the only legal party in Italy. Two years ago, Mussolini passed a law stating that he's only responsible to the king and the sole person to determine Parliament's agenda," Orlando said.

"I don't like Mussolini," Luigi said. "I read about his Blackshirts in the Italian newspaper *Il Progresso Italo-Americano*. A few years ago they beat up several of his opponents. The paper suggests that the fascists were responsible for killing the socialist, Giacomo Matteotti.

He accused them of using violence to gain votes in the 1924 elections. They sound like assassins and bullies to me."

"Who are the Blackshirts?" Appollonia asked. "And what does the fascist party want to do?"

"The Blackshirts are the military branch of Mussolini's political movement," Orlando said. "But I agree with Luigi, they're bullies who scare people into following their boss. The fascists say they want the people to have a national identity based on their culture and ancestry, but I think they're using violence and intimidation against Mussolini's opponents to gain a totalitarian state."

"What about King Victor Emmanuel?" Luigi asked.

"The King is only a figurehead now. As you know, after the war there was an economic depression. The working people like you and me were beaten down by the hard times. The country became politically unstable. Mussolini took advantage of this instability. It's why he was able to become powerful. There's no more democracy," Orlando said.

Giovanna didn't know anything about politics, but from what Orlando was telling them, she was relieved that they were no longer in Italy. "I think it's better that we live here in America," she said. Everyone at the table turned to look at her.

"Yes, your father did what was best for us," her mother said. "As much as I miss my family, I know it's better here. The thought of living under a dictator like Mussolini frightens me."

"They call him *The Leader*, but he's a tyrant," Orlando said. "You've done the right thing bringing your family to America, Luigi."

"What about you, Orlando? Are you planning to stay in America?" her father asked. He put his fork on his plate and studied Orlando.

"This is my home now. My business is doing well, and I like it here. I miss my family in Italy, but I've made many friends, nice people like you who are also from Italy, as well as Americans."

"Many Italians are ignoring the ban on alcohol. Making their own wine," Luigi said. "Are you a big drinker?"

"Pop," Giovanna said. Her face reddened at her father's bold query.

"It's a fair question," Orlando said with a smile. "I like a little homemade wine, but I don't want any trouble with the law, so I haven't made any. Most of the time, I don't drink anything but water. No ice, though. I don't like it the American way," he said.

"Too cold," Evelina said. She wrinkled her nose as if she smelled something rotten.

They all laughed, and Giovanna was relieved that Orlando had made light of the question. Her mother got up to clear the table. "Maria and Evelina, get water for the dishes," she said.

"Thank you for the delicious dinner. I should be getting back to the restaurant," Orlando said. "May I sit on the porch with Giovanna for a few minutes before I go?"

Giovanna looked at her plate where a meatball sat in a puddle of sauce. Her mother wouldn't throw it away, and she would eat it after Orlando had gone.

"Your sisters can help with the dishes. Go ahead, Giovanna," her father said. He surprised her by staying inside, instead of sitting on the porch with them to keep an eye on her.

They sat on the wooden swing and listened to the squeak of the chain as they rocked back and forth. She searched her brain for something to say, but then relaxed. The silence wasn't awkward. Orlando seemed content to sway on the swing without talking. It was warm and the cotton dress she wore fluttered as they moved. They sat together for several more minutes before Orlando broke the silence.

"May I visit you again next Sunday?" he asked.

"I'd like that. As long as it's okay with my father," she said.

He used his foot to stop the swing. Then he stood up and extended his hand to her. She placed her hand in his to shake it as she'd seen the men do, but he didn't let go of it after a moment. Instead, he put his other hand on the outside of hers and held it there.

"May I write to you in the meantime?" he asked.

"It will only be a week before I see you again."

"I'm better at putting my thoughts on paper."

"Ok, I'd like that. I'll look forward to your letter," she said. It was the polite thing to say, but she meant it. She had read his first letter so many times that it was committed to her memory word for word.

"Goodbye," he said, and walked down the sidewalk, turning to look at her with a smile on his face. When he drove away, she sat on the swing and kicked her feet into the air as her heart fluttered in her chest.

Later, when she was in bed, and Maria and Evelina were fast asleep, she closed her eyes and pictured Orlando at the dinner table, telling them about Italy. The easy way he explained what was going on in the old country and the fact that he owned a restaurant impressed her. Though he wasn't formally educated, she could see that he was intelligent. She liked listening to him talk, and he was handsome and kind. But the thing that intrigued her most was his desire to write to her. Her days would be filled with anticipation until his letter arrived. She looked forward to receiving it almost as much as she looked forward to seeing him again in a week's time.

Chapter 26

The backseat of the car was cold and cramped, but it was a free place to sleep. Zia Lucia had given Alessandro a blanket and pillow to keep in the trunk in case he needed it. He was thankful to have it. Spending money on a hotel was a luxury he could not afford. After leaving Isolde's apartment, he drove behind the local drugstore and parked in a spot where no streetlights would shine in his windows. Cafe Italia was next door. At daylight, he would meet Isolde there to talk again before she began her morning shift. The windows began to fog and a gust of air pushed against the glass. Though it was the middle of spring, the night was cold. He thought of opening the second bottle of wine he had hidden under the seat, but decided to save it for Isolde. It would help to warm him as he struggled to fall asleep, but using it as a way to encourage her to talk was more important than the warmth it might provide him now. Isolde was a cold piece of stone, and she knew where Giovanna and her family were. He was sure of it, but getting her to tell him where they lived might prove to be difficult.

Jesse was Luigi Falconi's son, and it seemed that the boy was an innocent pawn in her game to draw Luigi to her. He had never seen a mother so indifferent to her child. Even his patients in urban Detroit, many of them far from wholesome, showed more love and kindness toward their children. She was nothing like Giovanna's mother, who he remembered as kind and concerned more for her daughters' happiness than her own. He could not imagine Appollonia Falconi being so apathetic toward her children or using them to get something or someone she wanted.

Tomorrow he would be patient with Isolde. She had softened

just a little in the time he had spent drinking with her. He would buy her breakfast and do his best to charm her into telling him where he could find Giovanna and her family. He had enough money for a week's worth of meals, and then he would be out of cash, except for the twenty dollars he had stashed in his coat lining for an emergency.

He wasn't due back on duty at the hospital emergency room for a week. He hoped to find Giovanna within the next few days. Thinking of her, he relaxed and fell asleep.

At dawn, a man in a white lab coat tapped on his window. He rolled it down a few inches, and the man said, "Move your car. I'm opening the store in a few minutes. You can't sleep in my parking lot."

A layer of frost painted the windows, and he could see the frustrated face of the pharmacist through the crack. He didn't blame him for being angry. The fact that he was sleeping in a car in his clothes with a two-day growth of beard made him look and feel like a hobo.

"Sorry," Alessandro mouthed. "I'm going." He kept the blanket wrapped around him and got out of the backseat.

His boots were still on his feet to keep them warm. On the floorboard was a jar of water, his toiletries and a change of clothes. He cleaned his teeth and dressed in clean underwear, a sweater and corduroy trousers. If Isolde told him where Giovanna lived, he would take his razor from the glove box and go to the cafe's restroom to shave before he left to find her. Until then his beard could wait.

The sun was up and he checked his watch. In a few minutes, Isolde would arrive to meet him. If she hadn't been lying to him about drinking wine infrequently, she would be at least a little hung over. He waited for her in a booth near the front of the *Café Italia* and sipped a cup of black coffee.

His coffee was almost gone when she approached his table, wearing the same stained uniform she had worn yesterday. Her hair looked as if she'd combed it with her fingers, and she rubbed her temples and closed her eyes. His guess about her being hung-over was right.

"Did you order breakfast?" she asked.

"Just coffee. You go ahead."

She nodded and hollered to the cook at the grill. "Joey, make me the two egg special with bacon."

"I can only stay a few days," Alessandro said.

"Did you bring wine?" she asked.

He pulled the bottle out of the inside pocket of his coat, enough for her to see that he had what she wanted on the seat next to him.

"I thought about your proposition. I'll tell you where Luigi lives if you'll arrange for him to meet me here at the cafe on Saturday. It shouldn't be too much trouble to get him here. He comes to Wheeling on the bus with a friend two Saturdays, a month," she said. Then looking around the restaurant, she reached across the table for the wine.

"What's his address?" He stared at her and twirled the wine on the seat, letting his anticipation flow into the movement of the bottle.

"Main Street, Yorkville, Ohio," she said.

"The house number," he said.

"That's all I know," she said. "The town is about six miles from here. Luigi works at the steel mill. You'll have to find out which house is his. It shouldn't be hard. The town is small. It isn't even on the map. Someone at the store can tell you how to get there or you can ride the bus. That's how Luigi gets here, so I know it goes to Yorkville."

The cook brought her bacon and eggs, and she dipped her toast into the runny yolks before eating it. He watched her and finished his coffee. She appeared to be telling the truth.

"What do you want from Luigi?" he asked.

Isolde ate the last bite of her meal before answering. "I want him to meet Giuseppe. My son needs to know who his father is."

"That's all you want?"

"For now."

He shook his head, hoping she could see that he wasn't fooled. She pushed her plate aside and leaned across the table. The smell of bacon on her breath drifted toward him.

Her face flushed with anger. "I want to see if he still has

feelings for me."

"What if he doesn't want to be with you again?" he asked.

"If I see that, I won't try to force it."

"Do you want money?" he asked. "For Jesse?"

"I doubt he has any to spare."

"Then what? If he doesn't want to leave his family for you, you'll leave? Where will you go?"

"If he wants to see Giuseppe on the Saturdays he comes to Wheeling, I might stay," she said. Then she added without conviction, "For Jesse's sake."

She looked at her lap, smoothed her apron and readied herself to slide out of the booth.

"And what about you?" he said.

"Four years ago he chose his wife over me when he left town without telling anyone. If he doesn't want me this time either, then so be it."

Her dark eyes grew cold and she looked away. He wondered how she had finally found Luigi, but she cut him off before he could ask.

"Meet me here on Saturday at seven in the morning. I'll have Jesse with me. You can stay with him while I talk to Luigi outside."

Alessandro let go of the bottle as she pulled it from his hand. She wrapped her sweater around it, and then went to the kitchen, returning without it. He placed money on the table next to the check. Two men walked into the café, and Isolde took out her pad and pencil and greeted them. Her voice had a faraway quality and a friendliness that seemed false. There was nothing kind about her. The hatred in her eyes told him she wanted more than just a chance to see if Luigi would acknowledge his son.

He was certain she wouldn't play the silent other woman after all the trouble she had taken to get there. Unless Luigi gave up his family for her, Alessandro supposed she wanted revenge.

Chapter 27

Luigi held Appollonia in bed under the blanket. She had fallen asleep after making love with him for the first time in weeks. He didn't ask his wife for intimacy very often. She always seemed so tired at the end of the day. Today she had surprised him, by kissing him before dawn and telling him that she wanted him. She had worked hard to prepare dinner for Orlando's visit, and should have been exhausted, but the prospect of Giovanna's interest in a man from the old country had filled her with excitement. Orlando was the first man their daughter had taken any notice of since her arrival in America. Luigi knew a little about Giovanna's shipboard romance from his wife, but he figured it was only a brief first love that would fade. Appollonia felt it was more than that and had worried that their daughter would never get over the boy from the ship.

Both he and his wife were impressed with Orlando. His easy manner and the fact that he owned a business made for a good first impression, and his knowledge and interest in world affairs intrigued Luigi. Most of the men he spoke with at the mill or in the neighborhood didn't read or have any interest in what was going on outside of their own lives. He liked it that an intelligent man was interested in Giovanna. She was a bright girl and would enjoy a man who liked conversation. Orlando seemed kind and pleasant, and if he was telling the truth, didn't drink too much. Luigi wanted someone for Giovanna who would take care of her and love her. She deserved a good man. All three of his daughters did.

Giovanna had asked him if Orlando could write to her and visit again on the following Sunday. She was surprised when he replied with an immediate yes. Sometimes he wondered if he appeared stern and inflexible to his eldest child.

It was clear to him that Orlando wanted far more than a quick romance. He was looking for a wife and had set his sights on Giovanna. It made Luigi reflect on his own marriage, which had been less than perfect, mostly due to his restless desire to find a new homeland where he could raise his family to rise out of poverty. His biggest regret was the time he had left them alone in Italy, and what he had done to relieve his loneliness while he lived without them.

He stroked Appollonia's hair and kissed the top of her head. Orlando was right. Moving to America had been the right thing to do. When Appollonia had agreed, he was happy to hear her say it. Both of them knew their lives would be better here.

For a brief time he believed nothing could change the course of his life and that of his family, but he had been deluding himself.

He slipped out of Appollonia's arms and reached into the inner pocket of his coat for Vincente's letter. His wife turned away from him, rolling onto her pillow. A box of matches lay next to his pocket change on the bedside table. He picked it up, put on his coat and walked to the woods behind the house. If she woke up, she would think he had gone to the outhouse. It wouldn't take long to get rid of the letter. The air was still. The flame from the match burned the end of the paper as soon as he pressed it to the corner. The letter was destroyed, but the problem it warned him of wasn't going to disappear like the ashes that floated to the ground.

Isolde was in Wheeling. Even if he wanted to ignore Vincente's words, he could not. He had seen her with his own eyes, and he had a son. Some men would have questioned whether or not the child was theirs, but he didn't. His last transgression had been his most fatal. He had run away from his lover, but he couldn't run away from his child. A son. He had to meet him and be a father to him. It wasn't only his responsibility; it was his desire. With each day that passed he felt a longing to be with him that was like a starving man's need for food. If he could, he would find a way to do it without breaking Appollonia's heart. He would do anything not to hurt her.

Back in bed, he lay awake wondering how he could keep his child a secret from her. If he could convince Isolde to let him see the boy on the Saturdays he went to Wheeling, he might be able to have a relationship with him without hurting his wife. It was the only way he could think of to know his son. It had to work. Isolde had to do this his way. He would figure out how to appease her and keep her from coming near his family. Dealing with her would be complicated for she was unpredictable.

He would have to be patient with her and find a way to give her some money to take care of his son. If he did that, he hoped she would be logical. Once he explained that he had left West Virginia to take a new job, she would understand. After all, he hadn't known about her pregnancy. If he could charm her into forgiving him and promise to help her support their child, he might be able to carry it off.

With confidence that his plan would work, a feeling of relief quieted his fears. He went inside and got back into bed. Appollonia's body was warm and he lay close to her and fell asleep. When he woke up, she and the girls were making breakfast and laughing in the kitchen. Sunlight filtered through the open door. It was later than he usually got up for work.

Appollonia called to him from the kitchen. "Get up Luigi or you'll be late. I packed an extra sandwich for you to eat while you walk so you could sleep in."

He dressed, but there was no time to shave. The girls were ready to leave, so he took his lunch and coat and followed them outside into the crisp spring morning. Evelina was smiling as if she had a secret she couldn't hold in. Her book bag was dangling from her shoulder, and she reached into the front pocket to pull out a small white envelope.

"Here," she said, shoving the letter at her sister. Giovanna offered her hand. "It's from Orlando."

"He was just here yesterday. Did he leave this with you?" Giovanna asked.

"Pop gave it to me last night to keep in my bag. Orlando wanted you to have it this morning."

Orlando had left a love letter for each day of the week that he would be away from Giovanna. Somewhat embarrassed, he had given the stack of six letters to Luigi for safekeeping. They were labeled Monday, Tuesday, Wednesday and so on, in Orlando's neat handwriting. He had requested that Giovanna be given one on her way to work every morning. It was a very romantic gesture, one Luigi wouldn't have supported if he weren't fond of Orlando. Since he was in favor of him, he agreed to deliver the letters.

Giovanna blushed, tucking the envelope into her coat pocket without opening it.

"Aren't you going to read it?" Evelina asked.

"When I'm alone," Giovanna said, making a face at Ev.

"Will you tell us about it?" Maria asked.

Luigi smiled as he listened to their excited chatter. Evelina turned to take the road to school, and he, Giovanna, and Maria continued on to the mill. He knew Maria wouldn't push, but he thought that Giovanna would share the letter with her while they ate their lunch together. It was good to see his daughters happy. They had very little excitement in their lives. Most days were filled only with work and chores.

All three of them looked forward to Orlando's next visit. Giovanna and her mother were already planning the meal they would make for the coming Sunday. Pizza with tomatoes, onions, herbs and olive oil and an extra crust for sugar pizza. Evelina and Maria would help, too. His wife was teaching them to cook. They were growing up. Soon boys would be coming to dinner to court them.

Before receiving Vincente's letter and seeing Isolde in Wheeling, he would have hoped for a quick week as well. Instead, he now faced the prospect that on Saturday, he would most likely be paying a visit to the cafe in Wheeling to confront the mother of his son. He would have a lot to think about before then, like a reason to tell Appollonia why he would be spending Saturday in Wheeling again. It was his custom to go only every other Saturday, and though she said nothing, he knew she preferred that he stay home. His twice a month trip to town with a friend from the mill was an extravagance he thought he deserved after the long hours he toiled. His friend visited the brothel there, and he had gone with him once out of curiosity, but he had resisted temptation and kept the promise he had made to himself to remain loyal to his wife. It was easier with her and the girls here, and he didn't have the urge for sex as often now that he was forty-five. His friend called him an old man. Maybe he was, but he was content with his life and thought his troubles were behind him until he received Vincente's letter.

By his estimation, his son would be about three years old. He wondered if he had blond curls like the baby Maria or dark eyes like Giovanna and Evelina. Would he be pleasant in nature like his daughters, or sullen like Isolde? Blurred thoughts of Isolde filled his head. There was no denying her beauty and passion, but it was a faded memory compared to the harsh way she had treated him the last time they had spoken. In all fairness, he couldn't blame her. Their no-strings-attached arrangement had blossomed into a different flower for her. She wanted more from him than he could give her, but she'd gotten something more precious from him than being a part of his life.

As he worked, he contemplated telling Appollonia the truth. Hot sweat dripped down his face and back. It darkened the shirt his wife had washed with care. She was more fragile with each passing year. He didn't think she was strong enough to bear this news.

The last thing she deserved was a broken heart. Her family was her priority and she had never been anything but loyal to him and their daughters. He thought of all the years she had raised their daughters to love him, even though they didn't know him. The way she worked to make a nice home for her family and the love she showed them were the qualities that first came to his mind. How she took time each day to listen to her daughters and teach them how to be kind and thoughtful. Until this moment he hadn't thought about the cost of all the sacrifices she had made to live her life for the good of her family.

Somehow he couldn't picture Isolde being that kind of mother for his son.

The poem was written in Italian, printed in neat block letters on notebook paper. Giovanna read it, and the short letter that accompanied it, three times, before she slid it into the pocket of her dress. Maria watched, her eyes pleading as they began their morning clerical work. Of course she was curious, as Giovanna herself would be if a man had written to her sister. And she knew Maria would confide in her were the tables turned. But for a little while, she wanted to keep Orlando's romantic words to herself, a secret between the two of them.

Giovanna
Pretty young lady from the porch,
Who sat on a swing, looking at the blue sky and the leaves of the tree,
Listening to the golden bird chirping.

Turn your mind from those who dream of nothing but passion,
And look to me.
Oh, how I would be glad if I could hold you to my heart,
And say that I love you,
And embrace you passionately,
And kiss your lips.

She blushed and smiled thinking of the ardor his words conveyed. His poetic thoughts were so bold. It was flattering to be the object of Orlando's attention. The mystery of his first kiss was exciting to ponder. She liked him very much, but she wasn't ready for the language of his imagination to come to life just yet. She needed time to savor his words.

Thinking of a kiss reminded her of Alessandro and the most enchanting week of her life. She had only been a girl and was frightened by his show of affection. How she had been taken by surprise when he whisked her away from the dance floor to kiss her with a passion that took her breath away. It seemed like a long time ago, though she had thought of the moment many times since. In the past few months, her longing for him had waned, and she had begun to accept that she would never see him again. Maybe it was time to forget him and move on.

More and more Orlando replaced him in her musings. He was a handsome gentleman, full of life. Being with him made her happy. His infectious smile and kindness warmed the room around him. Still, she hoped he would give her a little more time. This time she wanted to be ready to accept a kiss without hesitation. The anticipation of his lips touching hers was as exciting as the thought of the actual moment.

Somehow the morning passed as Giovanna daydreamed and worked. Instead of going with the other girls to the lunchroom, she and Maria stayed at their desks to eat so they could talk in private.

She unwrapped her bread and cheese and cut up the apple she and Maria would share. Maria filled two glass jars with water and unwrapped celery and olives before she asked what Giovanna knew she had been waiting to say all morning.

"Well?"

Giovanna smiled at her. "It's a poem."

"May I read it?" Maria asked. Her face lit up

"It's romantic."

"You're blushing. Is it too private to share with me?"

"You can't tell Mama or Pop. And please don't let Ev see it. Don't even tell her you saw it. I don't want anyone else to see it but you," Giovanna said.

"Oh, I won't tell. I promise, but how will you keep Ev from seeing it? She knows all of your hiding places, and she'll be dying to read it. She won't rest until she finds it. Why can't she see it, too?"

"She's too young."

"Let me see it," Maria said, stretching her hand toward Giovanna. "Is it that passionate?"

"It's beautiful. I can hardly believe he wrote it for me." Giovanna took the poem from her dress pocket and gave it to her sister. Maria put her hand to her face as she read and breathed an audible sigh when she finished. Then she read it again.

"It's full of passion. What would Mama say? I think he'll try to kiss you the very next time he comes to the house," Maria said. She took a bite of her bread and passed the paper to

Giovanna. "If Pop knows what he's thinking, he won't let him in the door."

Giovanna laughed. "Pop can probably guess. I think he likes him."

"You're right or he would never have given you the letter. I heard him talking to Mama. They both like him," Maria confided.

"What did they say about him?" Giovanna asked.

"They think he's smart and full of personality and are impressed that he owns his own business."

"Can you believe Pop asked him if he was a big drinker?" Giovanna said. She popped an olive into her mouth and shook her head.

"I thought Orlando handled it well. And Pop likes it that he knows so much about what's going on in the world. Mama said he's sure of himself without being full of himself. And she thinks he has a nice smile and a good head of hair," Maria said with a laugh.

"I'll be dating a man whose hair is prettier than mine," Giovanna said, ruffling her sister's hair. She wondered what it would feel like to run her fingers through Orlando's soft waves.

"Does that mean you're going to see him again?"

"Yes. I like him." Just talking to Maria about him made her feel as if she'd been bathed in a ray of sunshine. She felt warm and pleasant inside and out.

"I think he's wonderful, and he's crazy about you. I'm happy for you," Maria said, putting her hands on Giovanna's.

"Thanks," Giovanna said. She knew her dear sister meant it.

"Oh, and one more thing," Maria said. "Pop told Mama that he thinks Orlando means business."

Giovanna stopped eating. "What do you think he means by that?'

Maria leaned close to her and whispered, "I think it means he's looking for a wife."

"But I've never even been alone with him. Yesterday was the only time I've been with him for longer than fifteen minutes."

"He's twenty-five, Giovanna. Pop thinks he wants to settle

down."

"I don't know if I'm ready to think about marriage." Giovanna sighed. Her happy mood suddenly dampened with the idea of matrimony.

"Then take it slow. Don't let anyone rush you," Maria said, getting up to clean her desktop and get back to work.

When the five o'clock whistle signaled the end of the shift, Giovanna walked with Maria and their father, happy that the workday was over. There were a few hours left of daylight, but it looked as if night was fast approaching. It had rained all afternoon and the sky was a dingy gray. She looked forward to changing out of her work dress and eating the meal her mother would have prepared. Giovanna knew they would have chicken soup or roast chicken for dinner as her mother always killed a chicken at the end of the month, an indulgence that was sometimes the culinary highlight of the month.

Evelina ran toward them when they reached the bottom of the hill that led to their house. If the weather was good, she played outside after coming home from school and met them before they started their walk up the hill.

She was out of breath from running and filled with excitement when she reached them. "You'll never guess who's here," she said.

"Is it Orlando?" Maria asked. Though it was unlikely he would be able to leave his restaurant in the middle of the week to travel to Yorkville.

"No, it's someone else who likes Giovanna." Evelina was bursting to tell them who it was, but she wanted them to play along.

Several boys in Yorkville were keen on Giovanna, but she paid them no attention. She would speak politely to whomever it was and excuse herself to wash up for dinner as quickly as she could.

"You'll never guess," Evelina said. "You'll just have to wait until you see him."

"Is it Ernesto from the store? He's kind of sweet on Giovanna," Luigi said.

"No, Pop. You don't know him," Evelina said coyly.

"Stop playing games and tell us," Maria said.

They passed *Comare* Rosie's house and she yelled a greeting.

"*Ciao*, Rose," Luigi said, waving to her.

The sun forced its way from behind a cloud as they reached the spot in the road where their house was fully visible. Giovanna saw him first. His back was to them as he stood on the porch talking to her mother, who sat on the swing where Orlando had sat the day before.

His hair was longer, and he wore a dark coat instead of a uniform, but she knew who he was by the confident way he stood with his shoulders back and the way his head moved when he laughed. She swayed to the side and her father caught her arm.

"Giovanna, are you alright?" her father asked. "Do you know who that is?"

"It's the boy from the ship." Giovanna's words came out in a whisper, and her father leaned in closer to her.

"Mama invited him to stay for dinner," Evelina said.

"What's his name?" her father asked, supporting Giovanna.

"Alessandro," Giovanna said. "Alessandro Pascarella."

Alessandro turned to face them and smiled as they came into the yard. Giovanna wished she could brush her hair and wash the smell of the mill away before she spoke to him, but there was no time for that.

His hand shot out. Her father let go of her arm, and Alessandro introduced himself. "I'm pleased to meet you Signore Falconi. I'm Alessandro Pascarella. I met your family on the *SS Roma*."

"Appollonia has told me about you. It's good to meet you," her father said. "Evelina says you're staying for dinner. Come in and we'll get cleaned up."

"I'm sorry for coming unannounced. I've been trying to find you for quite some time."

He was taller than she remembered and his hair fell over his eyes. When he pushed it away, she saw that he was brimming over with happiness. His face was practically glowing. She stared at him in wonder, and found that she was holding her breath. Her family hurried inside, but she stood frozen on the porch. She had dreamed of seeing him again, but now that he was here, she felt stunned and mute. He stopped in the doorway before going in, and she finally found her voice.

"I thought I'd never see you again," she whispered.

Alessandro put his arms around her waist. "I haven't stopped thinking of you since we said goodbye. As soon as I can be alone with your father, I'm going to tell him how much you mean to me."

"Giovanna," her mother called.

She shoved her hand into her pocket and felt the paper on which Orlando's poem was written.

"You can come back to Detroit with me. We can be together." He took her hands in his and looked at her expectantly.

"It's not that simple."

"Your father will see that my intentions are good," he said breathlessly. He let go of her hands and held her at her waist. She could see how happy he was to have found her.

"That's not it," she said. Her face darkened over, and she looked at the splintered boards of the porch floor.

"What's wrong?" he said. "Aren't you happy?"

With a deep sigh, she lifted her head and said, "There's someone else."

Chapter 28

Customers streamed into the café at a steady pace. On weekday mornings many of the employees of the downtown shops stopped in for coffee and a doughnut or pastry to take with them on their way to work. Isolde didn't have time to think about Alessandro and what he would be saying to Luigi until the breakfast rush was over. At ten o'clock, she filched a cigarette from the cook's extra apron that hung on a nail at the back door and went to the alley to smoke and collect her thoughts.

Alessandro was a determined young man. It wouldn't take him long to find Luigi and figure out a way to get him to Wheeling. He would be angry at first, but she had little doubt that he would be curious about his child. Whatever his reaction, she was glad Alessandro was breaking the news. By Saturday, Luigi would have had time to come to terms with the fact that he had a son.

A part of her fantasized that learning of Giuseppe's existence would make him happy. That he might look at her and remember their relationship with tenderness and want to take her and his child far away to begin a life together. But it was a fleeting fancy. She was no longer a naïve girl who dwelled on hopeless dreams. Four years had passed, and time had not been good to her. The voluptuous figure that had attracted Luigi was gone. Her face was full of misery and anger. She would fix herself up, but she couldn't afford make-up or a visit to the hair salon. The few dresses she owned were tight and unflattering.

The cook, Joey, dropped something in the kitchen and swore. His angry words floated through the screen door into the alley. He was the owner's son. His father wanted him to be at the restaurant to keep an eye on things, and Joey had his eye on Isolde. She wasn't interested and had ignored all of his subtle advances. If he hadn't tired of her indifference, he could help her. He was a bachelor with plenty of money.

She hesitated for only a moment, and then crushed what was left of the cigarette under her shoe and went back inside. In her kindest voice, she said, "Joey, could I have an advance on my pay? I've worked everyday since I've arrived. Sometimes two shifts."

"That's not up to me, but if it were, I'd say you deserve it. You're the best waitress we've had in a long time. Definitely the prettiest."

"I need a new dress. Do you think you could speak to your father on my behalf?"

"Sure," he said. He put down the spatula he was using to flip pancakes and leaned toward the window that separated the kitchen from the front counter. "Thought any more about going out with me?"

"Yes," she lied and stared at him like a fawn looking at the forest in wonder.

"Really?" His surprise and disbelief were apparent. She would have to convince him that she'd been interested in him all along.

"I wanted to get to know you first," she said and batted her eyes. "I would love to go out with you."

"Where would you like to go?" he whispered. He was so excited by her reply that he didn't even think to be suspicious of her intentions.

"Anywhere you like. I'm free any night except Saturday."

"How about tomorrow night? After the dinner shift?"

"I'd better get back to the customers," she said. Then she pulled a piece of her hair across her face. The smell of cigarette smoke that clung to it made her cough. It gave her a reason to back away from him.

"Maybe after dinner we could dance a little?" Joey suggested.

"That sounds nice, but I won't be able to do anything but dinner," she said.

A customer waved to her from the first table and she walked

toward him.

"Why?" Joey asked.

"My son will have to come with us. I don't know anyone who can babysit in the evenings." She took a plate filled with pancakes and eggs that steamed under the heating lamp, and turned to place it on the table nearest the counter.

The smack of the spatula on the chopping block startled her, but she didn't turn around. Instead, she asked the customer if he would like more coffee and poured him a cup with a smile. Two young girls came in and sat in a booth near the door. She walked up to them, her steps a little lighter than they had been earlier in the day.

When she returned to the window to give Joey their order, he pulled a bill from his wallet and said, "Here's a twenty. Get a nice dress and try to find a babysitter."

She took it without hesitation. It was more than she would make in a week of tips. "Maybe the lady who watches Jesse during the day will keep him while we go out."

"I'll ask around, too," Joey said.

"Good," she said and gave him her most seductive stare. He sighed and began to whistle as he poured more pancake batter on the griddle.

The twenty-dollar bill was crisp and smooth. She slipped it into her pocket. Going out with Joey wouldn't be so bad. She could endure a free meal and even a second date, but then it would have to be over. If she strung him along more than that, he might get the wrong idea. There was always the chance that Luigi might want to see her again. She didn't want him to think she was involved with Joey.

On the way home, she stopped at the department store and bought a red dress dotted with small white flowers. It was two sizes bigger than the few dresses that hung in her closet, and it camouflaged the flaws in her figure. The salesclerk commented that the color was a nice compliment to her raven hair and dark eyes. She hoped Luigi would notice. When she paid, her change was enough to buy cheese, bread, milk and a can of vegetable soup for dinner with a little money to spare. Jesse looked in the bag with excitement to see what she'd bought.

he was happy with the cheese as a treat. Their meals had consisted of day old bread and beans, or leftover soup from the café that she smuggled home in a glass jar.

Joey never questioned her about the missing crusts of bread or beans. They weren't fit to serve paying customers anyway and would be thrown in the alley for the mongrel dogs and feral cats. Sometimes she felt like a wayward animal herself, scrounging for the crumbs of others. At least tonight they would have a decent evening meal.

By the end of the week Alessandro would be back, but she wasn't patient enough to wait until then. On her way to pick up Jesse at the neighbor's after work, she used the remaining change to buy two bus tickets to Yorkville. Wednesday was her day off, and she planned to take Jesse to see Appollonia before Luigi met him on Saturday.

When Jesse fell asleep after eating the soup with the fresh bread and cheese, she stared at his untroubled face illuminated by the moonlight. He deserved something better than this, better than a mother who felt no tethered bond or ache in her heart for him. As she lay beside him on the bed, some of the weariness trickled from her tired bones. Contentment wrapped its soothing arms around her restless soul and a smile pulled at the corners of her lips as she fell asleep. She didn't think it would be hard to convince Luigi's wife that what she wanted might be best for all of them.

Chapter 29

The news that Giovanna was seeing someone else grabbed Alessandro's heart and twisted it. Anger and fear filled his thoughts, and he tightened his grip around her waist.

She backed away from him, and he let her go.

"I thought I'd never see you again," she whispered. Her body quivered as if she had been hit by a sudden gust of wind.

He sat on the swing and did his best to calm down and relaxed his shoulders with a sigh. "You're right. You need some time for this to sink in. I'm making too many assumptions. Of course lots of men are interested in you."

Evelina opened the door and gave him a curious look. She narrowed her eyes at Giovanna and said, "Mama says we're eating soon."

"Tell her we want to talk for just a minute. We're going to the pump to wash," Giovanna said, twisting a strand of hair around her finger nervously.

"Here then," Ev said, handing her the water bucket. "I'll tell her you're filling the pail."

Alessandro carried the bucket and walked beside her to the backyard.

"There aren't lots of men," Giovanna said. "Just one."

"How long have you been seeing him?" he asked. Again his voice sounded impatient and angry. He could see that she was upset, and he softened his tone. "I'm sorry. I'm not mad at you, just disappointed. I've been thinking of this day for four years. It was unrealistic of me to think I could sail back into your life as if no time had passed at all."

"If you had arrived a few months earlier, it might've been that way," she said.

"I came as fast as I could," he said. "Do I have a chance at all?

"I've thought of you and the days we spent together many

times," she said.

He smiled and looked into her eyes. His mood brightened.

She added, "But now I'm confused. I have feelings for the other man, and he's special to me, too."

"But you aren't promised to him yet?" Alessandro asked.

"No," she said. Her voice was so soft that he had to lean closer to hear her. She stopped at the pump and began to push the handle. Her arm barely moved. She seemed overcome with exhaustion. He reached forward to do it for her, but she shook her head as the water began to flow into the bucket.

"If you tell me to go away, that I don't have a chance with you, I'll do as you wish."

Giovanna finished pumping the water and began to walk back to the front porch.

Alessandro put his hand on hers and lifted the bucket as her fingers released it.

"I don't want you to go away, but I'm not sure what I want," she said.

"I have to be back in Detroit for work on Monday. Can I see you every day from now until Sunday?"

They reached the porch, and Alessandro set the bucket near the bottom step.

"I have to work at the mill until five o'clock. You can come here after that. Where are you staying?"

"In my uncle's car," he said.

Her lips puckered into a frown, but she didn't say anything. Even though they were miles from Italy, there was no chance she would consider asking him to stay with her family.

"It's comfortable," he added, with a wry grin.

For the first time since he'd laid his eyes upon her, she smiled. "I'll ask Pop if you can eat with us every evening." Hope filled his soul.

Together they walked to the door. Her family was placing the meal on the table. He opened the door for her, and she stopped him before they went in. "Where do you work?"

"The emergency room of a Detroit hospital. I'm a doctor, " he said.

"I'm glad for you. I knew your dream would come true."

Maria opened the door and they sat at the table with her family. The meal was simple and delicious. It reminded him of Italy and being at the table with his family. He liked Luigi Falconi at once, and fell back into joking with Evelina and Maria as if they saw each other every day. Giovanna was quiet. She listened as they talked and ate only a few spoonfuls of her chicken soup.

Appollonia asked what he had been doing since they waved goodbye to him on the *SS Roma*.

"I came to live with my Zia Lucia and Zio Franco in Detroit a short time after that day. My father and mother had saved some money for me to go to college and medical school in America. It was always my dream to study here, so that I could become a physician and live here in this country. I would never have been able to do it without the kindness of my aunt and uncle. It hasn't been easy for them to help me. They barely get by, but they took me in as if I were their son."

"Do you miss your family and Italy?" Luigi asked.

"Yes, *signore*. I miss so many things about Italy, and my family, but they will join me as soon as I have enough money to pay for their tickets."

"They want to leave Italy and live here?" Appollonia asked.

"It's always been our plan that they would do so once I was established. It'll be a little while longer though," he said. He ate a spoonful of soup and added, "My aunt and uncle are looking forward to having them close by. My mother says she'll have to cook dinner for them every Sunday for the rest of her life to repay them for what they've done for me."

Everyone laughed. "I'm sure they were glad to help you," Appollonia said.

"I'm lucky to have them." He finished his soup and turned to Appollonia. "Delicious. Thank you."

"*Prego,*" she said. "It's good to be able to do something for you after all you did for us."

Evelina touched his arm. "Remember the dance?" she asked.

"How could I forget? You stood on my feet all around the dance floor."

"We danced so long you almost didn't get to dance with

Giovanna," Evelina said. "And Maria danced with Mario."

"Have you seen him, Alessandro?" Maria asked. Her eyes sparkled.

"Not since my last day of work on the *SS Roma*, but knowing Mario, he's doing well. I miss him. He was a good friend. He thought a lot of you, Maria," he said, and patted her hand.

Maria blushed and Giovanna looked into her soup again as if it were more fascinating than the conversation. She hadn't spoken a word since dinner began.

"I'll clear the dishes," Appollonia said. "Maria and Ev, you can help me. Why don't you go for a walk and show Alessandro around the neighborhood, Giovanna?"

"She gets out of doing dishes again, tonight?" Evelina said.

Giovanna shot her a cross look, and Alessandro followed her out the front door.

"You're so quiet," he said.

"I couldn't wait to get away from everyone else. The music from the dance was playing over and over in my head. When Ev mentioned it, I could almost feel you spinning me past the other dancers and into the hallway."

"Where I kissed you," he said. "I wish that I could kiss you now."

"Are you asking me?"

"I'm afraid you'll say no."

"The last time, you didn't ask."

"I frightened you. I regret that. Can you forgive me?"

"I forgave you before we left the ship," she said. The kind tone of her voice that he remembered had returned. "Let's walk to the river. It isn't far."

He wanted to touch her, but she pushed her hands into her pockets without looking his way. They walked along the street and cut across a grassy patch of lawn between two houses. There they came upon the river. It's fast current caught his attention, and he paused to stare at it. Giovanna didn't seem to notice and kept walking along the bank. He hurried to catch up with her.

"Tell me about your life. Are you happy?" he asked.

"I work at the mill and sew and spend time with my family.

Maybe I'm getting a little restless for my life to move along. Some days I want to live on my own, but I'm happy with my parents and my sisters," she said. "What about you? Are you happy?"

"I am now, in this moment." He saw her smile, and kept talking. "After your departure from the ship, I was quite unhappy. Then when I started school, I focused on learning. I think until I finished my studies, I was only determined. Determined to get my medical degree and determined to find you."

"I suppose it's very rewarding being a doctor," she said. The earnest way she spoke made him feel as if she cared for him still.

"I wouldn't want to do anything else," he said. He stopped and put his hand on her arm. "Why are you avoiding talking about us?"

"I need more time to think. We should go back."

"Can't we walk a little more along the water?" he asked.

"For a few minutes," she said, looking toward the river.

Up ahead there was a tree close to the water with a patch of trampled grass beneath it. He pointed to it and asked, "Could we sit there for a moment? Then I'll walk you back before it gets too dark."

"Alright," she said, and walked ahead.

He took off his coat and spread it on the ground. Giovanna sat down and folded her hands in her lap. The hair around her face blew into her eyes, and she looked down when he pushed it behind her ears and touched her cheek.

After a moment, she took a deep breath and her words came out in a rush, as though she had to say them quickly or lose her nerve. "I haven't had a beau until recently. I've only had my fantasies about what love is. Most of my thoughts are probably silly romantic notions."

"I want to marry you Giovanna," Alessandro said, staring at her with longing. His emotions overtook him and the proposal came tumbling out.

"I can't answer you yet," she whispered.

The wind blew her hair again, but he didn't touch her. Instead he moved to sit across from her. All the things he wanted to tell her were swirling around in his mind like the wisps of hair falling across her beautiful face. What if a few days weren't enough to convince her that they belonged together? He didn't think he could stand losing her again.

"Though I haven't seen you for many years, I feel as comfortable with you now as I did then. The time we spent together on the ship was all I needed to know you're the one for me. That first day, when you came up the gangplank, I felt my heart beating in my chest. Each day after that just confirmed what I felt at the start," he said. "I might sound like a fool, but I believe I fell in love with you the first moment I saw you."

"I felt it, too," she said, looking up. Night was falling around them, but she was close enough for him to see the look in her eyes, and he saw that he might have a chance with her.

He leaned forward to kiss her. "Giovanna," he said.

She stood up before his face reached hers. Her words surprised him. "I didn't think another man could make me feel that way, until I met Orlando. I have to think. We should be getting back."

Alessandro shook his coat and put it on. He didn't look at her, and pushed his fisted hands into his pockets. They walked to the sidewalk in front of her house. Like a beacon against the dark sky, lights shown from inside the small kitchen where they had eaten earlier.

"I'm sorry I can't give you an answer," she said.

"I'll ask you again before I leave. If you say yes, I'll be the happiest man on earth. If you say no, I'll leave and never see you again." He was glad the darkness was there to conceal the anger in his eyes.

"Tomorrow then, for dinner," she said.

"Tomorrow," he said. He began to walk back to town where he was staying.

"I'm glad you're here," she whispered.

"Me, too," he said, and kept walking.

Chapter 30

The ticket seller at the bus station had cautioned Isolde to be on time for the 7:30 AM bus to Yorkville. It was the only bus that went there during the week, and it left promptly at 7:30 whether all ticket holders were there or not. He had also warned her that it would only leave the station if there were at least five passengers. The bus made two stops. If less than five were there for the trip, which frequently happened, as few people had the need to go to Yorkville or Steubenville from Wheeling on a weekday morning, the passengers would have to wait until Saturday or the next Wednesday to use their tickets. The Saturday bus always ran, he added.

Isolde hoped fervently she could go to Yorkville today. Saturday would be too late. Alessandro would bring Luigi to her that morning, and she had to speak to Appollonia before then. She and Jesse would have to leave soon to catch the bus. He was still in his pajamas, poking his spoon at the floating flakes of cereal in his bowl. His clothes were on the table next to his breakfast, and she pointed to them as she brushed her teeth.

"Your new red dress is pretty, Mama," he said and smiled at her.

She looked down to make sure no toothpaste had fallen on the dress she hoped would stay clean so that she could wear it again for Luigi on Saturday.

"Hurry, Jesse. We have to leave in a few minutes. Finish your cereal and get your clothes on."

He put his spoon down and took his bowl to the sink. Then he struggled into his clothes and shoes while she finished fixing her hair. She wanted Appollonia to think she was pretty.

"Tie my shoes, Mama," Jesse said. He had been practicing, but they were in a hurry, so she bent down to tie them. When she did so, he stroked her hair. It made her more determined to go through with the words she had been rehearsing to say to Luigi's wife.

"We're ready," she said. "Let's go." The minute hand on the clock above the stove in the kitchen made an audible *tick, tick* sound that she had never noticed until now.

"We have ten minutes to get to the station." She hustled her son down the stairs and pulled him by the hand. The bus was idling at the curb, and she could see three faces in the windows. Good, she thought.

"Cutting it a little close there. Aren't you, Missy?" the driver said.

"We're on time," she said.

"Cute kid," the driver said. "Sit wherever you like."

The ride to Yorkville took less than fifteen minutes. Isolde and Jesse were the only passengers who got off. The others stayed on the bus for the ride to the next stop in Steubenville.

"Pick up is at three o'clock," the driver said. "Same spot."

Isolde took Jesse's hand and glanced at the storefronts and the people walking on the sidewalk. Smoke poured into the sky from the smoke stacks of Wheeling Steel. Most of the building was hidden from view by rows of houses. Luigi and his two eldest daughters would be at the mill already. His youngest would be at school. She counted on being able to speak to his wife alone.

Severini's Grocery Store was behind her. She went inside and asked the man behind the register if he knew the Falconi family. He gave her the address.

"Three houses up from *DelVecchio's Furniture Store*," he said. Then he gave Jesse a caramel wrapped in wax paper.

"Wow," Jesse said. "Thanks, mister."

They began the walk up the hill to the small house he had described. Rain drizzled down from the gray clouds that hung in the air. In the side pocket of her purse, she kept a large scarf, which she wrapped around her hair.

Jesse pulled the hood of his jacket up over his head and

asked, "Where are we going, Mama?"

"To see a lady," she answered. "We'll talk for a little while. Then we'll take the bus back home."

"Does she have toys?" Jesse asked.

"Maybe. We'll see when we get there."

"I hope she has a dog," he said, as he took two steps to her one to keep up with her.

They passed *Piciacchia's Drug Store and DiNapoli's Gas Station*. The attendant pumped gas into a car and stared as they walked past him. In a town this small, she was sure he knew she was a stranger. Across the street was *Del Vecchio's Furniture*. The front window was dark. A man in a long trench coat fumbled with a ring of keys and unlocked the front door. She counted each house after that. Luigi's porch had a swing that moved as the wind blew. It was painted white. A broom stood against the doorframe, and the wooden front door was open. A soft light filtered through the screen door. She walked down the path and up the steps, dragging Jesse along.

"You're holding my hand so tight," Jesse said. She let go of him and knocked.

Appollonia wiped her hands on a towel and came to stand at the door.

"I'm Isolde Caldara and this is my son, Giuseppe."

"I know who you are," Appollonia said.

All morning, Luigi felt as if something bad was about to happen. At lunchtime, he went to the offices of the mill to check on Giovanna and Maria. They weren't at their desks, and he panicked until he found them eating in the cafeteria with the other clerical workers. By mid-afternoon, he was overcome with worry and almost burned his hand on a machine. He wanted to run from the mill to Evelina's school and then to see Appollonia to make sure nothing was wrong, but to do so would mean losing his job. His only comfort was the knowledge that if something had happened to them, Rose would come to the mill to tell him. A headache and a feeling of dread overtook him just before the five o'clock whistle. When it blew, he ran to the office and found Giovanna and Maria putting on their coats. When he saw their looks of concern, he took a deep breath and wiped his sweaty hands on his pants.

"What's the matter, Pop? Are you sick?" Giovanna asked.

"A little," he said. "I'll rest when I get home."

Maria took his lunch pail and looked inside.

"You didn't eat your lunch, Pop," she said.

"My stomach is upset, but I feel much better now that I'm with you."

When they reached Main Street, Evelina didn't meet them. Luigi quickened his step and the girls followed. Ev was taking bread out of the oven when he opened the door of their home.

"Mama's been resting. I was just going to wake her up," Ev said.

"Is she feeling bad?" Luigi asked.

"She says it's her asthma. She's been lying on the bed since she made the pasta."

Luigi took another deep breath. "I'll wake her. You girls get water and set the table."

As soon as they went outside, he opened the bedroom door. The room was dark. Luigi sat on the bed next to Appollonia and took her hand.

"I'm awake," she said.

"Is your breathing bad today?"

"She was here, Luigi."

Her voice was full of sorrow and he leaned closer to her. "What's wrong, Appollonia? Should I get the doctor?"

Her breath was labored and she wheezed when she spoke. "The girl from the restaurant in Covel. Isolde. She came to see me today with a beautiful little boy."

Her words struck him as forcefully as if he'd been punched by a prizefighter.

"I'm sorry," he said.

"I had a feeling about her. I thought I could forget when we left, but it's impossible now." Her words were a surprise to him and floated toward him in slow motion as if he were in a dream.

"You knew about her before we left West Virginia?" he asked.

He had not spared her feelings as he had hoped he might.

"The night you went to the restaurant and brought home the pie, I had my suspicions then. I pretended it was nothing, because I didn't want it to be so. But when we moved so suddenly..."

"She doesn't mean anything to me, Appollonia," he said with anguish. "She was company to me..."

Appollonia sat up and he touched the tears on her cheeks. She moved away from him. "The child is yours, Luigi. There's no mistaking that he's a Falconi."

"I'm sorry. I would do anything to take back what I've done. You and the girls are everything to me," he begged and hoped she would forgive him.

Tears began to flow down her cheeks and her shoulders shook. "Did you know about him? About Giuseppe?"

"A few days ago I got a letter from Vincente. He told me Isolde was in Wheeling and that she had a child. I didn't know before that. I didn't know his name."

"I guess she was telling the truth."

"Alessandro is taking me to meet him on Saturday. I was going to tell you after we returned," he said. There was no reason to hide the truth about his plans to meet Giuseppe now.

The creaking of the front door startled him. It was the girls.

Giovanna came to the door of the bedroom.

"Where is Alessandro taking you?" she asked.

Luigi was glad the room was dark.

"We're going to Wheeling together on Saturday." He paused and tried to speak in an even tone. "We'll be out in a minute. Shut the door."

Appollonia sat up as Giovanna closed the door. "What does Alessandro have to do with this?" she asked. Her hands shot up to her face and she wiped her tears.

"His search for us led him to Isolde in Wheeling, and she told him where we were. I did my best to keep our whereabouts a secret, but she found out anyway. It's why she moved to Wheeling."

"Yes, she told me everything."

Her words were like a knife in Luigi's side.

Evelina knocked on the door. "Are you feeling alright, Mama? Should we put the food on the table?"

"Yes," Appollonia said. "We'll be right out. Close the door." She lowered her voice. "I don't want the girls to hear us."

"Why did she come here? Did she hurt you in any way?"

"Only you have hurt me," she said. Luigi touched her shoulder and his eyes filled with tears. She moved away from him again, and his hand dropped to the bed. "She wanted me to meet Giuseppe. She didn't think you would have the guts to tell me."

He felt sick and distraught. The secret he had tried so hard to bury had been laid bare for her in the worst way. From the first moment she had arrived in America, the voice of his conscience had told him to tell her everything. The best way would've been to start fresh and confess all he had done that went against their vows to one another. If he had told her right away, he might not have had a lapse in judgment. The lapse that led to his last night with Isolde and the son it had produced. It dawned on him that she had hoped for a pregnancy as a way to tie them together. He knew from the start that being with her could spoil what he had with Appollonia, but he had done it anyway. Now it was time to pay for his mistake.

What a fool he had been, to think he could keep Isolde and a child hidden forever, a secret that would choke him more each day. She had done what he was too much of a coward to do. Tell the truth. But he knew her well. She wanted more than just to hurt him by telling Appollonia everything.

"What else did she say, Appollonia?" he whispered.

"She wants to see you on Saturday. I think she wants you to choose between her and me."

"I've made my choice. There's nothing she can say or do to change my mind," he said. "If you'll have me."

"Go and see her. For the sake of our daughters, I'll do my best to forgive you," she said. Her voice was cold and angry now.

"I'm sorry, Appollonia," he whispered.

"I'm tired. We'll talk about the child after you've seen him. He's a beautiful boy," she said. "Giuseppe. He's named after her brother. His American name is Jesse."

Appollonia turned away from him. He wanted to hold her and tell her everything could be the way it had been for them when they were young in Italy, though he knew it was too late for such a false promise.

She had seen his son. A part of him had always wanted another child. He was sorry that it hadn't been with Appollonia.

Chapter 31

Her parents had been shut up in their room for much too long. Giovanna put her ear to their door and listened. Their voices were too soft for her to make out what they were saying, but she had heard the tremble in her mother's voice in the few words she'd spoken before her mother had instructed Ev to close the door. Her mother and father seldom fought and never closed themselves up in their room until it was time to retire for the night.

With measured steps, she went to the table and stared at the food. Something was wrong. After work and on their walk home, her father had been acting agitated, almost fearful, as if something terrible was about to happen at any moment.

Footsteps echoed outside, and she remembered that Alessandro was coming for dinner. Through the screen door she saw him pause when he placed his foot on the boards of the porch.

"Cover the pasta, Maria," she said, released from her thoughts. "I'm going outside to meet Alessandro. Set the table, Ev."

"What's wrong?" Evelina asked.

"I think Mama and Pop are feeling a little sick. Maybe this isn't the best night to have a guest for dinner. I need to talk to Alessandro. I'll be back in a minute."

"Please don't send him away. Where else will he eat dinner?" Maria asked.

"I'll figure something out," Giovanna said. She grabbed the water bucket and took Alessandro's hand. "We have to talk. My parents are upset, and I think you might know why."

"What's going on?" he asked. His face was filled with concern.

"I heard my father say you're taking him to Wheeling on Saturday to meet someone. Who is it?" She kept walking and pulled him along.

He wasn't surprised by her question. His knowing look told her that he understood what was going on.

"Did you ask him who it is?" Alessandro said.

"I don't think he wants me to know. Somehow my mother knows and she's upset about it. I can think of only a few things that might upset her like this. You seem to be involved somehow. Please tell me what's going on."

"It's not my place to tell you. You'll have to ask your father," he said.

Giovanna stopped walking when they reached the water pump and dropped the bucket. Her legs were tired from her long day of standing at the filing cabinet in the mill office. Her sisters were waiting to eat dinner and her parents were in their room with the door shut. Alessandro looked up into the trees and didn't speak.

"I think you should leave," she said.

"Giovanna, this is between your mother and father. It isn't any of my business," he said firmly. They had reached the pump and Alessandro stood next to it facing her.

"Then why are you going with my father to Wheeling on Saturday? And why does it upset my mother?"

Alessandro lifted the pump. He didn't answer her until the water gushed onto the ground and muddied the dirt and grass. Giovanna watched the brown water run to her feet before she held the bucket under the spigot.

"I've been trying to find you since you left West Virginia," he said. "I wrote to you and the letters were returned. Then my uncle and I drove to Covel. No one knew why you'd left in such a hurry or where you had gone. Just before I left, I spoke to a waitress at the restaurant."

Giovanna began to feel dizzy and sat on the cement blocks that surrounded the pump.

He sat next to her and continued his story. "Her name is Isolde. She said she didn't know where you'd gone, but she gave me her address and asked if I would write to her if I found you. She was desperate," he said. He took Giovanna's hand. "Last week, I took the train to Covel again. A woman named Signora Limone told me that Isolde had moved to Wheeling. She thought that Isolde might have gone there to find your family."

"You mean my father," Giovanna said. "Something happened between them while I was still in Italy." All the dark fears she had known the moment Isolde had mysteriously appeared in the field came to the surface.

"I found her in Wheeling and convinced her to tell me where you lived," he said.

"Now she wants to see my father," she said with resignation. It was as though she had known this moment was bound to come.

"I thought it would be easier if I told him before she surprised him with a visit. Your father must have told your mother. Maybe that's why she's upset."

"There's more," Giovanna said. She stood and steadied herself. "I heard my father say that you were going with him to meet someone. He said him, not her. Is there someone else with Isolde?"

"You'll have to tell your father that you heard him say that. He'll have to explain."

"I think it's better if you don't stay for dinner. I'll make you a bowl of pasta that you can take with you," Giovanna said. Anger and fear burned through her. She began to walk back to the house. Tears filled her eyes and blurred her vision. Alessandro put his hand on her arm and she pulled away from him. Water splashed her legs as she lifted the pail with a jerk of her hand.

Alessandro stood and pleaded with her.

"Don't be angry with me."

"Why did you have to get involved?" she asked, as though he were the one who threatened to tear her family apart.

"Giovanna," he said. "I was trying to help, but I can't erase what happened in the past."

He was right. Whatever her father had done wasn't Alessandro's fault. It was wrong to take her anger out on him.

She closed her eyes and tried to calm down. "I'm sorry," she said. "I knew she might turn up. She seemed so determined."

"What do you mean?"

"She spoke to my sisters and me one afternoon shortly after we arrived in West Virginia. I had a terrible feeling about her then. She doesn't care if she hurts my family," she said.

They walked to the porch. Giovanna stopped when she saw her sisters sitting on the steps instead of rushing about the kitchen to place dinner on the table. The house was ominously quiet.

"We should all be eating dinner together now," she said.

He wrapped his arms around her, and she held onto him. "Please tell me who he is?" Giovanna whispered into his shoulder. She didn't lift her head and he stroked her hair with one hand and held her around the waist with the other.

"Go inside and ask your father who he is," he said.

Her sisters watched them with troubled faces. She knew they were even more confused than she was.

"I'm afraid of what he might say," she said. It began to rain. Drops of water fell on Alessandro's face and hair and dripped onto her cheek.

"I'll come back tomorrow," he said, releasing her.

"Wait," she said, as he let go of her. "Maria, bring a bowl of pasta and a fork for Alessandro to take with him."

Maria went into the kitchen and Evelina followed her. They returned with the pasta, two slices of warm bread wrapped in a towel, and a glass jar. Alessandro dipped the jar into the water bucket he was still holding, and thanked them for the food.

"I'm sorry you have to go," Evelina said.

"I'll be back tomorrow," Alessandro said. "This will all be sorted out soon."

Giovanna watched him walk to his car and place the food on the seat. He stood and leaned across the roof of the car. For a moment it looked as if he were reaching for her. His face was full of sadness as he paused there in the waning light. Then he got in and drove away. She didn't know where he was going.

As she opened the screen door, she reached into her dress pocket for Orlando's letter. Her father had given her two more letters, one yesterday and another that morning. Monday's and yesterday's letters were in her room. She told her sisters not to bother her parents and that she was feeling sick as well. For once they didn't question her when she told them to eat without her and clean up the kitchen. Her head ached and her body felt as if she'd climbed a mountain. She slipped off her wet shoes and unbuttoned her damp dress, letting it fall to the floor. The cotton gown she had folded into a neat square that morning was still on her pillow. She finished undressing and slipped on her gown. Overcome with weariness, she got under the covers and opened the letter to read it. The room was dark, so she reached for the matches on the nightstand and lit a candle.

Dear Beautiful Girl,
I will not be able to resist the impulse to kiss you and to express all my good intentions not with words but with the affection that my heart feels for you, my beloved Jennie.
I love you. I hope someday you'll be mine, and I'll be able to say with pride that you belong to me. If that day comes I will never be away from you again.

Affectionately, with my whole heart,
Orlando

Reading his letter calmed her fears, and she closed her eyes and pictured his gentle smile and the way she felt sitting next to him on the porch swing. Jennie. He was the only one who called her that. She liked the American version of her name. The second poem he'd written for her, the one her father had given her yesterday, was titled *Jennie*. She folded the letter and exchanged it for yesterday's poem that she had pushed deep under the mattress. This poem was longer. She felt he knew her well already as he had composed it with references to nature and feelings of longing that touched her heart. She opened it with care as though each page were a fragile flower petal that might fall apart with the slightest touch.

The room was so dark that she had to hold it close to the candle's flame to see the words Orlando had written in pencil.

Jennie
O pure heart, divine child, infinite light, sweet Jennie
Oh bright sunshine of my life,
Oh life of the sun,
Oh eternal spring,
Oh immaculate and fragrant flower.
My soul is a prisoner for you.
My heart beats with passion.
When I dream of you, Jennie, Your head lies on my chest.
The sublime ecstasy of affection makes me suffer,
But I still dream of your true love.

Her eyes closed and tears fell onto the poem Orlando had written with such tenderness. She knew that once her father had felt this kind of passion for her mother.

"Giovanna," Ev said.

The sound of the door opening caused her to sit up and wipe her eyes with the sleeve of her gown. "Did you eat dinner?" she asked Evelina.

"Yes, were you sleeping?"

"No. Where's Maria?" Giovanna asked.

"I'm here," Maria said. Both of her sisters stood in the doorway. The light of the candle cast its shadow on them.

"Are Mama and Pop asleep?"

"We think so. We don't hear them talking," Ev said.

"Come get under the covers with me," Giovanna said.

They crawled into the bed, one on each side of her, and she wrapped her arms around them. Having them close was a comfort to her.

"What's wrong?" Maria said.

Though her tears were on the sleeve of her gown, her sisters didn't need to see her crying to know when she was sad.

"We'll talk about it tomorrow. Remember what Mama read to us from the Bible when we were leaving Italy?" Giovanna asked.

"That was so long ago," Maria said. "Tell us."

"Weeping may endure for a night, but joy cometh in the morning. It's from Psalms."

"What does it mean?" Ev asked.

"Anything that is troubling you at night will seem a little better in the morning. Now say your prayers and go to sleep."

"Giovanna," Ev said.

"Yes?"

"Will you choose Alessandro or Orlando?"

"I don't know."

"But you only have until Saturday."

"I guess I'll have to make a choice by then, but for now, I'm going to sleep."

"Goodnight," Maria said.

"Joy comes in the morning," Ev said.

Giovanna blew out the candle and closed her eyes. The image of Alessandro's retreating figure on the dark road in front of her house was the last thing she thought of before she fell asleep. On Saturday morning, she would have to give him an answer.

It was a short drive to Wheeling. Alessandro hadn't planned on going there again until Saturday. Some of the money he had set aside for food would have to be spent on gas, but he could get by with eating only the food Giovanna gave him each day and use the money for this extra trip. The road was deserted, so he ate the pasta and bread while he drove, and washed it down with the water that splashed over the edge of the jar.

When he reached Isolde's street, he parked the car close to the curb. A light shone from the picture window of her apartment, her silhouette highlighted in front of it.

Seeing Giovanna so upset had made him angry. It would be better if Jesse were still awake when he spoke to Isolde. Having the boy there would keep his temper under control.

He lifted his hand to knock on the door, but Isolde opened it before he could do so. She didn't seem surprised to see him.

"What do you want?" she asked. Dark circles ringed her eyes and she wore a tight faded dress and no shoes.

Jesse jumped up from the sofa where he sat looking at a book. "Did you come to take us for a ride in your car?"

"Not tonight," Alessandro said. He smiled at Jesse, and gave Isolde a somber look. "May I come in? I won't stay long." Isolde opened the door wider and he stepped inside.

Jesse looked up at him with Giovanna's eyes. "We rode on the bus today to a town with a funny name," he said.

"Yorkville," Alessandro said. "I thought you might have visited there today."

Isolde went to the kitchen and came back with a glass of water. She took a sip and didn't offer him anything. "I wanted to speak to Luigi's wife," she said. "She needed to meet Jesse."

"Why? Why didn't you wait for Luigi to come here on Saturday?"

"I have my reasons, and it's really none of your business." She bent down and patted Jesse's leg. "It's time to get your pajamas on."

"Ok, Mama. Can I come back in and say goodnight to Alex?"

"After you brush your teeth."

Jesse went into the bathroom and turned on the water.

"You've upset his family," Alessandro said. His voice was filled with anger.

"I had to speak to her myself, to see what she's like," she said. She restlessly paced the living room, as though trying to release some of the hostility he could hear in her combative tone.

Alessandro sat on the sofa and watched her walk from the kitchen to the living room. "She's a good person," he said. When she didn't respond, he added, "Maybe Luigi didn't want her to know about Jesse yet."

She stopped and glared at him. "I wanted her to know. After Saturday, Luigi won't be able to hide his son from her." Her reply was controlled and harsh.

"Are you satisfied? You've caused his family a lot of pain," he whispered.

She walked to the door and put her hand on the knob. "I did

what I had to do," she said quietly. The fight in her tone was gone.

He got up and stood across from her. "Don't expect to win him back."

"I only want what's best for Jesse," she said, and opened the front door.

"Tell him goodbye for me," he said, as he walked down the steps. He wondered if she was capable of caring about what was best for anyone but herself.

Chapter 32

Luigi dipped his shaving brush into a cup of foamy shaving cream and lathered his beard. His straight edge was next to the sink. He picked it up and used his left hand to steady his shaky right hand as he drew the blade across his neck and face in slow strokes. He had slept very little and stumbled through his morning tasks in a fog. Today he was going with Alessandro to meet Giuseppe. Tears filled his eyes when he thought of the moment he would see him for the first time.

Isolde had asked that they arrive at seven in the morning. They would meet her and Giuseppe at the *Café Italia*. He hoped she would be reasonable. He wanted to be a part of Giuseppe's life. Alessandro cautioned him that she might be dangerous. She was still in love with him and might do anything to convince him that he should come back to her. It wasn't what he wanted. In the four years they had been apart, he hadn't missed being with her. Fear of what she might do to his family was the only emotion he felt when he thought of her.

Appollonia hadn't spoken more than a few words in the last two days, though she'd cleaned his house, cooked his meals, cared for his daughters, and slept in his bed. After she told him of Isolde and Giuseppe's visit, she didn't cry again or raise her voice to curse him for his betrayal. When she completed her chores, she sat alone in the chair and stared out the window, her eyes vacant like a wounded animal's. He craved her forgiveness, but it would have to come when she was ready, if at all. Was it possible that the hurt he had caused would ease with time? The thought that she might never recover filled him with despair.

A car engine rumbled on the street. He placed his razor and shaving brush in the cupboard and wiped his face and hands on a towel. No one was awake to tell him goodbye. With sadness, he looked at the closed bedroom door, and went to the street, where Alessandro waited for him.

He opened the car door and got in. "Good morning, *signore*," Alessandro said.

"*Buongiorno*," he answered. "I'm missing Italy today."

"I miss it, too, sometimes," Alessandro said, as he began to drive.

"My life was less complicated there."

"Mine, as well. Are you ready?"

"Yes," he said. As Alessandro drove, Luigi stared out the window at the closed stores and quiet homes of Main Street. Their blurred shapes disappeared at the edge of town where the sun rose in the sky above the plowed fields and farmhouses.

They rode in silence. When they reached Wheeling, Alessandro parked across the street from the *Café Italia*. Through the front window of the café, he saw Isolde in a booth with his son. He walked up to the boy and sat down beside him.

"Does he know who I am?" Luigi asked, staring at his son. Isolde pushed her hair away from her face, and put her hand on the table near his arm. Luigi kept his eyes on their child.

Giuseppe nodded his head and touched Luigi's face. "You're my Papa."

"Yes," Luigi said, his voice caught in his throat. His eyes filled with tears and betrayed the longing and regret he felt in his heart. "And you're my boy."

He hesitated for a moment. He wanted to take the child into his arms, but he turned to Isolde instead. Her face had softened and was full of tenderness. He was suddenly overcome with the memory of how he had once been swept away by her. He thought she looked happy to see him and their son together.

Alessandro stood at the end of the booth and reached his hand out to Giuseppe.

"Come with me to the counter, Jesse," Alessandro said. "We'll get you some eggs for breakfast."

"Is it okay, Mama?" Giuseppe asked.

"Yes," Isolde said. She touched his face and kissed him. "I'll be outside talking with your Papa."

Luigi followed her to the sidewalk in front of the café. She stood near the edge of the street and held on to the streetlamp on the corner. The early morning air blew her red dress and her hair whirled about her head in the wind. She held his gaze with her hypnotic eyes, but the power she had once had over him was gone.

Time stood still for Isolde as she watched Luigi. She wanted to remember this moment when there was still a chance for a life with him, still a chance that she could have a family of her own. The early morning sunlight shone on his face. His hat was down low over his forehead, and his dark eyes watched her intently. She thought of his mouth on hers and all the times he had made love to her. She stepped toward him. Her mind was made up. If he rejected her again, she knew what she had to do. She wouldn't beg.

"The only time I've been happy in my life was when we were together," she said.

He looked down and took a deep breath before looking up at her. His eyes were filled with pity. She knew then what his answer would be. She took a gulp of air and held her breath.

"I want to be a father to Giuseppe," he said. "But you and I can't be together again."

His body stiffened, and the gentle countenance he had shown their son turned to stone. He stared off into the distance, as if she were no longer there. She steadied herself against the streetlamp and stepped closer to the curb. The bus was coming. The next stop was several blocks past the café. She looked at the clock on the iron post behind Luigi. Seven-thirty. It was on time, just as it had been on Wednesday morning when she took Giuseppe to meet Appollonia.

"Promise me you'll take care of Giuseppe. He's a good boy. He deserves someone who will love him," she said.

"I will," Luigi said. "You'll let me be a part of his life?"

"Yes," she said.

The bus was just behind Luigi. She looked longingly at him, at his face now filled with relief. He opened his mouth, just as she turned to look at the oncoming traffic.

"Goodbye," she said, and stepped out in front of the bus.

A blur of red flashed in front of the café window, and Alessandro saw Luigi reach for Isolde's arm. He dropped the menu in his hand and rushed to the door to look upon the scene in the street.

"Hey," he yelled to the cook, as he threw open the door of the café. "Stay here with the kid. Don't let him come outside and keep him away from the window. There's been an accident."

Outside the sun filtered through the clouds. Its rays lit the sidewalk and the street for only a moment before it returned to the cover of a haze that had begun to darken the sky. Alessandro shivered and his face turned ashen as he stared at Isolde in disbelief.

He found Luigi slumped on the sidewalk with an envelope in his hand. Isolde's body had been thrown into the middle of the road. He went to her and knelt beside her. His heart raced in his chest. Her face was oddly serene and unharmed, but her body was twisted and wounded. Just like her soul, Alessandro thought. He placed his fingers on her neck to feel for a pulse. She was very still. He took off his coat and covered her with it. Then he made the sign of the cross.

The bus driver sobbed into the sleeve of his coat.

Alessandro patted his shoulder. "It wasn't your fault." It was all he could think of to say. He walked to Luigi and took him by the elbow to help him stand. Luigi's knees buckled and Alessandro steadied him.

Luigi looked up at him overcome with emotion. "She gave this to me," he said, looking at the envelope in his hand and then at Isolde's body that was hidden by Alessandro's coat. He began to weep.

Alessandro took the envelope. People ran into the street and stood over Isolde's body.

A policeman put his fingers to her neck. "She's gone," he said.

"Did anyone see what happened?"

"She jumped in front of my bus," the bus driver said slowly. He turned to Alessandro with a stunned expression. "I couldn't stop in time."

Alessandro felt Luigi's body go limp and he kept his arm around his waist to keep him from falling to the sidewalk.

"She did it on purpose?" the policeman asked.

"She looked right at the bus and jumped in front of it," the driver said. "She knew I was going too fast to stop before I reached her. How could she do this?"

Alessandro took Luigi inside the café. Joey had taken Jesse to the kitchen. While Isolde's body was being moved into an ambulance, he opened the letter she had given Luigi and read it aloud to him.

> *Dear Luigi,*
>
> *When I met Appollonia I knew she would be a better mother to Giuseppe than I could ever be. I want him to live with you, his father, and be a part of your family. It's the best decision I've ever made. I'm finally at peace. Take good care of him. He deserves to be loved.*
>
> *Isolde*

Alessandro drove Luigi and Jesse back to Yorkville. Luigi was silent and stared out the window. Jesse's fingers were intertwined with his on the seat between them, and he wept softly, his head buried in Luigi's arm. Alessandro glanced in the rearview mirror at the child whose life was about to change forever. Jesse lifted his head. His face looked innocent and confused as he stared up at his father.

When Alessandro stopped the car in front of the house, Appollonia opened the front door and stood on the porch, her arms crossed, her face sullen. Alessandro got out of the car and walked to her. He sighed deeply and took her hands in his. Her eyes changed from angry to confused. A strong breeze blew and the porch swing lifted into the air as though an unseen specter had decided to take a ride.

Appollonia searched his face and waited for him to collect

his thoughts.

"Isolde is dead. She jumped in front of a bus. The driver couldn't stop."

"Oh," she sighed, and her knees gave way. "*Mio Dio.*" Alessandro braced her until she was steady. When he released his hold on her, she went to Luigi.

Luigi got out of the car, and she surveyed his face with concern. Jesse slid along the seat and reached for her hand. She bent down and pulled him close, wrapping her arms tightly around him. He began to cry, and she stroked his hair and murmured words of comfort as she gently rocked him back and forth. Alessandro's heavy heart was lifted when he saw that she treated him as though he were one of her own children in need of solace.

Chapter 33

A faint grayness painted the sky and low clouds hung suspended and full of rain. Giovanna felt as dreary as the weather as she watched from the window as her father lifted his head out of Alessandro's car and into the mist that had begun to fall. She wondered why he hadn't been riding in the front with Alessandro. Then she saw a little boy step onto the sidewalk. He reached his hand toward her mother, who stood next to the car.

She began to cry as soon as she saw the gentle face framed with auburn curls. He was her brother. She vaguely remembered twirling Maria's curls around her finger when she had been a little girl. His hair was just like hers.

Just a short time ago, she had heard the creak of the screen door and the muffled sound of a car engine. Rising up from her pillow, she lifted the curtain and saw the red glowing taillights as her father and Alessandro disappeared down the hill. Her eyes had just fluttered shut again when her mother came into the room. Giovanna opened her eyes and found her sitting on the edge of the bed staring out the window with tears welling in her eyes. She sat straight up and took her mother's hand. The tears had startled her more than her mother's presence.

"Tell me what's wrong?" she had asked. Her sisters woke up at the sound of her voice, and her mother told them about Giuseppe and Isolde.

Somehow Giovanna knew Isolde would come back into their lives, but she never imagined having a brother. She could hardly take in what it would mean for all of them. Her mother didn't say that he would be coming to Yorkville today, but for some reason he had.

Her heart was full of sorrow and happiness at the same time

as she watched her mother embrace him. She wiped the moisture from the glass and stared as he buried his face in her neck, and she gently rocked him.

It was still early in the morning, but the dark sky made it seem like late afternoon. Giovanna held the door open for her mother and Giuseppe as they stepped onto the porch. Then rain began to pour from the sky. Her father stood oddly still on the sidewalk as though he couldn't feel the sudden change in the weather.

"This is Giovanna," her mother said.

She turned from staring at her father and bent down on one knee.

"Hi, Giuseppe," she said.

He smiled at her. He seemed confused, as though he wasn't quite sure why he was there.

"You can call me Jesse," he said, in English. "It's my American name."

"Okay," she said. "I will, and you can call me Jennie."

"Come inside, Jesse," her mother said gently, in Italian. She stroked the top of his head. "I want you to meet Maria and Evelina." Then she turned to Giovanna. "Alessandro is waiting for your answer. It's time for him to go back to Michigan."

Giovanna pulled the shawl from her shoulders and wrapped it around her head. With a nod to her mother, she walked out into the rain.

Her father passed her on the sidewalk and grabbed her hand. His hair and coat were drenched. He looked down, but she could see that he had been crying. He squeezed her hand and let it go without looking up. The door slammed behind him as he entered the house.

Alessandro got out of the car and opened the door for her. Water dripped from her hair onto her face. She closed her eyes as she waited for him to sit on the seat beside her. The rain on his eyelashes fell to his cheeks.

She had lain awake until after midnight thinking of what she would tell him at this moment. At first, she wished for more time. But it wouldn't have changed her feelings for Alessandro or Orlando. She cared for both of them, but her feelings for

Orlando were deeper. Her heart ached to be with him. She longed for him to hold and kiss her. She wasn't unsure of him the way she had been with Alessandro, whose intensity frightened her, even though it drew her to him as well. She had been a child when she met him, and her feelings for him were merely infatuation compared to the love she felt for Orlando.

If Alessandro hadn't come back into her life, she might have continued to romanticize everything about him and their time together, like a hazy dream to be relived in the first moments of the day. But now that he was here, she knew leaving with him wasn't what she wanted.

She wanted to be with Orlando and her family. She couldn't leave them now. This was where she belonged.

The Falconi family circa 1927:
Appollonia, Evelina, Maria, Giovanna, Luigi

Giovanna, Appollonia, Maria & Evelina,
Passport photograph 1927

Giovanna's future daughter, Eliana, mid 1940's

Orlando, early 1930's

Giovanna, Evelina & Maria as young adults,
late 1930's

About the Author

Christine Simolke is the granddaughter of Italian immigrants. She was inspired by her grandmother's life story to write a novel of the immigrant experience. Christine has traveled to many countries all over the world and is thankful that her ancestors chose to settle in the United States. She is a former language arts teacher with a degree in special education from Texas Tech University and a master's degree in English/reading education from The University of Houston. She currently resides in North Carolina with her loving husband, and they are the parents of two wonderful young men. When she is not writing, she's active in non-profit work at her local YMCA, animal welfare society, children's charities, church, library and is an elementary school tutor and group cycling instructor.

The idea for her book, *Children of Italy* was formed many years ago when she wrote a research paper in graduate school based on an interview she'd done with her grandmother, Giovanna and stories her great aunt, Evelina told her. Her grandmother and her family immigrated from Italy to America in the 1920's, and Christine and her parents, aunts, uncles and cousins were always fascinated with the stories her grandmother and her sisters told of leaving Italy and their early life in the United States. Their tale of hope, struggle, perseverance and love of family was an inspiration to all of the generations after them. *Children of Italy* is Simolke's first novel. She currently resides in North Carolina with her husband Greg.

CPSIA information can be obtained
at www.ICGtesting.com
Printed in the USA
LVOW12s1920230516

489547LV00002B/307/P